RUDE AWAKENINGS

THE PARANORMAL INVESTIGATOR
BOOK 9

CHRISTOPHER CARROLLI

RUDE AWAKENINGS
Copyright © 2023 by Christopher Carrolli

ISBN: 979-8-88653-148-0

Melange Books, LLC
White Bear Lake, MN 55110
www.melange-books.com

Published in the United States of America.

Cover Design by Caroline Andrus

As always, for my mother, Gladys (1937-2011), and since it's been a while, there are a few people to remember. I would like to dedicate this book to my first avid reader and number one fan, if you will. To Burma Gergeley (1946-2021). She waited patiently to read this book but never got the chance. Thank you, Burma, for being there every step of the way. And also, to my lifelong pal, Amy Ramsey (1963-2020) for encouraging my writing for many years. She left us much too soon.

I would also like to dedicate this to another avid reader and lifelong family friend, Mr. John O'Neil (1939-2023) Also to Jackie Ramsey (1957-2023) RIP, with love always. And for others taken far too soon, Ashley Risko (1987-2023) and to my cousin Alan "Lenny" Emanuele (1957-2023) whose support had been unending from the very beginning.

1

JAMIE

THE DREAM WAS HAPPENING AGAIN. IT *was* JUST A dream, wasn't it? Either way, she experienced it again, and every time it happened, it was all too real. Like the other times, she lay in bed, completely rested as though she were sedated, lingering in that moment of half-sleep that occurs just before total unconsciousness. Inexplicably, her body felt paralyzed, and she glimpsed around her bedroom through half-closed eyelids. She could see her dresser and mirror, her TV, and the bed beneath her as she rolled her eyes to the side. It had to be a dream because she felt and saw herself levitating upward from the bed, rising up toward the ceiling.

Then, the great starry expanse of nighttime sky spread out before her, and she felt herself ascending up toward it. That's when she saw Mother. Mother had been gone for two years. Cancer. Mother called out to her, her hand outstretched.

"Jamie! Give me your hand! Jamie!"

But a strong magnetic pull yanked her away from Mother. Jamie felt her body rising upward higher and higher toward a great green flood of light. The light, so green, so bright, it blinded her half-closed eyes. She glimpsed something gray and metallic within the green light, and then the green light was gone, replaced by bright white rectangular lights that moved above her. Only the lights weren't moving; *she* was moving. The soft, warm plush of her bed had been crudely replaced by a cold, hard metal beneath her, a frigidness that made the dream even more vivid, if that's what it really was.

Finally, she stopped moving. She lay on some type of gurney. Shadowy gray figures scurried around her. One of them moved his hand over a surgical lamp above her until it flooded her eyes with bright light, and like always, sent a sharp pain through her head. She tried to move, but a suctioning force pinned her back down to the cold, hard gurney.

One of the gray figures lifted the bottom of her nightgown up above her hips. This was the moment when she panicked. A soft, soothing, female voice entered her mind, assuring her that everything would be all right. Two of them stood on each side of her. She could never quite make them out, as if a shadowy veil protected them from being fully observed, but Jamie could see the wide shape of their heads and the frailty of their seemingly gaunt yet tall bodies. Black eyes pierced through the shadowy veil, eyes that appeared large with no pupils or irises.

But the one thing Jamie could clearly see was the thin, pointed needle that descended from above. She cried out as it neared her exposed stomach, the female voice once again caressing her. The needle made a whirring, drilling sound, fueling her suppressed hysteria. The needle entered through her navel, producing sharp pain and pressure inside her stomach. Jamie screamed. Then, the needle lifted out of her just as quickly as it entered. The pain disappeared, as though it had never occurred.

She was left alone for what seemed like hours. The dream had never been this long. Something was different this time. Jamie's eyes moved to the foot of the gurney and beyond. Only feet away from her was a set of double doors. A small rectangular window was set in each door. Gazing beyond the windows, Jamie could see only shadowy dimness. Abruptly, a female face appeared in one of the windows. Jamie clearly saw the woman's face and her auburn hair. She tried to move, to call out for help, but the invisible force continued to restrict her. The woman's face was gone as quickly as it appeared in the window. Fear burgeoned inside her. This was the furthest the dream had ever progressed, and she wasn't waking.

Soon, two shadowy figures returned, wheeling some type of metallic cart in front of them. Nearing the foot of the gurney, they clasped her legs and spread them apart. Two stirrup-like contraptions emerged from the sides of the gurney, and her captors locked her legs in them, one on each side. One of the shadowy figures held something up and examined it under the light. It wasn't a needle, but an injector of some kind.

"No, no, NO!" she cried out, but the female voice shushed her once more.

She felt another pressure inside her, one that entered through her womb. She fought, but to no avail. The suctioning force suppressed her. The pressure was quick and gone, just like the pain in her stomach. The female figure stroked her forehead, and she felt herself drifting.

Jamie awoke in her bed, like always, throwing the covers from her and glancing around her bedroom. It was just a dream, or was it? The dreams began two years ago, only a few months after Mother died. Each time, the dream progressed further. She'd experienced the needle before in these strange and sporadic dreams, but this time, she was invaded. She knew it; she'd felt it. She'd often wondered if the dreams were some sort of psychological response to her mother's death, but she was no longer convinced of that. The dreams were unlike any other; they were real, so real she could recall the cold touch of the metal gurney beneath her.

The most disturbing part of the dream was seeing Mother. Mother had tried to intervene. Mother had tried to stop what was happening, but some unearthly force pulled Jamie away from her, as if it held dominion over not only the Earth but the Heavens as well. She sat up in bed, still reeling from the trauma the dream inflicted. She felt like she was losing her mind. Maybe she should see someone about this recurring dream that had turned nightmarish, a psychiatrist maybe, but who? Jamie felt less and less convinced that the whole thing was a dream. Some odd notion churned inside her, one she felt ashamed and afraid to confront or even articulate.

That had been nearly three months ago. She hadn't dreamed since. This morning, she ran her fingers through her shoulder-length dark hair and looked around her room, thankful to be in her own bed, just as she was when she slipped into it the night before. She rose up out of bed and showered, then trudged downstairs to the kitchen for a light breakfast. Jamie faithfully read the morning news online as she ate, and today was no different. She read the national news first, and then the local news, where today, a special hometown item caught her eye. She stopped eating as she read the article's headline.

Paranormal Investigator Pens Shocking Memoir of Eagle Rock Experience

Jamie recalled a local controversy regarding Eagle Rock Mountain. There were claims of a mass UFO sighting at Green Valley University. It had been in all the papers and the news. Someone had gone missing. Jamie now read how that someone was Dylan Rasche, a paranormal investigator from the university. Apparently, Dylan Rasche wrote a memoir about that event, and today was the book's release day. Jamie sat stunned, her eyes attached to the screen. She never realized the incident occurred almost two years ago, around the same time her dreams began. She read the words Rasche told the reporter covering his book's release.

"I was abducted by that UFO up on Eagle Rock. My memories of that night have returned."

Jamie sat speechless, her heart pounding. Could there be someone else who might actually listen to the details of her recurring dream without deeming her crazy? She could never tell Sam about the extent of her dreams. He knew she suffered through nightmares, but she never felt comfortable going into the details. She didn't think he would understand. After all, they'd only been seeing each other for less than a year. Sam always seemed straightforward, not the type of guy to be chained to someone with such overbearing issues. It wasn't that she didn't trust Sam, but she felt sure she would drive him away and declare herself a basket case in the process.

She finished reading the article. Dylan Rasche was signing copies of his book, *Abduction from Eagle Rock Mountain*, later today at the university. Jamie sat contemplating. The book signing began in two hours, more than enough time for her to go, get a signed copy, and read the book for herself. Jamie decided to do just that.

She arrived at Levin Hall just in time. In the reception area, a line had formed to Dylan Rasche who sat behind a long table with a stack of hardcover books in front of him. Jamie could tell by looking at the people in line that many of them were UFO enthusiasts, researchers, and possibly, Jamie thought, other abductees. She read the pamphlet-style program given to her at the door. Dylan Rasche was not only a GVU professor, but the chief-investigator of the Paranormal Research and Investigative Society. Standing in line, she leaned to the side to get a better glimpse of him. Handsome, with dark curly hair, approximately thirty-five, and he sounded polite.

Finally, she stood in front of him. He greeted her.

"Hi, Dylan, I'm Jamie Cohen." She could hear the nervousness in her voice.

"A pleasure, Jamie," he responded. Then, he asked how she wanted her book signed.

"To Jamie, is fine," she said. "So, as an investigator, have you spoken with other abductees?"

She hoped her question didn't sound out of line. He looked at her curiously.

"I hadn't before I wrote the book," he said. "But I have a feeling that's about to change."

Her heart pounded.

Dylan signed her book and handed it to her. She shook his hand and thanked him. Nervously, she turned away. Feeling the need to say more, she hesitated and turned slightly back toward him. Then she caved. Jamie quickly turned around and kept walking, paid for the book, and then left the university.

At home, she curled up on the couch with her cat, Misty, and began reading. A knot formed in her stomach as she read the inscription. It felt like a sign, a loud answer to her silent prayer.

To Dr. Susan Logan, for being instrumental in recovering my forgotten memories and helping me through this experience every step of the way.

Before continuing, Jamie grabbed her phone and searched the internet for Dr. Susan Logan of Green Valley. Items about the UFO controversy flooded the screen. One item showed Susan Logan standing behind a lectern and speaking to the Press. Of course, Jamie thought, Susan Logan was the woman who held that press conference, the one who exposed the hidden facility at Eagle Rock. So, she was not only a psychiatrist, but a parapsychologist as well. Jamie set her phone back down on the end table and resumed reading.

She read about how a friend of Dylan's, Ursula Masters, had witnessed a UFO and suffered radiation exposure as a result. Soon, other eyewitnesses came forward with their stories about that night. Dylan, Susan, and the team began to investigate. Even local newsman, Marv Kincaid, became involved after witnessing the strange sighting. Jamie remembered something of his involvement back then. She was astonished to read of the Men in Black and their threatening presence. Born and raised in Green Valley, Jamie heard stories of the Kecksburg UFO incident most of her life, and how the MIB became involved back then. But not long ago, they returned to this area in hopes of silencing those who saw the strange "phantom in the sky" or those who threatened to expose the secret Eagle Rock facility.

Jamie sat, turning page after page. Finally, the author detailed the night of his abduction. Devastated over the knowledge that his father had been murdered, Dylan drank heavily that evening, and then made his way to Eagle Rock Mountain to investigate on his own. At the top of the mountain, he'd seen the great metallic-shaped object and became immersed and strangely hypnotized by the green light it emanated. The next thing Dylan knew, he was wandering aimlessly at the bottom of the mountain, unsure as to what had happened.

"At first, I had assumed that I'd drunkenly passed out somewhere at the top of the mountain," he wrote. *"I assumed I walked to the bottom during a drunken blackout. That's when I phoned Sidney to come and get me. Shortly after, I discovered how wrong I was in my assumptions. Never again will I assume."*

Sidney revealed to Dylan that he'd been missing for twenty-four hours. Jamie couldn't take her eyes from the page as she read about Dylan's missing time. Not only had Dylan been missing time, but his memories of those twenty-four hours were wiped out. He'd endured several hypnosis sessions with Susan Logan, all of which failed. Then, nine months ago, Dylan experienced and saw quick passing images in his mind. He began having vivid dreams. Jamie's eyes froze upon the word "dreams." She read the next words closely.

"I saw bits and pieces. Random pieces of a puzzle I could not remember slowly came together in my mind. In visions and dreams, I felt myself laying on a cold hard surface, a gurney of some kind. I saw bright-white rectangular lights above me. They moved, only they weren't moving, I was moving. Faceless beings wheeled me into a shadowy sterile room, where I was experimented on."

Holding the book, Jamie's hands began to tremble. Her heart restarted its incessant pounding. Dylan's description of the sterile room matched the room she dreamed of so often. He wrote about a mechanical arm with a suctioning device at the end that came down upon him and extracted from him with a caressing, flowery motion. Then he'd felt release.

Jamie closed the book and set it down on the end table next to her phone. She couldn't read any more. Dylan's Rasche's memory coincided with her dreams, down to the rectangular lights that moved swiftly above him. The one terrible unspoken thought that lay buried inside her was the notion that these dreams were not dreams at all, but horrific events that were actually happening to her. Dylan's accuracy in his descriptions was too hard to ignore.

She breathed harder and faster. Runaway breath, she was hyperventilating. Her shaking hands turned numb, along with her nose and cheeks. She was having another panic attack. In her mind, she saw the shadowy figures with misshapen heads looming over her. She heard the female voice shushing her. The sweat began to drench her.

Breathe, Jamie, she told herself, *breathe.* She breathed in through her nostrils and out through her mouth. She'd learned how to calm her heart rate and her rapid breathing. Those two issues, once accelerated, made her panic attacks worse. She grew calmer, fanning herself with both hands to break the sweat that slicked her face.

Calm now, she felt slightly embarrassed, as usual, even though she was alone with the exception of Misty. She overcame this latest panic attack, yet that did nothing to eliminate the fear she felt. She remained frightened at the thought that the dreams could be real and also confused at the prospect of how such a thing could be possible. Abducted from her bedroom in the middle of the night? It sounded preposterous, even to her, but she'd always known the dreams were too real, too vivid, and she was able to recall everything that occurred within them, unlike most dreams.

Jamie picked the book back up from the end table. Having only fifty pages left, she would finish reading later. She had to pull herself together and get ready for work. But one thing remained certain. She needed to know the truth, and there was only one way to find out. She needed to meet with both Dylan Rasche and Susan Logan.

2

NADINE

NADINE PARKS HAD BEEN THE FIRST PERSON IN LINE TO get a copy of Dylan Rasche's book. She left an hour early this morning and waited inside Levin Hall for the book signing to begin. Nadine remembered well the Green Valley UFO incident. She was an eyewitness who had remained silent out of fear, fear of not being believed and even ridiculed. Then, rumors and sightings of the Men in Black were enough to keep her silent. She remembered how the mass UFO sighting occurred right here at Green Valley University, and how the news of it spread nationwide in only hours. She also remembered how Dr. Susan Logan gave a stunning press conference, one that not only unveiled the nuclear facility within Eagle Rock Mountain but exposed the Men in Black. That day, Susan Logan confirmed the rumors surrounding these strange men as certain and undeniable facts.

Nadine had followed the headlines closely, keeping quiet her own experience with what the local news deemed the "phantom in the sky." She paid close attention to any headline regarding Dylan Rasche, not that there were many of them. He had disappeared for a brief period and inexplicably returned. Rumors abounded that Dylan had experienced missing time, although after his return, much of his story was kept quiet from the public. The prospect of missing time is what fueled Nadine's interest.

Back then, Nadine worked as a bartender at "One-Eyed Jack's," a bar and grill not far from Eagle Rock Mountain. The Friday night crowd dwindled early that evening, so Nadine announced last call at 1:00 am. By 1:30, she was out on the road, on her way home to a hot bath, her couch, and late-night TV. She'd always taken the back road home, the one that ran behind Eagle Rock Mountain. It was quicker.

She'd been listening to a local late-night radio show that discussed and debated politics and current events when the radio began flipping stations on its own. Baffled by the back and forth barrage of voices and sounds, she turned the knob, attempting to steady it, but to no avail. The haywire radio transmission continued to jump from station to station of its own accord. Slightly spooked, she pressed the button that turned the radio off, and drove through the silence.

Then a burst of green light engulfed her car. So vivid was the light, it appeared as though the world had suddenly been bathed in green luminescence. Blinded, she couldn't see the road ahead. Nadine swerved the car off to the right and assumed she'd pulled over to the berm of the road, but the green light made it impossible to see. She stopped the car and got out.

Nadine glanced above her. The light was coming from the sky. She remembered gazing through a sea of green and spotting something gray and metallic. The next thing Nadine knew, she was heading towards I-70, way past Eagle Rock Mountain and far from Green Valley. Immediately, she pulled into an all-night convenience store. She checked the time on her phone—3:04 am. Over an hour and a half had passed. How was that possible? She'd just left the bar only minutes earlier. Something was wrong. Something had happened.

Nadine had seen the headlines, as well as Susan Logan's press conference. Still, she remained quiet. After all, she couldn't remember anything beyond the flood of green light, and the gray metallic object she'd failed to clearly see. The mayhem that erupted in Green Valley after the so-called "phantom in the sky" events was not something Nadine wanted to get wrapped up in. She wanted to reach out to the investigators at the university, but she'd had an eight-year-old boy at home and an aging mother. She couldn't risk bringing any negative attention toward them. She couldn't risk their safety or the steady stream of their lives.

Months after the incident, talk of the Green Valley UFO and Eagle Rock Mountain had died down, outside of private talk and barroom conversations. As time went on, just when she thought all was forgotten, Nadine began to remember. One such barroom conversation took place right in front of her, at work, while she wiped the bar free of water rings left behind by wet glasses. A regular customer pondered the possibility that all of it had been a hoax perpetrated by those paranormal investigators out of the university.

"So, how do you explain the different video footages and pictures?" Another determined customer's adamant rebuttal caused a stupefied silence. "All those people saw the same thing at the graduation ceremony. They can't all be liars!"

The debate had triggered something in Nadine's mind. A flash of memory overwhelmed her. She saw the flood of green light. She saw herself moving toward the gray metallic object. Then she saw rectangular white lights moving above her, but they weren't actually moving; it was *she* who was moving. She saw shadowy figures scurrying about.

"Grab me another, Nadine!"

The customer who countered the skeptic rudely brought her out of the reverie. The images she saw in her mind stopped. She gazed around her, realizing what had happened. She took his empty Budweiser bottle and fetched him another without saying a word. The missing memories of that night had been coming back to her, and she wasn't sure that was a good thing.

After work, in the wee hours of the morning, she'd finally slept. In her dreams, the memories came to her, replaying in her sleep, as if the incident occurred all over again. She'd been on a gurney, a suctioning force pinning her down to it. The shadowy figures had strange looking heads, with frail and somewhat emaciated bodies. One of them stuck his face right up to hers. She flinched but couldn't move from the invisible weight, forcing her down to the gurney. The eyes were round and opaque, no pupils, no irises, just wide black ovals. Then the figure quickly whisked his face away.

They'd moved her into a room, a sterile room, seemingly gray everywhere. She'd seen the figure's face clearly. It had made sure she did. But she found it difficult to see the rest of the shadowy figures. It seemed like some sort of veil protected them from being seen by her. She breathed hard, heavy, her mind slipping into panic mode. That's when they injected her with something, and within seconds, she felt tranquil, at peace, and unafraid.

Stirrup-like contraptions emerged from the sides of the gurney. They fit both of her legs into them, left and right. What were they doing? Where were her clothes? She felt her cold nakedness beneath the sheet that covered her. She wanted to cry out, but she felt at peace. A female voice soothed and assuaged her. More shadowy figures hovered at the end of the gurney. One of them held something up to the light, a tubular-shaped instrument, and then the doctor-like being used it to enter her. She felt an intense pressure, all the way to her stomach. Then, the instrument was removed. The pressure dissipated. She felt herself floating, floating back down to her car parked on the right side of the road.

She'd awakened, nearly jumping out of the bed. She'd whisked the covers off of her, the sweat drenching her, her heart hammering. She remembered what had happened. The dream had brought it back to her.

They'd experimented on her.

"Excuse me. Is this the reception area for the book signing?"

A young man's voice brought her out of the past and back into the present. For a moment, she'd forgotten where she was. The young man looked older than a student, but still younger than herself.

"Yes," she replied. "It is, but we're both early. No worries."

The young man thanked her, took a program from the student handing them out, and then sat in one of the chairs set up for the occasion. *He's almost as early and just as determined to meet Dylan Rasche.* Nadine wondered why. She checked the time on her phone, still a half an hour until the book signing began. Nadine couldn't help but slip back into the past, back to the worst part of the whole experience.

It was nine months after the Green Valley UFO incident. She had clearly recalled her own encounter in a dream only three months before. An arctic January cold spell, much like this year's, along with winter's early darkness kept most people inside for quite some time, Nadine among them. The bar had closed early one night due to the harsh winter weather. They'd had four customers all day, all of whom left after 8:00 p.m., leaving an empty barroom behind. Arriving home by ten o'clock, Nadine decided to call it an early night.

She fell fast asleep, the frigid cold having taken a tiring toll on her body. As the dream state took over, she saw it all again: the flood of green light, the gray metallic disc-shaped vessel, and the rectangular lights above her. The same shadowy figures scurried about her as they wheeled her gurney into a sterile room. But this time, something was different. The room was not the same. It had the same gray tile, but it was the opposite of the other room, left sided, rather than right. The same stirrup-like contraptions emerged from the sides of the gurney, and once again, her legs were positioned accordingly inside them.

Nadine squirmed and writhed as a long, pointed needle descended upon her exposed stomach from above. She squealed as the needle penetrated her navel for a moment, and then removed itself. All the while, the same female figure as before soothed and caressed her, massaging her forehead with long, slinky fingers.

This hadn't happened before. There was no needle last time.

This was not the dream recurring over again as a nightmare. She was not remembering what she'd blocked from her memory nine months ago. This was real.

They'd left her alone for what seemed like an hour. Then, three of them returned, the female among them. Another doctor-like shadowy figure stood at the foot of the gurney. This one was slightly taller than the last one, examining the same tubular-shaped injector under the lights above. Then it entered her again. She felt the same pressure as before for just a moment longer. The pressure ceased as the object was removed.

The female's elongated fingers stroked her face and forehead, until she felt herself floating. Soon, the sudden warmth of her bed and the blazing heat radiating from the furnace had rudely awakened her. Her bed's softness had abruptly replaced the cold, hard metal she'd endured for what seemed like hours. She glanced at her alarm clock—3:04 a.m.—the same time she'd found herself wandering near I-70. What just occurred was no dream. She still felt a slight chill against her back from the gurney. Had she been abducted from her sleep? How on Earth was that possible?

Nadine knew it was an altogether different experience. She saw and felt the dissimilarities. She remained awake on that cold gurney for at least an hour. Now, was she supposed to believe that she'd been asleep in her warm bed the entire time? Nadine knew better. Whoever they were had experimented on her. They had invaded her. But who in the world could she tell? Who would believe her?

Days passed. Sleep remained dreamless. Nadine made a conscious effort to forget the latest dream, only it wasn't a dream. She knew what had occurred had been real, but it was best to try and move forward as if nothing had happened. What else could she do? The days had turned into weeks, six to be exact. One morning, Nadine suddenly became ill.

After fixing her son, Todd, his breakfast, her stomach suddenly turned. All of her senses seemed overwhelmed. The smell of morning food sickened her. She ran into the bathroom and hurled

14

into the toilet. It would be the first of two occasions that day and three the following. Her mother looked at her, as if she knew what was wrong.

"Best to get yourself to the doctor, Nadine," she said. "Whatever it is doesn't seem like it's going away."

She took Mom's advice and went to see Dr. Wilson. After checking her over and withdrawing her blood for testing, she waited in the small exam room in his office. He returned within fifteen minutes. She noticed his sideways glance and the slight grin on his face.

"So, what's wrong with me?"

"Nothing's wrong with you," he said. "You're pregnant."

Nadine felt her face and ears burning. Pregnant? How was that possible? She hadn't been with anyone since the last time she was with Carl, and they divorced a year ago. It had been way over a year for her. Pregnant was not possible. She kept her mouth shut as something stirred in her mind.

"Pregnant?" She paused, trying to keep her emotions in check. "How far along am I?"

"Six weeks to be exact."

She saw sudden images: the shadowy figures scurrying around her gurney, the doctor-like figure holding the injector, the pressure inside her as he invaded her with it. She said nothing, feeling as if this very moment was not real. They'd impregnated her. No other explanation existed. For a passing second, she wished she would die.

"I take it this isn't a happy occasion?" Dr. Wilson picked up on her mortification.

She laughed lightly, unsure of what else to do or say.

"It's not that. It's just a little unexpected is all."

"Understandable, it happens that way all the time."

He prescribed her prenatal vitamins and rescheduled her for another appointment in six weeks, at the end of her first trimester. He also scheduled her Ob-gyn appointment shortly after that time.

She left the doctor's office quietly, and then cried all the way home.

———

TWO FEMALE STUDENTS ENTERED THE RECEPTION AREA, carrying boxes which they began to open. Nadine noticed they were unpacking copies of *Abduction from Eagle Rock Mountain* and placing them on the various tables for purchase. A male student began to set the long conference table in the middle, where Dylan Rasche would sit. He hooked up a microphone, set down a legal pad and a box of pens, and stood two water bottles nearby.

Nadine had read the article on Dylan Rasche's book in the local newspaper. Rasche hadn't gone into elaborate details prior to the book's release, but he did reveal to the reporter that he was not only abducted from Eagle Rock Mountain but experimented upon. His abduction occurred at the same time hers did, that is, the first time. She had to find out the details of his experience. She had a distinct feeling that their stories were not far apart. If she was right, she had to talk to Dylan Rasche. He would be the only person who would believe her.

She took a seat as close as possible to the table where Dylan would sit, ensuring her status as first in line. During the brief quiet, Nadine slipped back into the cloudy realm of reverie. She'd been nearing the end of her first trimester. Her next appointment with Dr. Wilson was two days away. Having left "One-Eyed Jack's" on a so-called "maternity leave," she'd decided to collect unemployment compensation. Now free to watch more late-night TV and binge on Barbeque Potato Chips, she stayed up late one night. Shortly after 2:00 a.m., she went to bed.

Sleep loomed closer than she thought, and before long, her mind and body slipped into restful oblivion. A flood of green light interrupted her slumber. Bright and encompassing, it obliterated any possibility of her entering the dream world. She floated closer and closer toward the gray, metallic object. *Not again.* Those two words had entered her mind but didn't quite register as everything happened so fast. She'd felt the cold metal of the rushing gurney on her back once again. The rectangular lights shined down, always appearing as if they moved above her. She'd been brought back to the sterile room. During this occasion, she cried out, but one of the misshapen shadowy figures scrambled toward her and placed a plastic mask of some kind over the lower part of her face. That was the last thing she remembered before she woke on the gurney some time later.

Time had passed, but how much, she wasn't able to tell. Strange, she'd been left in the room alone. Her non-human captors lingered nowhere in sight. She'd risen up from the gurney and glanced around her. Not only had she been alone, but the double doors of the sterile room were inexplicably open. Nadine saw her chance. She needed to find out where she was, who these beings were, and whether or not a way out of here existed. She swung her legs over the side of the gurney, which had been propped up higher than she imagined. She'd dropped to the floor with a small jump. Then she ran out between the open double doors.

Nadine had found herself running down pristine metallic hallways. Shiny, yet industrial-like, the surroundings appeared almost immaculate. Her feet pounded a greater clamor upon the floor that frighteningly felt like tin, but of a more durable, indestructible type. Left and right, Nadine spotted great constructed metal beams patterned like metallic lattice and protruding upward from indiscernible lower depths. Another room, like the one she'd been kept in, loomed ahead of her on the same side of the hallway. She ran toward it.

The room's double doors were closed, yet the same dual windows were set in each door, allowing a view of the room inside. Nadine had pressed her face to one of the windows. A young woman laid on a gurney like she had, her legs trapped in the stirrup-like contraptions. They, whoever they were, were doing the same thing to this younger woman as they'd done to her. She caught the young woman's attention for a moment, shoulder length dark hair, big frightened brown eyes. Nadine had sought to intervene. She planned to grab the young woman, and they would try to find their way out of here. She attempted to push the door open but felt a pair of strange hands on her shoulders, light hands that gripped her strongly and whisked her away.

Nadine had awakened in her bed, thrusting her body upward and throwing the covers up and away from her. She'd glanced at her alarm clock—5:12. Not her usual time of 3:04, but this instance was not like the others. They hadn't experimented on her this time; at least, she didn't think so. She remembered floating through the flood of green light toward the gray metallic object. She recalled the gurney, but this time, her captors had placed something over the lower part of her face, something that put her back to sleep. The young girl in the other room was an abductee, just like her. She was sure of it. She would probably never see the girl again, but she would never forget her or the look of absolute fear on her face.

Nadine got out of bed. No way would she sleep now, not after this instance. She'd only had a little over three hours of sleep, but maybe she would make up for it later this afternoon. She'd brewed a pot of coffee and read the morning paper, silently realizing that she felt slightly different since waking.

Two days had passed before Nadine sat in one of Dr. Wilson's exam rooms again. He'd felt her stomach and then stared at her solemnly.

"How do you feel?" he asked.

She shrugged. "Fine, I have no complaints."

Perplexed, he continued to stare at her. "I want to order more blood work for you."

"Why, is something wrong?"

"I just want to make sure everything's okay. You're getting older, Nadine. Always best to take precautions."

She did feel age creeping up on her. Although Dr. Wilson never said it, Nadine knew what he meant; thirty-nine was pushing it, age-wise, to have another baby. If he only knew the real circumstances behind this pregnancy, he would probably commit her to the mental health facility. How would she ever tell him she'd been abducted during the Green Valley UFO incident, experimented upon, and impregnated against her will by beings unknown?

Wiseass responses took turns in her mind, signals of her extreme apprehension and nervousness. There was something Dr. Wilson wasn't telling her; she could see it on his face. Again, she walked down a hallway to the testing room and had her blood withdrawn. She returned to the exam room and waited another ten minutes before Dr. Wilson returned, seemingly anxious.

"Nadine, I want you to go straight to Dr. Houseman for your sonogram. It's a little early, but I want to get this out of the way now. I've scheduled you to be there tomorrow at 10 a.m.."

"Dr. Wilson, is something wrong? Please tell me."

He sighed. "I'm not sure, Nadine. That's why I've scheduled you to see Dr. Houseman." He paused. "It seems your blood tests are slightly different than before. I just want to make sure everything is okay."

"Different? How?" Nadine persisted.

Wilson sighed again, somewhat defeated. "According to your blood work nearly three months ago, you were pregnant. According to these new tests, you are not."

"What?" Nadine couldn't believe what she was hearing.

"I've run the tests twice, but Nadine, we'll get a better idea of what's happening after your sonogram. There doesn't seem to be any reason to panic, so stay calm, rest, and see Dr. Houseman tomorrow morning. Believe it or not, there could be any number of reasons for this discrepancy. Let's let Dr. Houseman be the judge of what's going on, okay?"

The rest of that day had remained a blur. The next day she arrived at Dr. Houseman's office early and sat nervously fidgeting in his waiting room. Finally, she got into the exam room. The chill from the cold lotion spread across her belly broke her out of her inner frenzy, if only for a moment. Dr. Houseman, renowned for being one the best in his field, moved the ultrasound transducer over her stomach.

"You don't appear to be showing much for someone as far along as you are, but we'll get to the bottom of this."

Nadine watched the monitor screen as he moved the device, straining her eyes and attempting to see beyond the gray haze of images. Dr. Houseman remained silent for an agonizing eternity, moving the device back and forth across her stomach. Finally, after what seemed like more than five minutes, he bluntly shattered the silence.

"No, there's no fetus here." His tone was direct and to the point. "I'm sorry, Nadine, but you are not pregnant."

"No!" Nadine wailed, pushing herself upward on her haunches. "They took the baby! THEY TOOK MY BABY!"

She remembered the nurses pushing her back down as her screams continued. Her arms flailed in futile attempts to combat restraint. The next thing she knew, she felt a pinch as a needle jabbed her upper arm. Dr. Houseman had sedated her.

———

A COLLECTIVE ROAR OF APPLAUSE WHISKED HER OUT OF the past and back into the present. Nadine turned her head toward the front, watching the young man who'd set up the conference table now speak to a crowd that had gathered in healthy numbers while she'd lapsed into a painful memory. The young man, a student of Dylan Rasche's, talked about what a great professor and friend he was and offered background details on the UFO incident that took place right here at GVU almost two years ago. Finally, he introduced his mentor.

"Here to launch and sign copies of his newly released book, *Abduction from Eagle Rock Mountain*, my friend and professor, the author, Dylan Rasche."

Nadine quickly rose from the chair and stood as the roar of applause erupted again behind her. Dylan Rasche entered through a door behind the conference table. He stood behind the table, held up his hands, and addressed the crowd.

"First off, I want to thank you all for being here. It's been a long road of therapy, as well as mind and soul searching, but I believe writing this book has helped me through it immensely. You're being here today makes it well worth the fight I've endured." Again, the room erupted in applause. "I'm going to start by unveiling the cover." He turned to a large poster board situated on an easel-like structure and covered by a large cloth. "Jacob, whenever you're ready."

Jacob, his student, walked over to the covered poster board and pulled back the cloth. More applause rippled through the room at the sight of the cover. A close-up picture of the top of Eagle Rock Mountain absorbed most of the cover. Then, a photo of the so-called "phantom in the sky" was superimposed to appear at the top of the mountain. A splash of green shaded the cover's images, representing the green light the strange craft emitted.

Nadine stared at the object looming above the mountain on the cover. She'd seen it in the newspaper and on the local news. One of many photos taken that day on Commencement Field, the image was regarded to be one of the clearest and most precise. The craft was exactly what she'd seen that night, driving home from work. It's also the same object she'd seen in her dreams, if that's what they were.

Dylan spoke about the events leading up to that night, and how he drunkenly ended up alone on top of the mountain. He talked about his father and the search for answers to his strange and untimely death.

"That first night, I saw it through a telescope," he proclaimed. "I hadn't been sure what it was, but I knew I'd seen something. Then, witnesses started coming forward, one of which was a good friend of mine. You'll read about Ursula Masters' ordeal in the book. But when it became clear that something of a UFO nature was going on in Green Valley, it led me back to my father's journals. That's when all of these events, past and present, seemed to come together at the same time, as though someone somewhere was sending me a silent message. All of it was overwhelmingly troubling, traumatic, and beguiling, to put it mildly.

"What happened to me that night? I could stand here and fill you in detail after detail, but I would be spoiling the book for you." He laughed. The audience laughed with him. "Besides, I want you to read this in my words, and understand how it all felt to me at the time, what it meant to me afterwards, and the frustration I endured while futilely trying to remember. That's why I wrote this book, for you to experience it with me. So, I'm going to let you do that, right after I sign a copy for you."

Nadine applauded with the rest of the room, then walked over to the table, took one of the hardcover books, and paid for it. While everyone else stood skimming through the pages, Nadine hurried over to the conference table, first in line as she'd hoped. Dylan Rasche was now seated, and she slid the book across the table to him. He greeted her and asked how she wanted it signed.

"Hi, Dylan, I'm Nadine Parks. 'To Nadine,' please."

"Nadine. Thanks for your support." He spoke to himself as he scribbled on the title page.

"Dylan, I wanted to make sure I came early today. I wanted the chance to mention something to you. You see, I also had an experience with the phantom in the sky. I was abducted by that thing also." He stopped scribbling and looked up at her. "I was hoping I might be able to come by sometime and discuss it with you. I don't know who else to turn to or who else would believe me, but I know what they did to me, and I have a feeling you know what I mean."

He swallowed hard. She couldn't help but notice something in his eyes, something that looked like not only surprise, but a little like relief. His eyebrows lifted and arched. She got her point across. He hadn't taken her as a crackpot.

"Why don't you come by room 208 at your earliest convenience?" He took a card from the wallet in his back pocket. "Here's my card. Call me, so we can set up a time. It would be great if you could tell your story to the whole team, if you wouldn't mind."

"Not at all," she said, taking his card. Finally, someone she could tell this nightmare to, someone who would listen and not judge. He finished signing the book and handed it to her. She thanked him and promised to be in touch.

He nodded. His face was a somber mask. "I'll be waiting to hear from you."

Again, she thanked him, and then left Levin Hall. Arriving home, she lounged back on her recliner and began to read.

3

BRAD

THE SOUND OF HIS VOICE SEEMED TO SNAP THE WOMAN out of a daydream. He knew he'd entered Levin Hall, but being early and unfamiliar with the campus, he wasn't sure if he had the right room. He'd asked the woman with auburn hair. Like him, she also arrived early. She sat up front, close to a long table, seemingly lost in her thoughts.

"Excuse me; is this the reception area for the book signing?"

He'd shaken her out of her reverie.

"Yes," she replied. *"It is, but we're both early. No worries."*

He'd taken a pamphlet from the young student who assisted with the setup. Then he sat in a chair a few rows behind the woman. After reading most of the program-style pamphlet, his eyes moved upward to catch a quick glance of her. She sat staring at nothing, lost once again in her daydream, or possibly a nightmare. Brad could tell from the woman's blank and listless stare that her mind wandered somewhere in the past. Whatever she sat remembering is what brought her here—just like him. He remained certain of it. She'd arrived even before he did. Brad wondered what kind of story she would tell if asked. Could her story be even bigger than his?

His eyes roved back over the pamphlet. He began reading the blurb for *Abduction from Eagle Rock Mountain*. So, through his book, Dylan Rasche would reveal to the world that he was abducted by aliens. Finally, Brad felt a connection, someone who would understand and believe him. He, too, had been abducted by the phantom in the sky, but telling the world had not been an option. He finished reading the pamphlet, and like the auburn-haired woman a few rows up ahead, Brad began remembering.

He'd always had a love of night fishing. He'd spent most of his youth fishing, discovering early that the best time to fish was after the sun went down. At night, fish were more prone to bite since the darkness hid human shadows which, during the daylight, frightened fish away. Dad had passed this theory on to him, and it became one he maintained frequently. Now that Dad was gone, Brad liked to fish alone by the river and listen to the sounds of the night intermingle with the river's soft thrashing. He found peace and quiet by the river at night, soothed by the water and the dim glow of city lights in the distant background. Fishing season had just begun, but only for limited trout fishing. Yet that didn't stop Brad from packing up his gear and heading out to the river a few miles from Green Valley.

Brad sat on the riverbank, watching the tip of his fishing pole that was propped in the makeshift stand he'd rested it upon. It jerked to the right rather than in an up and down motion like it would if he'd had a nibbler somewhere at the end of his line. A sudden and unusual current yanked his pole from the stand and dragged it a few feet away from him. He leaped to the right to catch it.

Grasping the pole's handle firmly in his hand, he gazed out at the water. Something was wrong. Something unseen disturbed the river. This was no tide. Whatever it was parted the river into halves, creating two sides, a left one and a right one. Brad heard the rush of the water as the unseen force obstructed the river's natural path and sent it thrashing and crashing just above the riverbank.

Then, he gazed up at the sky, up to a flood of green light that painted the murky twilight a shimmering emerald. Something within the green luminescence hovered above him, a craft of some type. Brad felt the wind turn hot around him. He made an arch with his hand and bridged it above his eyes, shielding them from the brightness that grew in intensity. He felt his pole drop from his hand, yet he stood oblivious, unable to bend down and pick it up. Mesmerized, his unblinking eyes felt paralyzed, fixed in a frozen gaze upon the gray metallic object rotating within the green light. The object appeared to come closer and closer.

The next thing he knew, he stood off to the left, a few yards away from his fishing spot, feeling an intense head rush as he watched his pole wade in and out of the water lapping at the riverbank's edge. He stumbled back toward his spot, wondering what had just occurred. He remembered the water parting and rushing, but that was all. The water was calm now, as if it had all been his imagination. But why had the sky suddenly grown darker?

Not wanting to be bothered while fishing, Brad had left his phone in his truck. He kept an old strapless watch face in his tackle box to tell time. He opened the box, found it, and pressed the button on the side. The watch face glowed for nighttime viewing—12:16. Past midnight—how was that possible? He'd arrived at the riverbank shortly after 8:00 and sat for at least two hours before noticing the strange current. Over two hours had passed since then; something was wrong.

A rush of restless inner frenzy swept him. His body reacted to the urgent feeling of time having slipped away. Reeling his line back in, Brad set his pole on the ground and dashed into a thicket of wild weeds. The urgency burst from him in a torrent of piss he'd unleashed just in time. Proof that time had passed, time for which he could not account, made a pitter-patter sound as it flooded the thick brush before him.

He zipped up and scrambled to the spot where he'd stood. Gathering up his pole and tackle box, Brad hurried to his truck and threw his gear into the back, and then hopped into the driver's side. Within seconds, the truck's tires screeched as he barreled down the highway.

Brad glanced at the digital time on the dashboard—12:23. He couldn't have fallen asleep. He'd been standing in one spot, one moment, and then a few yards away the next. In his mind's eye, he kept seeing the rushing river and how it parted into halves. Then, the water became calm and unaffected. Yet *something* had transpired—something he couldn't remember.

He'd only had two beers before arriving at the river. He hadn't been sick. Never touched drugs. Yet two hours had passed. He'd stood on the riverbank, confounded and unable to recall his actions, while above him, the sky had visibly darkened. Now he didn't quite feel the same as when he'd arrived at the river; he felt tired and confused. A strange foreboding overwhelmed him, one he could not identify. He felt as if everything he'd always known had been challenged and couldn't explain why he felt the way he had in that moment. He'd just wanted to get back home.

Brad arrived home in less than thirty minutes. He keyed off the ignition and hopped out of the truck, experiencing an overwhelming instinct to get indoors. He charged down the sidewalk and through the front door.

"Wow, you're late tonight. Somebody must've caught *something*." Sheila reclined on the couch, watching a late-night movie and waiting for him to come home. She often teased him when he'd stayed out fishing a little later than normal, but tonight was a night he could not explain.

He shut the front door and locked it. Sheila must have noticed something about him, maybe the way he burst through the door, perhaps a look on his face of which he remained unaware. At that moment, he hadn't been sure. She bounded up from the couch and hurried over to him, planting her hands on the sides of his face.

"What's wrong?" The worried tone in her voice reminded him of how perceptive she was. "You're pale. Did you get sick? Look at you, you're shaking." He hadn't even noticed the slight tremors of his hands. She took his hands in hers, squeezed them, and then wrapped her arms around him. "Did something happen?"

Brad waited a moment before answering. He took a deep breath and exhaled.

"I don't know." He felt dirty, soiled, more than he normally did after a fishing trip. "I need to take a shower. We'll talk about it when I get out."

Afterward, he plopped down on the living room couch next to Sheila, silent, his mind reeling after failed attempts to remember what he could not. Sheila pressed the mute button on the remote, silencing a seven-minute string of commercials that cut into her movie.

"Is everything okay?" she pressed. "What happened tonight?"

Brad sighed and took a deep breath. "Like I said, I don't know. Something happened tonight, and as a result, I'm missing almost two hours." She stared at him, her eyes wide with more than just concern. Brad wasn't a storyteller; this she knew. He told her what he remembered: standing on the riverbank, the quick jerking of his fishing rod, and then watching as the river parted into halves. "It looked like some kind of current, a force like a tide, something I couldn't see. It parted the river. That's the last thing I remember."

He described waking from what felt like a daydream and standing a few yards away from his fishing spot. Suddenly, the water appeared normal. Then he scrambled to retrieve his fishing rod before it became swept out.

"When I looked at my watch face, it was past midnight."

"Do you feel sick?"

He shrugged. "Not really sick. I feel somewhat strange and of course, confused."

Brad and Sheila had been married for seven years. Their son, Adam, slept soundly in his bedroom down the hallway. Something inexplicable caused Brad to feel a loss of control, as if he no longer possessed the ability to protect his family. Something had happened to him tonight, and whatever it was had been erased from his memory. No longer did he feel like the father, the husband, the protector. Something greater than him had changed all that, and he remained unable to recall it in his mind. What he couldn't remember now silently reduced him to a frightened child.

Nearly leaping from the couch, Brad trudged down the hallway to Adam's room and opened the door. The boy lay sleeping on his right side, just like always. Sheila kept a fast pace behind him. He felt her hands ushering him away from the door.

"Shh, don't wake him," she warned with a whisper. "He's fine." She closed the door and wrapped her arms around him. "Brad, what's wrong?"

He couldn't explain his sudden sense of paranoia, the overwhelming need to protect his family. He grasped her, immersing himself in the familiar. Whatever happened was over now. He was home with his family. He needed to move on, to forget what he couldn't remember. That night, he put the unexplainable behind him and moved forward.

Almost a year had passed, and then the dreams began.

———

A BURST OF GREEN LIGHT INTERRUPTED THE nothingness of sound sleep, and the first of the dreams began. Surrounded and swept upward by the green light, Brad could see the riverbank below and the spot where he'd stood fishing. The river rushed and strangely parted. His body remained listless, drawn by a forceful magnetic pull that lifted him up into the air and toward a gray rotating object. The green light nearly blinded him, but through squinted eyes, he saw himself gliding closer and closer toward the gray metallic craft.

One by one, white lights flashed above him. Coldness touched his bare back, making him brutally aware of his own nakedness. The same magnetic pull pinned him down to a table of some type, a gurney maybe. Shadowy figures rushed the gurney through odd metallic surroundings. He could see his captor's heads, large and somewhat deformed. Eyes, but the eyes were not human. Large black orbs peered through a seemingly translucent veil shielding their faces.

They transported him to a room, gray tile, sterile and immaculate. The gurney stopped moving, the suctioning force evaporated, and Brad acted quickly. He leapt up from the gurney and nearly stumbled, planting his feet on the strange floor. He sprinted, sending something he didn't notice crashing to the floor with a metallic clatter. Cold, hard hands strong beyond his understanding dug into his shoulder blades, inflicting a painful pressure down to the base of his neck. Another pair of hands clutched his legs. Together, the two beings tossed him into the air. Drifting like a feather, he landed gently back on the gurney.

The suctioning force, stronger this time, enwrapped him and clutched him tightly, nearly squeezing the air from him. Brad struggled futilely, unable to move his neck, all the way down to his toes. Above him, they gathered around the gurney, two on each side, and one at the end. Solid black eyes stared intently, reducing him to nothing more than a specimen.

He felt himself hyperventilating, his breath heaving uncontrollably. Desperate cries and moans escaped him. He heard a voice in his mind.

"Calm yourself. Everything will be alright."

The shadowy female figure to his left leaned over him. Her voice spoke, yet her mouth didn't move. Her large, black eyes bore down on him. Then she moved upward and away. In her place came a robotic arm that held a sharp needle. Brad fought again, but to no avail. The needle penetrated his left shoulder, pricking sharper than a normal needle, yet the pain lasted less than seconds. The needle removed itself, as did the robotic arm. Then tranquility washed over him in waves. Calm replaced agitation. Curiosity overwhelmed fear. The figures scurried around the gurney as another device moved over him.

It descended from above, another robotic arm eliciting a whirring noise as it lowered to his waist. A suctioning device ejected slowly from it, throbbing and pulsating, and then gripping his privates. He felt the device's flowery suction, a rush like ecstasy, and then a discharge. He cried out in both painful exhilaration and release. Then, the device lifted upward and away.

The next thing he knew, he was floating down to the riverbank, his body warmed once again by the thickness of his clothes. His feet landed gently on the riverbank, where he rushed to catch his fishing rod before it became swept away.

Brad bounded up from the bed, his eyes wide upon waking. He'd been dreaming, but it was more like a memory being replayed. The dream had restored the memory of what had happened that night on the riverbank. He remembered everything. Now, he wished he hadn't.

Later that night, once Adam was asleep, he told Sheila everything. They kept no secrets between them.

"I recalled everything in the dream last night. I know that's what happened. I remember it, but when my feet touched the ground, it all became wiped away. The dream brought it all back to me."

Sheila held both hands over the lower part of her face and heaved a troublesome sigh. The look in her eyes expressed a combination of both fear and doubt. She let her hands sink to her chin, where she held them in deep thought.

"So, there's no chance it was just a nightmare?"

He shook his head, adamantly. "No. It was like it was happening again. I saw myself being pulled upward to that thing in the sky by some force, a magnetic pull. Then, I saw myself being lowered back down to the riverbank. I even grabbed my fishing rod out of the water again. Then, I woke."

"You know, stories exist all over the world, especially on the internet, of these types of abductions."

"I saw them again," he interrupted her. "I'll never forget their odd-shaped heads and frail bodies now that I've remembered them. I think they're why I wasn't supposed to remember. I know I wasn't supposed to see their faces." He described the shadowy, translucent veil that somehow protected their identities. "But I saw their eyes, big, round, black and opaque. No irises, no pupils, just eyes."

Sheila got up from the couch and walked over to a desk where she kept her laptop. She sat and internet searched the words "alien abduction." The quick typing of keys and a click of the mouse produced a multitude of hits regarding the subject. Brad sat down next to her and glanced at the screen, silently startled to realize that his fears and suspicions were not so unfounded. Abduction accounts spanning decades were published all over the world, not only on the internet, but in books, magazines, and newspapers. Brad and Sheila read about different types of abductions, everything from unexplained takings, to medical testing, to the two words that made them stare at the screen in silence—reproductive testing.

Brad abruptly broke the silence. "Enter 'Green Valley UFO incident.' The day I went fishing was a day after that mass sighting at the university. What happened to me is connected to the Green Valley UFO. I know it."

Sheila's fingers rapidly tapped the keyboard, and within seconds, articles and photos of the Green Valley mass UFO sighting and subsequent scandal flooded the page. Brad and Sheila sat reading articles about witnesses who saw the elusive gray metallic object and were exposed to radiation. They read about newsman, Marv Kincaid's involvement, and how he worked with the paranormal investigators out of Green Valley University to expose a secret nuclear testing facility within Eagle Rock. Then, articles about Dylan Rasche repeated throughout the listings.

Dylan Rasche was one of the GVU paranormal investigators. After disappearing, he was discovered twenty-four hours later, wandering around Eagle Rock Mountain. Whatever happened to Dylan had been kept hushed, but Brad soon realized that like him, Dylan Rasche may not have even known what happened to him the night he disappeared.

As they sorted through news items and images, videos of a blonde-haired woman infused the electronic page. They both remembered watching the press conference the woman gave, warning everyone about the infamous Men in Black, and then exposing the secret Eagle Rock facility. Dr. Susan Logan was her name. Brad and Sheila watched the video of the news conference a second time through its internet posting. Then, Sheila read a side article about the woman.

"It says she's not only a parapsychologist, but a psychiatrist as well," she pointed out. "She knows about this thing. She's part of it. Maybe you should speak to her. From the looks of things, it's not like she'd dismiss you."

That day, Brad shrugged off Sheila's suggestion, still reeling from the shock of the restored memory, not to mention the embarrassment. That was before the second dream began.

Six months had passed without any recurring memories or dreams. Brad secretly kept the idea of talking to Susan Logan tucked away in the back of his mind, but the longer time passed without a single recurring memory, the likelihood declined by the day. Brad hoped the memory remained behind him forever. He had no other choice but to forget it and move on for his sake, Sheila's, and most of all, their son's.

One night, as quickly as sleep overcame him, he slipped into the dream. He saw himself standing in a vast field. The winter wind whipped a light flaky snow into a frenzy. Freezing weeds and brush blew wildly in the wind's icy wrath. In the beyond, Brad glimpsed a figure walking across the field toward him. Curiously, the figure moved forward faster and faster at a pace only a dream could provide. Now, standing only feet away from him, Brad could see the figure was a girl, at least twelve years of age. She wore a zippered gray hoodie, khaki jeans, and bright white shoes. Her hair, a dirty dishwater blonde, hung loosely down the sides of her face, which remained slightly hidden from the downward tilt of her head. Brad spoke to her softly.

"Little girl, who are you? Where is this place?"

Slowly, she lifted her head. Brad's heart leapt when he saw her pale gray face. Her black eyes were rounded orbs, opaque and devoid of irises and pupils. Brad had seen those eyes before. Watching her, he felt an overwhelming sense of dread, as if his insides were suddenly being ripped away. She lifted her right hand in a beckoning gesture toward him.

"*Daddy.*" She spoke, yet her lips hadn't moved. Brad heard her clearly.

"*I'm sorry, but—*"

"*Daddy!*" Her telepathic voice grew louder, angrier this time. She pointed a long, lanky finger adamantly at him. Her eyes widened into large black pits nearly swallowing her head. Brad's heart pounded. His breath heaved faster and heavier.

Again, he bounded upward from his bed, startled awake. Sheila slept soundly beside him. He glanced at the digital clock on the nightstand—3:57 a.m. He'd been dreaming again, and he rudely awoke, remembering every vivid detail of it. Brad whipped the covers off of him, walked to the bathroom, and splashed cold water on his face. He peered into the mirror, somehow knowing that from this latest dream, there would be no waking.

Now, the idea of seeing Dr. Susan Logan no longer seemed like an option but a necessity.

———

MAKING THE CALL TO DR. LOGAN TOOK ANOTHER TWO months. Brad remembered how awkward he felt, talking to her on the phone. He should have just gone to her office at University Hospital, but he hadn't wanted to make a wasted trip if she wasn't there. He remembered her friendly, pleasant voice.

"This is Dr. Susan Logan, how may I help you?"

"Hi, Dr. Logan, my name is Brad Byers. I'm from Green Valley." For a second, Brad hesitated. "I believe I may be in need of your services," he paused, "as a psychiatrist and a parapsychologist as well."

"I see." She sounded curious. "So, Brad, how about you tell me what the problem is, and let's see if I can help you."

Brad sighed. The sound of her voice made him want to tell her everything. She would either believe him or not.

"Dr. Logan, I've kept this between myself and my wife for almost two years now. I didn't know who else to turn to. My wife, Sheila, suggested I contact you." Brad told her about finding her on the internet. "You see, Dr. Logan, I was abducted by the phantom in the sky. I didn't remember at first, but I knew I had missing time. Then, I began to remember everything in my dreams. I read about Dylan Rasche. I don't know his whole story, but they abducted me. They experimented on me. My dreams have brought this nightmare back to me."

Brad heard a dead pause on the other end of the line. Unsure of what her response would be, he could almost hear his own heart pounding.

"Brad, I'd like to see you immediately. How does one-o'clock sound?"

Brad affirmed he would be there, and within hours, he was on his way to her office. He took deep breaths as he rode the University Hospital elevator up to the fifth floor. His fingernails dug into his sweaty palms as he clenched and unclenched his hands. He really shouldn't have been so nervous; if anyone had reason to believe him, it was Susan Logan. It was just that he'd never seen a psychiatrist before or a parapsychologist, but fortunately, this one would know more about what he was talking about than he did.

The elevator doors opened, revealing the fifth floor with a nurses' station in the center hub. One young nurse stood attending the station, her attention fixed on the desktop screen in front of her. Other nurses hustled and bustled to and fro between the station, the long hallways, and patient rooms. As he approached, Brad noticed the young nurse's name tag—Ashlee.

"How can I help you?" she asked without taking her eyes away from the screen.

"I'm here to see Dr. Logan at one o'clock."

Ashlee looked up from the screen. "You're Brad Byers?"

"That's right."

Ashlee picked up the desk phone and pressed a button. "Dr. Logan, your one o'clock has arrived." She replaced the receiver. "She's waiting for you. You can go on ahead, down the hall, last door on the right."

Brad thanked her and walked slowly down the hallway. At the end of the corridor, the last door on the right suddenly opened. Out stepped an attractive mature woman, somewhere in her late sixties or early seventies maybe, with blonde hair and soft blue eyes.

"Brad?" She stuck out her hand. "Please, call me Susan."

He shook her hand. "It's nice to meet you, Susan, and thank you for seeing me."

"Likewise, Brad. It sounds like we have much to discuss." She motioned to her right with a nod of her head. "Right this way."

Following her into her office, she invited him to sit in the chair opposite her desk, while she closed her office door behind her. Then, Susan sat in her desk chair and folded her hands in front of her.

"So, Brad, before we begin, let me just say that since the Green Valley UFO business, I've heard from quite a few eccentrics, researchers, and people in general, fishing for information. You said you discovered me on the internet. Then you know about the press conference I gave and the ordeal I went through regarding the Men in Black. These factors are why I'm sometimes cautious when someone seeks me out and mentions the 'phantom in the sky.' But number one, you sounded authentic to me, and secondly, we as a team have long suspected that other witnesses remained out there, waiting to come forward." She paused, examining every aspect of his face as though she were sizing him up. "And so now, one has. Let's just say that certain aspects of your story rang true: missing time, dreams, and certainly experimentation."

"So, I'm not crazy?"

Susan scoffed and chuckled. "Brad, we're all crazy in our own way. Don't tell anyone I said that." He laughed with her. "But are you mistaken? Brad, you and others like you would also have to be mistaken about the same damn thing. You've read up on me and the paranormal team. Every word of that press conference was true. Believe me when I say there isn't much at this point that I will disbelieve. Brad, I want you to relax, take a deep breath, and begin at the beginning."

And so, he did. Brad told her everything from the riverbank to the missing time, and the dream that brought back what he failed to remember. He spoke timidly about the reproductive experimentation and the full realization of it.

"Don't be embarrassed, Brad. I realize it may be stranger for you being a member of the male species, but what they did to you was beyond your control."

"*They?* So, they're real?" Brad wasn't sure if he felt relieved that he wasn't crazy or worse because the unthinkable had just been confirmed.

"What do *you* think, Brad? Do you think you made them up in your head for no reason? Has your mind ever reached that level of fantastical creativity before?" Brad lowered his eyes and humbly shook his head. "I know this, Brad. I've never met those who manned the craft that Green Valley calls the 'phantom in the sky.' But I know the Men in Black are very real, and they have made their presences known in Green Valley and the surrounding areas for a reason, a reason we are never supposed to discover. I also know that I've listened to you, watched you, and examined you closely enough. I believe you, Brad. I know when someone's bull-shitting me, and when someone's scared to death of what they're saying. Unfortunately for you, you fit the part of the latter."

Brad glanced up at the ceiling and took another deep breath before resuming his face-to-face with her.

"There's more. It involves the second dream I had."

Brad watched her expression closely as he told her about the field and the girl walking toward him. Susan's face hardened into a more serious mask, as if he'd struck a silent chord. When he finished detailing the dream, she spoke.

"You said you read about Dylan Rasche. Obviously, like you, I am bound to Dylan by doctor-patient confidentiality. But Brad, you need to meet and talk with Dylan. I can tell you that you both have many things in common, things you both need to discuss. Next month, Dylan will release a book he's written about his experience. This would be a good way for the two of you to connect. Naturally, Dylan is working twenty-four-seven until then. So, here's what I want you to do. I want you to take this next month and keep watch over yourself and your home, like always. Be mindful of your dreams. If you dream again, write it down in detail, and call me. Either way, I want you to attend Dylan's book signing. I'll notify you of the exact date."

———

BRAD REMAINED SEATED NEARLY TWENTY FEET AWAY from the table where Dylan Rasche sat signing books. He watched the auburn-haired woman scurry over to the table, hell bent on being the first in line. She spoke to Dylan Rasche about something, something that provoked his curiosity. Brad realized by her persistence that he wasn't the only one with a story, a memory, an account no one would believe. Still, he sat patiently, waiting until the room cleared. It took almost an hour, but Brad didn't mind. He remained reluctant, even squeamish over the prospect of anyone else overhearing what he had to tell Dylan.

Finally, the last of the book groupies and aficionados staggered out of the room's double doors. Dylan Rasche's assistants wandered back and forth, in and out of the auditorium. Brad felt more comfortable now as Dylan stood, gathered his belongings, and glanced out as he approached. He'd even made an attempt at a joke.

"Ah, last but not least."

Brad couldn't tell if that was a failed joke, or if Susan had already notified Dylan that he would be there. Brad extended his hand in a handshake.

"Hi, Dylan, I'm Brad Byers. Susan Logan sent me."

Dylan wagged his finger, remembering a name that sounded familiar.

"Yes, Susan mentioned you. She said we have things in common we need to discuss."

Brad's response matched the graveness of Dylan's expression.

"More than you and I could possibly imagine."

4

PARAGON

"A FEW CAME FORWARD TODAY. BRAD BYERS WAS THE last." Following the book signing, Dylan treated Brad Byers to lunch at the campus café and listened to a story nearly identical to his own. Now, he sat in Susan's office across from her desk, conveying the events that transpired as a result of his book's release. "He told me everything."

"So, you see, Dylan, as we suspected, you were not the only one abducted by the Green Valley UFO. We knew there would be others who would come forward. Now, it looks like their stories are beginning to surface."

"Yes, but why now?" Several possibilities tumbled around inside Dylan's head, yet frustration stopped him from corralling them into a cohesive thought pattern.

"It seems as if your book has triggered some kind of an awakening to others who were affected by the Green Valley UFO. I believe you've made them feel compelled to come forward. You're now somewhat of a paragon for those who've been abducted. I assumed this would happen."

"So why didn't you just tell me about Brad? I would've liked to have talked to him immediately."

Susan reiterated her obligation to doctor-patient confidentiality. "I'm bound to both of you, Dylan. You know that. Besides, you were busy with the final wrap-up of the book, and I wanted you to hear his story for yourself, *from him*, not from me. What would be the point in hearing it twice?"

"He had the same dream of the black-eyed kid in a field, only he dreamed of a girl. The girl called him 'Daddy.'"

Dylan remembered his own dream of a black-eyed boy. The boy walked toward him from across a vast field, wearing a red hoodie sweatshirt. Black bangs jutted out beneath the hood. Black eyes glared at him, eyes that had no pupils, no irises.

"Papa!" the boy had cried out in the dream. Dylan had rudely awakened in bed, remembering every detail of the night he was abducted from Eagle Rock Mountain. The dream occurred the night the team saved Susan from the wrath of the malevolent spirit. That night, as angst and mayhem winded down, peacefulness took over, and silent relief washed over them in waves. Dylan had been able to sleep well for the first time in nearly two weeks. Then during his restful sleep, something unlocked his subconscious mind, releasing memories never before allowed to the forefront. That was nine months ago. Now, the makings of a newly brewing storm swirled around them in a spiraling invisible eddy.

Susan nodded. "So, tell me about these others who came forward."

Gripping the sides of his chair, Dylan sat up straighter as his thoughts gathered into orator mode.

"First, a woman named Nadine Parks, auburn hair, somewhere in her late thirties. She sat in front and hurried over to the table, wedging herself forward to be first in line. She told me she was abducted around the same time I was. She also hinted that she was experimented upon. She said she didn't know who else to turn to or who else would believe her. I could sense she was telling the truth. I gave her my card and asked her to come by headquarters. She agreed to tell the team the whole story, so I'm waiting to hear from her."

Thinking back, Dylan wagged a finger at Susan.

"Then this younger girl came up to me. I signed her book as she sheepishly asked if I'd heard from any other abductees since the book's release. It felt like she wanted to say more but wouldn't or couldn't. She even lingered for a moment before turning away. Then along came Brad. Those three were the only ones who stuck out to me."

Susan studied his face, sneakily trying to get inside his mind.

"So, do you think there are others besides them?"

He shrugged. "I don't know. That remains to be seen."

"I wouldn't be surprised if we become inundated with witnesses and abductees, all of them referring back to the 'phantom in the sky' and coming forward now because they'd been embarrassed or afraid before. Remember, after announcing to the world that the Men in Black were real and dangerous people, my press conference may have stopped many from coming forward. If so, I regret that, but there was no other choice at the time. You had disappeared without a trace. The team and I were frantic. I didn't know what else to do. I stood up to the MIB, and we haven't encountered them since, but that doesn't mean they're not right around the corner. For all we know, they could have been watching us this entire time. We need to remain watchful, especially since others are now coming forward."

"That shouldn't be a problem. We as a society will maintain their privacy and keep their anonymity. That's our practice."

"Yes, but you know how the MIB have an uncanny way of knowing things. We also know how they work, threatening and blackmailing others, break-ins, even hacking into computer systems. We can't allow that to happen again."

"It won't," he insisted. "Everything will remain off the electronic record."

"Good. The last thing we need is a repeat of what happened back then." Susan leaned forward. "But on the other hand, I want to congratulate you, Dylan, not only on this book but on all the hard work you put forth in trying to remember, and then putting your life back together after this nightmare. You remembered everything. You did it on your own. I'm extremely proud of you."

Dylan thanked her, insisting he couldn't have done it without her. Then, the loud electronic bleating of Susan's desk phone stirred him away from the moment. Susan answered the phone, and a familiar voice blared from the speakerphone, which she'd forgotten to turn off.

"There's a call for you, Dr. Logan, from a young woman claiming it's urgent she speak with you."

"Thank you, Ashlee," Susan responded. "You can put her through." Susan turned off the speakerphone. "Don't go anywhere, Dylan. I'm going to handle this as quickly as possible."

"Take your time."

Dylan rose from his chair and turned toward the back wall of Susan's office to examine a new painting she'd acquired. A recently discovered Russian artist she now claimed as her favorite had depicted a young woman walking through a downpour, shielding herself with an umbrella, with her back turned away from the observer. Reds, blues, purples, and yellows shimmered in the painting, as the artist was known for his vivid use of colors. Dylan immersed himself in the painting as Susan spoke in the background.

———

"THIS IS DR. LOGAN." SUSAN ANSWERED THE INCOMING call.

"Dr. Logan, my name is Jamie Cohen. I'll make this quick since I'm at work and on my ten-minute break."

"What can I do for you, Jamie?" Susan noticed Dylan abruptly turn away from the painting.

"I attended Dylan Rasche's book signing today and got a signed copy of *Abduction from Eagle Rock Mountain*. I've read most of it, specifically the inscription, and about how you helped Dylan. I convinced myself to call you."

Susan raised her index finger and used it to gain Dylan's attention. He hastened back to his chair across from her desk and sat back down.

"I see," Susan said. "So, let me guess, Jamie. In the recent past, you were somehow affected by the Green Valley UFO, am I right?"

Dylan watched her intently. Susan would've liked to turn the speakerphone back on for Dylan's benefit, but then thought of Jamie's privacy.

Jamie sighed and told her about her dreams. "Each time, I awake in my bed. But I see that thing clearly in my dreams, disc-shaped, metallic and emitting a blinding green light. And unlike most dreams, I remember everything. I'm hoping you might be able to help me."

Susan glanced directly at Dylan but spoke into the phone. "Yes, Jamie, I'd like to try and help you. I'm curious, though, as to why you didn't mention any of this to Dylan. I know he would've liked to have spoken with you more."

Jamie described her constant feelings of uncertainty and how at the book signing, she'd felt that right then and there with others gathered around would not have been the best place to talk.

"I was planning on contacting him again though," Jamie explained. "But I thought maybe I should call you first."

"With that said, Jamie, do I have your permission to tell Dylan that you contacted me and the nature of your call? I believe that both of us together will be able to help you immensely, rather than you and me working alone."

"Of course, please do."

"Great, when can you make it to my office?"

"Friday is my day off. I can make it then."

Susan scheduled her for Friday at 10:00 a.m.

"I'll see you then, Jamie." Susan replaced the receiver and glanced at Dylan, who had already put the pieces together.

"Jamie," he remembered. "She was the girl who asked if I'd heard from any other abductees, and then hesitantly turned away."

"She says your book nudged her to come forward. She's having dreams, or should I say vivid nightmares of being abducted and experimented upon, but then she wakes in her bed. She claims to have seen the UFO in her dreams, described it exactly, down to the bright green light."

"Interesting," Dylan said. "I could tell there was something about her, but do you think she might only be dreaming?"

Susan shrugged. "That remains to be seen. I've studied reports about abductions through sleep. This isn't the first time I've heard of it. Plenty of reports exist about this kind of thing. People, predominantly women, claim to have been abducted from the safety of their own beds. One can never tell if it's real or a dream because it was not an incident that occurred in the every day, out in the open, if you will. As a result, the level of shock and terror involved tends to be more psychological than physical."

Dylan had that look in his eyes again, that faraway look that clearly showed how his myriad thoughts moved in multiple aimless directions.

"I say we meet with Jamie first and try and judge the validity of her story," Susan continued. "But I have to say, just from the phone conversation, she sounded authentic. She spoke with timidity. I could almost hear the fear and the embarrassment."

Dylan nodded. "Yes, that's how she came across, timid, or shy."

"After we meet Jamie, I say we gather these three witnesses together and let them tell their stories to the entire team. After all, we were all part of the 'phantom in the sky' controversy. We need to help these people as a team."

Reflecting, Dylan shook his head and sighed. "Brad Byers, Nadine Parks, Jamie Cohen." He glanced up at Susan. "How many more of them are out there?"

"I don't think we'll ever truly know the answer to that question, Dylan. It's a secret reality that remains plainly hidden within our everyday world. But I have a feeling we're about to get another glimpse into that which lies just underneath."

5

TROY

THE TUMOR WAS GONE, VANISHED, INEXPLICABLY.

Troy Adler's mind reeled with both joy and confusion as he sat and listened to Dr. Brighton stumble through speechless bewilderment.

"Troy, to be perfectly honest with you, I don't know what to say. I've never seen this type of thing before, though I have heard of it in extremely rare occasions. Three months ago, you came to me complaining of headaches and dizziness. The MRI showed a small brain tumor on the frontal lobe. Your biopsy concluded it was benign. Now, the tumor is just not there anymore. I can't explain it."

The young Dr. Brighton shrugged, his eyes a deep blue sea of wonder. Troy felt his stomach turning. He couldn't say that he had equally met Dr. Brighton's perfect honesty. While Brighton didn't have an explanation, Troy couldn't say the same.

Troy listened as the young neurologist rambled on about "spontaneous remission" cases and the rarity of them, catching merely words as his mind backtracked through time. He remembered the devastation he felt after the first MRI, the insurmountable stress, the fear of not knowing, all of it eventually alleviated only by the revelation that the tumor was benign. After the biopsy results were revealed, Dr. Brighton insisted on waiting, and then seeing him again in three months. Another MRI would be taken at that time to monitor the benign tumor's growth and size. Then, the young doctor would determine the best way to go forward.

Troy had taken a few days off work before returning to his office. But then, being a renowned local attorney, he'd felt the need to dive back into his case load. It would relieve his thoughts of the burgeoning growth in his head. Alone in his office, he'd stayed well into the night, wrapping up long overdue paperwork. His secretary, Nicole, had left hours before. Finishing up, he gathered up his briefcase and donned his coat and gloves. He turned off the lights, and then locked the door behind him.

The parking garage was just a jaunt across the street. Troy groped around in his coat pocket for his keys as he crossed. The glow of the traffic lights to his left had cast a crimson shine off the wet October pavement. Wrenching his keys stubbornly from his pocket, his hasty hand dropped them to the ground. Troy bent over to pick up his keys, noticing how the red glimmering of the pavement had changed to green. Then, something happened. Green light exploded all around him, much too bright to be a changing traffic light.

The next thing he knew, he stood next to his car inside the parking garage, keys in hand. Yet he clearly remembered never making it inside the garage. He'd dropped his keys in the street outside, and then bent down to pick them up. Then, green light surrounded him, but it was gone now. The garage's glowing fluorescents radiated yellow light all around and emitted the sound of a thousand gathering flies. He turned and looked out at the street. Troy saw no one, but still, something felt off. Experiencing an odd sensation, he scratched the back of his head, and then glanced at his watch.

12:16, over a quarter past midnight. How was that possible?

He'd left the office at 10:30. Reaching inside his inner coat pocket, he retrieved his phone and glanced at the time. No mistake. His phone wasn't broken and neither was his watch. It was well past midnight, and Troy was missing approximately an hour and forty-five minutes.

He turned and walked back out of the garage. Looking up, the sky appeared somewhat darker than before. Only a few cars lumbered through the streets in the late hour. Time had definitely passed. Troy hurried back to his car and unlocked it. He hopped inside and fired up the ignition. The brakes of his Lexus screeched as he barreled out of the garage.

He'd nearly driven himself crazy trying to recall anything within that missing time frame. His mind drew a complete blank each and every time. Sweat slicked his forehead as his efforts would end in frustration and anger. Oddly, the issue of missing time seemed to overshadow the fact that a benign brain tumor resided in his head and could turn malignant at any given moment. Then, one night about a month later, the dreams began.

Oblivious that he'd fallen asleep on the couch, images played out in Troy's unconscious mind. He saw himself in the street, bending over to pick up his keys. The vivid green light engulfed him, blindingly iridescent. He felt a force of some kind, something swiftly lifting him upward and pulling him with the heavy draw of a magnet. He felt motionless, defenseless, as the ground he once stood upon grew more and more distant. The world lay forsaken below him.

In his dream, Troy drifted closer and closer toward a gray, metallic, disc-shaped craft. Unexplainable warmth washed over him, calming him with waves of peace and serenity. Suddenly, white lights seared above him. He felt himself moving on a gurney. Surrendering to the peacefulness, he allowed himself to be shepherded and tended to. The shadowy figures knew what they were doing. He couldn't see them clearly, but their lithe bodies were gray in color. Their heads appeared larger than normal, but maybe it was just the dream.

He'd been transported to a room, where an even brighter white light obliterated everything. Heat exuded from the light, warm heat like the sun. He felt his body tilting backwards on the strange surface beneath him. Cool, lanky fingers stroked his forehead. Lost in abandon, he drifted into a sea of oblivion. Suddenly, his legs were moving. He was walking toward his car in the parking garage.

Troy had awakened with a start, nearly rolling off his living room couch. The dream had shown him what he failed to remember. Troy recalled seeing the metallic disc-shaped craft. He remembered his immobility and the odd beings that scurried around him. They'd made him not remember. He felt sure of it. Troy knew what had happened. He'd read about this type of thing often enough. In fact, something local made the news not long ago.

Brighton's fervent astonishment snapped Troy out of it. The memory was suddenly lost as he continued to listen.

"Troy, I just don't have an explanation," the young doctor continued. "But you have every reason to be thankful. The tumor we found three months ago is no longer there."

Troy's surprise was even greater than Brighton's for a reason Troy could not explain.

"I don't know what to say, Doc." Being a lawyer, Troy knew well how to spin the truth while not revealing his hand. Though his shock was real, Troy did his best not to show that while the young doctor didn't have an explanation, he did, and it was one that not a soul would believe.

A smile spread across young Brighton's face, an expression seemingly bursting with joy.

"You're a lucky man, Troy! I'm so happy for you right now. But I still want to see you again in three months, just to make sure everything stays the way it appears right now."

Troy had no doubt that in three months, everything would still be normal. The tumor would not return. He shook Brighton's hand and assured him he would be back for his follow-up in three months. Throughout the next week, Troy remained speechlessly lost in his own amazement. One thought recurred over and over again—*why him?* He'd been singled out by beings unknown, shadowy misshapen figures that cured him of a brain tumor. Who were they? Why had they chosen him? Were they able to extract the tumor because it was benign? What if it had been malignant, would he still have been a candidate for their mysterious experimentation?

Somehow, Troy understood that he would probably never know the answers to these questions, but his mind would forever ponder them. He began to research online, and a part of him did not want to confirm the best possible key search words, yet after silent moments, he relented and typed them into the search field —*alien abduction.* After reading hundreds of abduction stories, he clicked on a link that led him to articles on alien experimentation. He read for twenty minutes, until four words outlining a section of accounts practically jumped from the page to his eyes—*The Removal of Tumors.*

For nearly an hour, he read accounts from all over the world by people who claimed to have been abducted by aliens who removed all forms of tumors, both cancerous and benign. He wondered about the authenticity of certain claims, yet many had given their accounts using their real names and whereabouts.

Then, a familiar item caught his eye. He remembered the headline from nearly two years ago. It was about the local UFO scandal that occurred right here in Green Valley. Troy began to recall the event sitting in the doctor's office, but his thoughts had been distracted by the raving young neurologist. He read the headline again.

Local Paranormal Investigator Reported Missing

Now, he sat and remembered what little he knew about what had occurred back then. Dylan Rasche, a local paranormal investigator, had been reported missing not long after a mass UFO sighting at

GVU. Whispers of UFO abduction abounded. Troy remembered something about a cover up at Eagle Rock Mountain. Then, Dylan Rasche was found, but nothing regarding his whereabouts was revealed.

Not long after these events, a young woman paid Troy a visit at his office. Ursula Masters was her name. She'd suffered radiation poisoning after witnessing an unidentified craft, spent a few days in the hospital, and recovered. Then, she arrived at his office wanting to sue someone for her exposure, whether it was those who operated the secret facility at Eagle Rock, or whether it was the government for allegedly knowing and covering it up for years. Troy got nowhere with Ursula's lawsuit. Soon after her exposure, Ursula, a friend of Dylan's, was among the thousands who witnessed the UFO hovering over Commencement Field at GVU. But it could not be proven that the Eagle Rock facility and the unidentified craft that exposed Ursula were connected in any way. Troy knew well that suing the government would get them nowhere. He'd felt for Ursula, but as time passed and talk died down, the incident had soon been forgotten.

The old headlines were trending again because Dylan Rasche released a memoir regarding the incident. In an article published only yesterday, Dylan claimed to have been abducted by the Green Valley UFO. *Abduction from Eagle Rock Mountain* was now available at bookstores everywhere.

Even though Ursula was an insider in the paranormal investigative society, Troy never asked her about Dylan Rasche's incident. Dylan's story was not Troy's concern at the time. His main concern had been Ursula, even though his legal pursuits on her behalf had led them nowhere. Now, Troy had every reason to envelop himself in Dylan's story. Troy's experience did not occur during the Green Valley UFO mayhem. It occurred within recent months. Troy didn't believe in coincidence, and now he suspected his experience and Dylan Rasche's, as well as Ursula's, were somehow connected to the same thing. Was Troy recently abducted by the same 'phantom in the sky?' He took the first step in finding out more.

Using his laptop, he signed into his Amazon account and purchased the Kindle edition of Dylan Rasche's book. Within seconds, he watched it download into his Kindle. He pressed a button and began to read.

6

DREAMS OF BLACK-EYED CHILDREN

Speaking to Susan Logan on the phone had set Jamie's mind at ease, at least for now. Susan assured her that she wasn't alone, that there were others just like her, including Dylan Rasche. She felt more relaxed, not having given the abduction dreams a single thought in over twenty-four hours. Nightfall arrived early, as it always did in late January. The sky darkened to a deep indigo, and the furnace heat radiating through her small apartment sent Jamie into a sleepy spell. She slipped into bed with Misty curling up beside her, and then absorbed herself in her plush pillows until sleep rendered her unconscious, and the strange dreams began.

The world around her appeared colorless, plunged in a drab grayness just enough to make the hazy surroundings indistinguishable. She recognized the figure coming toward her—Mother. Frantic, Mother called out to her.

"Jamie! My Jamie!"

Mother ran to her with arms outstretched. Jamie embraced her. Mother was crying.

"Mother, what is it? What's wrong?"

Mother pulled back from her.

"Jamie. Oh, Jamie." Jamie knew that sound, the desperate worrisome moan her mother made over bad news she couldn't change. Mother placed her hands on her stomach. *"Jamie, you can't keep it. Do you hear me? You can't keep it!"*

"What? What are you talking about?" Feeling the familiar pair of hands on her stomach, Jamie looked down and noticed her swollen belly. Pregnant, no, she couldn't be.

Mother cried out in horror. Then, Mother closed her eyes, opened them, and then gazed into hers. *"They're going to come and take it from you, Jamie. It doesn't matter. Let them take it. Let them take it!"* Mother's face contorted into a mask of fear and terror. Her eyes widened as her lips parted and quivered. She sobbed again. *"You don't want it, Jamie. You don't want it!"*

Jamie bolted upward from her all-too warm bed and whipped away the stifling covers. Sweating profusely, her nightgown stuck to her skin. Again, the dream was real, too real to be just a dream. Jamie clutched her flat stomach, relieved that no bulging pregnant belly protruded from her, yet this dream frightened her. She thought of the experiments and the needle, and the pressure inside her womb. She was pregnant in the dream, and Mother was terrified.

It looked like her mother, sounded like her mother, except for her words. Mother never condoned abortion. She would never have told Jamie to get rid of her child. It wasn't something she believed in. Jamie recalled Mother's exact words.

"Do you hear me? You can't keep it!" Then, Mother claimed that "they" would come and take the baby from her. *"You don't want it, Jamie. You don't want it!"*

This was no dream. Mother was trying to tell her something. Fear gripped Jamie in what felt like a wave of fire that suddenly and endlessly engulfed her. Her mind imagined the fear of having no recourse, no way of knowing what inevitable fate could be. Jamie's breathing became harder and faster. Her heart raced. She felt terror in the air around her, thick and descending like a dark, invisible cloud and stealing her breath. Her hands shook.

Breathe, Jamie, breathe, she told herself. Jamie took a deep breath, inhaling through her nose. Then, she expelled air through her mouth, and repeated her actions. Jamie stopped shaking, but now her hands curled with crippling Charley Horses. She breathed again through her nose.

Breathe, Jamie, breathe.

––––––

NADINE FOUND HERSELF WALKING THROUGH A STRANGE and unfamiliar field. The winter wind whipped all around her, yet she couldn't feel it. She could hear it, though, a ghostly howling through a wintery landscape no one would dare tread through in such weather. How and why was she here? Where was this place? She glanced around her, seeing no one. Then, a flashing glimmer against the white powdery snow caught her eye. Someone or something moved in the distance. Someone was walking toward her.

Straining her eyes to see, Nadine discerned a light-gray sweater, possibly a hoodie, and khaki pants. The figure's head remained down, watching its own feet make tracks through the snow. The closer the figure approached, Nadine noticed reddish-hair jutting out and hanging down from the sides of the hoodie—a girl.

Then, the girl stopped and turned. She stood waiting for someone, someone whose same plodding gait mimicked hers. Nadine watched as the other figure joined the waiting girl. Now, they both turned and walked together in unison. Nadine could see them more clearly now. The pair had to be in their early teens. Like the girl, the boy had reddish-hair jutting out from underneath a hoodie that seemed to match his counterpart's in color, yet he wore what looked like black, faded sweatpants. Nadine found their attire strangely drab, not to mention inappropriate for such weather. Cautiously, she took a few steps toward them.

"*Excuse me,*" she called out. They stopped walking but kept their heads lowered and their eyes to the ground. *"I'm sorry. I seem to be lost. Can you tell me where we are?"*

The girl remained mute, immobile, keeping her eyes to the ground. With a swooping motion of her head, Nadine glanced inward a bit closer. Seconds passed before the girl lifted her head and glared at Nadine with the blackest of eyes. The girl had no pupils, no irises, just black oval pits of nothing. Then, the boy lifted his head. His eyes were the same, his face nearly identical to the girl's. Fear gripped Nadine; an inner wrenching, a turbulence that erupted into a tempest inside her. Frozen from the shock, words died on her lips as her mind went blank.

Nadine studied them closely, her eyes absorbing their appearances. Their clothes seemed old, faded, perhaps in need of a wash, yet their bright-white shoes appeared new, no marks, no scuffs. Something seemed off about their complexions. Their skin shined but not quite of a flesh tone, more like a sleek whitish-gray. Nadine's apprehension skyrocketed. Something was wrong with both of them. The girl eyed her with what felt like uncertainty, almost waiting for Nadine to do or say the wrong thing. The boy's glare appeared somewhat soft with skepticism. Nadine wanted to speak, but the words failed her, her lips seemingly paralyzed. Abruptly, the boy lifted his right arm, and with his index finger, pointed at her accusingly.

"Mother!" The boy's voice sounded warped, almost mechanical, commanding a strange timbre that haunted Nadine. The girl then raised her arm and repeated the boy's actions. She tilted her head to the right and spoke with a lower cadence. *"Mother."*

Twins. The word formed automatically in Nadine's mind.

Nadine woke up in bed, her legs kicking and swishing under the sheets. She sat up, breathing hard but recognizing the safety of her bedroom. She wrestled herself out of bed and flicked on the light switch. Catching her breath, she wiped the sweat from her forehead with the back of her hand. She recalled every moment of the dream, just like the others; although this time, she couldn't say she'd been abducted. Not like before, anyway.

The strange twins had called her "Mother." Who were they? Where had they come from? Nadine thought of the baby stolen from her womb. Was she supposed to believe that the twins in the dream were hers? How was that even possible? Nadine's stolen child would be not quite two-years of age. The twins in the dream appeared to be at least pre-teens.

As the blue light of dawn peeped through the curtains, night began to dissipate, and a back and forth birdsong ushered in the morning. Sleep would be futile now. The dream had shaken her awake into full and thriving reality. She brewed coffee and retrieved Dylan Rasche's card from her purse. She would wait a few hours and call him. It was time to talk. She needed someone to know what was happening to her, before she lost her mind.

———

SUSAN HAD TOLD HIM THAT IF HE DREAMED AGAIN, TO write down the details and call her. Since then, Brad kept a pad and pencil on the nightstand next to the bed. He hadn't dreamed within those past few days, but as the winter's day and a warm night by the fireplace wooed him to sleep, tonight turned into a dreamy occasion. Sleep overcame him, and so did the sudden dream.

He stood in the living room, tossing a red plastic ball back and forth to Adam, the one he and Sheila bought for the boy at the supermarket. Sheila breezed quickly through the room, chastising them over Adam's joyful laughter.

"I wish you both would play catch outside before you knock something over."

Sheila's sarcastic sing-song tone was meant for Brad.

"Seriously, Sheila? It's twenty degrees outside."

Adam's laughter continued as Sheila disappeared into the kitchen. Then, the cheerful, *ding-dong* of the doorbell echoed through the house. Adam ran to the door before Brad could stop him.

"I'll get it!"

"No, Adam, let me or your Mother get it."

Unsuccessfully, Brad had instilled this into the boy over and over again. He felt that five-year-old Adam was too young to answer the door. Anyone could be on the other side of that door. Not to mention that Adam was not yet old enough to understand why he and Sheila turned away solicitors or Jehovah's Witnesses. On two occasions so far in his young life, Adam had admitted several such persons into the house, while bellowing, *"Mommy, Daddy, there's someone here to see you."* Brad and Sheila would enter the living room, only to be greeted by someone trying to sell them all day passes to a festival sixty miles away, or someone preaching their slightly altered version of the Good Book. Now was no different.

Adam had his hand on the doorknob before Brad could stop him. The boy twisted the knob and opened the door. Brad felt his heart stop beating. Standing on the doorstep was the girl from the field, her long, dishwater blonde hair hanging down the sides of her face. Brad could see her opaque eyes from across the room.

"No!" he yelled. *"Adam, shut the door!"*

Adam noticed her eyes as well. Brad watched as the boy took a step backward. In her strange, mechanical tone, the girl spoke.

"Hello, Adam." She held out her hand. *"Do you want to play?"*

Adam turned to Brad, a slightly convinced look on his small, round face.

"Adam, shut the door, now!"

Adam turned back to her, saying nothing.

"Come and play with me, Adam. I'm your sister."

Adam stepped closer toward the door, mesmerized by the girl.

"NO!"

Brad cried out in his sleep, the sound of his own voice rendering him fully awake. He jolted up in bed, realizing it was a dream. Quickly, he reached over and grabbed the pad and pencil. Scooting himself upward, he set the pad in his lap and wrote as fast as possible. Sheila had heard him cry out in his sleep. Now, the rapid scrawl of the pencil on paper, stirred her awake.

"What's wrong?" she asked.

"Nothing, it was just a bad dream."

Sheila sighed before turning over and falling back to sleep. Brad depicted the images in the dream, word for word, as he freshly recalled them. He would call Susan Logan later today. The time had come to discover exactly what was happening.

7

PHOENIX FROM THE ASHES

Tahoe Manoa stared at himself in the bathroom mirror, still mesmerized by the mystery that had been unfolding for the past nine months. Rejuvenation, that's what he was beholding in the mirror, a process that played out on his face, body, and mind. A Soul Sharer, that's what he was now since his soul had merged with that of the warrior chief who had once been his great-grandfather. Their two souls became as one after Tahoe battled the shadows, a feat that allowed him to conjure the chief's soul, which then produced a sort of give and take. Tahoe needed the chief's soul to defeat the looming shadows; the chief needed Tahoe's body to live once again, to see the world through Tahoe's eyes, even if only on a shared and somewhat limited basis. The end result was that Tahoe became like a phoenix rising from the ashes of age. From the moment after that fateful confrontation with the shadows, Tahoe felt a new and unexplainable vibrancy. His mind became clearer, his body more limber, his movements faster.

Rejuvenation is what he marveled at now in the mirror. Tahoe stood proudly as an eighty-one-year-old man, but the man in the mirror appeared only fifty-eight. This was how he appeared at that age, many years ago. For the past nine months, he and the investigators watched as his white hair diminished and turned gray again. Then, his more youthful black hair overwhelmed the grayness, leaving behind only gray streaks at his temples.

Nine months ago, the skin that had begun to sag, leaving pouches of puff under his eyes had grown tighter and tighter until they were no more. The few liver spots that once appeared out-of-nowhere had vanished. Little by little, the lines of Tahoe's face faded and became finer and finer. Nine months ago, Tahoe woke one morning and noticed that a decade seemed to have left him. Now, it looked as if he'd discarded another, as the age regression was not limited to his face; Tahoe's body had changed as well. The withered skin of his torso had tightened. The muscles in his chest, arms and shoulders inflated, rendering his body back to a more youthful age. After becoming elderly, his complexion had waned. Now, his skin tone returned to its original nut-brown hue, a proud aspect of his Native-American heritage.

An eruption of laughter broke from him. Not even Tahoe's renowned third eye had shown him such an extraordinary visage. He heard how his own laughter sounded full and hearty, like it used to be. He saw the wide beaming smile that, for so long, he'd remembered only in his memories. The shock he felt was a welcome one. Still, he wondered how long this would go on. Since his great-grandfather, the chief, had lived only as far as his mid-fifties, Tahoe assumed that this strange reversal of the aging process would not last much longer. In a way, he hoped he was right. Tahoe shuddered at the thought of being a small boy again.

Returning home to Arizona was no longer an option. Tahoe had no immediate family, only scattered great nieces and nephews he rarely saw. He had friends back home and many of them. Tahoe had resided in Arizona for over fifty years. It pained him to leave, but he could not go back home and face his friends and acquaintances. He'd shed almost twenty-five years from his identity for a reason he could never explain. What would he say? News of such a thing would travel fast in this day and age and place him back in an unwanted worldwide spotlight.

Tahoe remembered the words spoken by the malevolent spirit when it possessed Susan. The spirit had gazed inside him and likened him to a phoenix, a mythical bird that rises from the ashes of death and lives again. Tahoe seemed to be rising from the ashes of age, but nine months ago, a swarm of cicadas surrounded him. Cicadas were said to represent rebirth, rejuvenation, and immortality. Immortality. Was that possible? Was that what was happening? Tahoe doubted it. While he may be regressing in age, Tahoe knew all too well that death was a stranger to no one. This past summer, cicadas swarmed western Pennsylvania in multitudes. Tahoe knew well that it was no coincidence. He was the one who'd been attracting them.

He enjoyed life here in rural western Pennsylvania. The country air did him good. Living in Brett Taylor's farmhouse afforded him a peace and quiet he could enjoy without the blazing sun and the desert heat he began to feel too old to endure back home. He also relished being around people who cared about him, even if he was now the object of their paranormal studies. Tahoe insisted that what was happening to him must remain between the six of them. He didn't want to deal with the publicity when the masses discovered that world-renowned psychic, Tahoe Manoa, was getting younger. His plan was to retire into a life of quiet seclusion here at the farmhouse.

Tahoe stroked his chin, continuing to marvel at the man in the mirror when the bathroom door opened. Brett stepped inside.

"At the mirror again, I see."

Tahoe laughed. "I still can't get used to this."

"I'm afraid it's going to take more than a little getting used to," Brett said. "Come downstairs. I've got something to show you."

———

"Sit down. I want to show you the pictures I've taken of you since this all began."

Brett directed Tahoe to a chair at the kitchen table, where Brett's laptop lay open. Brett's job in the team's study of Tahoe was to photographically record his age regression. The pictures he'd taken of Tahoe would remain part of the society's archives. Many were regular photos taken at different stages of time. Brett had captured them with his digital Nikon. Then, he took more photos of Tahoe using the thermal camera he often used in ghost hunting. The thermal camera sensed heat and other factors of temperature in the photograph's setting and was capable of capturing ghostly images. As a result, Brett picked up something in those photos. After uploading all of the images into his laptop, he was now ready to reveal them to Tahoe.

Brett sat in the chair next to Tahoe and retrieved the slideshow of images. The first set of images included three side-by-side photos of Tahoe; one from a short distance away, the second was a close up shot, and the third was a split image of a left and right profile.

"This was taken a week after Susan was released from the hospital, nine months ago." Brett pointed at the images. "As you can see, there was still gray in your hair at that time. But what we never got to record was how it turned from white to gray, literally overnight."

"The lines in my face were much deeper also," Tahoe noticed.

Brett clicked on the next set of images. "This is a month later."

The next three photos showed Tahoe with even less gray hair and finer, tighter skin. Month by month, Brett clicked through the photos, and the result was the same each time. Tahoe appeared years younger with the passing of only months. Each set of photos showed the eighty-one-year-old man becoming younger, and younger. By the time Brett reached the last set of photos taken with the Nikon, they were looking at a man somewhere around the age of sixty.

Tahoe sighed. "I wonder how much longer this will continue."

"I would guess as far back as the chief wants to go."

Brett noticed the expression of sudden alarm on Tahoe's face.

"Let's hope not, my friend. One way or another, I am too old for the sock-hop."

Brett laughed. "Well, these photos are just the tip of the iceberg, as they say. Wait till you see what I picked up on the thermal stills."

Brett clicked on an image, and on the screen a thermal photo of Tahoe appeared. It depicted merely a sitting figure facing the camera. Tahoe's semblance was absorbed in a splurge of fluorescent blue color. The background was awash in a sea of equally fluorescent green.

"This is the first of the thermal images of you," Brett explained. "This was taken inside, in the living room. As you can see, there is nothing specific or unusual about this photo. But then, I took another outside on the patio."

Another click produced the nighttime thermal shot in slideshow fashion. In this photo Tahoe stood on the patio, the fluorescent blue had been replaced by a bright orange hue, while the nighttime background was drenched in deep purple. Brett explained that the difference in colors between the two photos had much to do with the outside temperature, as well as the nighttime setting. But Brett drew Tahoe's attention to something else in the photo, something obvious that Brett could not explain. He pointed to a shape; a misty form of a person seemingly emerging from Tahoe's left side. The thermal photo made Tahoe appear as a two-headed monster.

"You see this?" Brett pointed to the shape. Tahoe moved in closer to the screen. Having studied the photo long before showing it to Tahoe, Brett could make out enough details about the strange shape to explain what he saw. Brett moved his finger over the shape. "This is clearly a head. Do you see it?"

Tahoe nodded.

"And this," Brett continued, running his finger above the top of what appeared to be the shape's head. "What does this look like to you?"

Brett wanted to get Tahoe's opinion first. What Brett saw was an exuberant crown of what appeared to be feathers. Tahoe's expression seemed to melt away. Brett could see that they observed the same thing, and the shock of it turned Tahoe's gaiety into a sobering stare.

"A headdress," Tahoe replied. He closed his eyes, moved even closer to the screen, and opened them again. He turned back to Brett. "It is the chief's headdress."

"Then you and I see the same thing," Brett said. "There are several more shots like this." Brett clicked through the more random mundane images. "Check this one out." Another blue and green thermal shot showed Tahoe standing in the kitchen and a figure rising out of him from the front. "It's like we're looking at a photo of conjoined twins."

Brett noticed how Tahoe no longer peered through squinted eyes to look at something up close. Little facts like these Brett would take note of and submit them to the study.

"So, there is the proof," Tahoe said. "The chief and I are one."

"And there's one more." Brett clicked the mouse again, but Tahoe reached out and clasped his hand.

"That's enough, my friend. What I see in the photos is something I already know. I need not see any more."

Just then, the doorbell chimed through the house.

"That's what else I had to tell you," Brett informed him. "The team is outside. It's time for their random check-in on you."

Tahoe laughed. "Ah, yes, time to go under the microscope again."

"Yes, but this time, there's another reason they're here. Dylan and Susan have called a meeting. Something's come up, and it has to do with Dylan's book. Apparently, our next case has presented itself, and according to Dylan and Susan, the details are quite disturbing."

———

IN THE LIVING ROOM, TAHOE STOOD AND WATCHED Brett open the front door. Through the doorway stepped Dylan, Susan, and then Sidney, and last but not least, Tahoe's protégée, Leah Leeds. They were dressed warmly against the cold in thick coats, scarves, and gloves, all of them anxious to get near the roaring fire Brett kindled in the fireplace only moments ago. It had been a month since he'd last seen them, and as they noticed him, they ogled at the amount of age regression that had taken place in only thirty days.

Dylan laughed. "This is amazing!"

"I told you, you were immortal," Sidney joked.

"Very handsome, Tahoe," Susan said.

"I agree." Leah stepped forward and cupped his face in her hands. "I don't believe this. You look just as you did when I was a little girl."

"And physically I'm about that age again," Tahoe said. "Let's just pray I don't go back too far."

"Tahoe's afraid that the age regression will continue until he's a child again," Brett said. "I don't believe that will be the case."

"Well," Susan said. "That's what we're here to find out."

They all took seats on the couches in front of the fire. At Susan's suggestion, Tahoe sat in the loveseat as her makeshift patient. Brett started the video camera rolling. Susan had brought her black bag with her. She retrieved a stethoscope from it and listened to Tahoe's heart and lungs.

"Your heart is beating stronger every time," she said. "That slight wheeze you had in your lungs is gone."

Brett stood while recording Susan's mini exam. She took her pen-shaped flashlight and shined it in Tahoe's eyes. Then, she touched his face, examining the tightness of his skin, the texture, and how the lines under his eyes had become less visible.

"I'd like to show you all the pictures from last time," Brett said. He set his laptop on the coffee table and showed the team the pictures and the thermal shots he'd shown Tahoe. Brett traced his finger around the shape seemingly attached to Tahoe in the thermal photo.

"Tahoe and I have concluded that this is an image of the chief. This looks like the shape of a headdress as you all can see."

"Remarkable," Sidney said, looming close to the laptop.

"I'm going to have to agree with Brett," Susan said. "I think this age regression is about to taper off, if you will. Look at the first picture of you, taken last month. We all agree that you appear about sixty. Tahoe, you claim that you now appear as you did at age fifty-eight. From what I can tell, you are no longer shedding decades, but years. It has slowed down by my estimation. So, I don't think you have to worry about going back to elementary school."

"Or being adopted by one of us." Sidney sniggered with his usual sarcastic air.

"Sidney, stop teasing," Susan calmly scolded. Tahoe laughed. "Tahoe, tell me how you feel both physically and emotionally."

Tahoe told her about the changes to his body, how he felt his muscles ballooning inside him, how everywhere his skin felt tighter and more alive.

"The energy and vigor I feel is greater every day. My eyesight is what it was at that age. I no longer feel my arthritic pains. Even my voice is younger, as you can hear. Emotionally, I'm in shock, but an exciting shock. I also feel somewhat blessed in a strange way. Yet at the same time, fear of the unknown still exists within me, regardless of who I am or what I've seen and faced."

"That's understandable," Susan replied. "Brett, go ahead and take another round of photos for this month."

Brett quickly situated the video camera within its tripod and kept its focus on Tahoe. He adjusted the lighting to a more appropriate setting, and then strapped the Nikon around his neck. Tahoe sat up, and Brett took several shots of him from different angles. Then, using the thermal camera, he took a few more thermal photos as well.

"I don't know what else we could see from more thermal shots, but just in case."

"Well, that concludes my examination," Susan announced. "Dylan, I think it's time to tell everyone about what's been happening."

Susan sounded grave, yet Tahoe felt slight relief at anything to take his mind off his own predicament, anything to take the spotlight off of him. Something big was happening. He sat forward and listened intently. Dylan sat closer to the coffee table from his seat on the couch, so that everyone could hear him.

"It looks like our next case has presented itself, and I'm afraid it's all because of me. As you all know, after I was abducted by the Green Valley UFO, we all assumed there had to be others. We even predicted that these others would come forward one day. As a result of my book, our predication has come true."

8

A NEW CASE

"So, that's it," Dylan concluded. "Nadine Parks, Brad Byers, and now Jamie Cohen, they all came to my book signing claiming to have been abducted by the Green Valley UFO, or the 'phantom in the sky,' as they called it."

Dylan explained everything from Nadine's claims of abduction, to meeting Brad and sharing their similar stories, to Jamie's eventual call to Susan.

"Jamie called me while Dylan sat in my office. I'm meeting her on Friday. She's been having what she calls nightmares. She wants to know if the dreams are real or not. I suspect that Jamie may have been a sleep abductee, those who are taken right from their beds."

"I've read a lot on that," Leah claimed. "The person can never tell if it's real or a dream."

"Exactly," Susan said. "Jamie's dreams may not be dreams at all. She described the details of the Green Valley UFO perfectly."

"There could be any number of reasons for that," Sidney countered.

"Well, Sidney, I'm definitely going to find out. I also got a call from Brad this morning."

"And I got a call from Nadine," Dylan said.

"Apparently, they are all having dreams of these black-eyed children, not necessarily children, they claim, but pre-teens," Susan explained.

"And if you recall, I've had the same dream several times, about the young boy in the field, wearing a hoodie and walking toward me." Dylan paused. "He even called me, 'Papa'."

Sidney wagged his finger. "You know, I've been thinking about that ever since you told us. I've read many articles about these 'Black-Eyed Kids,' as they're called. We've all heard of them, but we've never had the chance to really study the subject." Sidney stroked his chin, as if he wanted to say something, but then thought better of it. "Many theories exist about them, but I can't seem to recall them all right now. I'm going to make that my assignment for the next meeting."

"Good," Susan interjected. "Because I'm hoping that will be Saturday, after I meet with Jamie on Friday. The three of them are invited. They've agreed to tell their stories to the entire team. I'd like us all to be there."

The investigators consented, confirming a meeting on Saturday at their headquarters, room 208. Dylan turned his attention toward Sidney.

"Sid, you seemed like you wanted to say something. What's bothering you?"

"Quite a few things," he replied. "But mainly this, what is it about this place?" They all gazed at him, not quite understanding. "Seriously, what is it about western Pennsylvania, specifically Green Valley? It's almost as if Green Valley is the heart of all paranormal activity in the country, or at least one of. What is it about this town that attracts that which is unseen, unexplained, and haunted? What is it that lies beneath this strange ground? What is this strange air that surrounds us?"

"As someone with my history," Tahoe interrupted, "I've found Green Valley to be extremely interesting, and the air has done me wonders."

Susan laughed. "I doubt we'll ever know the answer to those questions, Sidney."

"I don't mean to sound philosophical," Sidney continued. "But this small part of the country has had more than its fair share of paranormal activity, as far back as the late nineteen-sixties. I think that's something that someday, we should get to the bottom of."

"Yeah," Brett scoffed. "Good luck on that one."

Concluding the meeting, they ended work with pizza and beer. No more UFO talk or mentions of soul sharing and age regression. They would work again on Saturday. Yet Dylan could see that something was bothering Sidney, something he didn't want to mention.

———

THE BOY WITH THE SHINY BLACK HAIR AND THE RED hoodie sweatshirt stood across the road from the Taylor farmhouse, hidden by the trees of a wooded copse, watching as four people exited the big white vehicle. As he'd always been instructed, he stood with his counterpart. They were not to travel alone, not in this world. They must stick together and travel all together or in pairs. He and the red-haired boy stood oblivious to the icy temperature and the bone chilling wind while watching the black-haired man. That was his father, his Papa. That's what the main parents, the guardians, had told him.

He'd been following him. He'd tracked him to a huge domicile, where the man entered after pushing a few buttons, a place where he lived all alone. Then, he watched as the big white vehicle picked him up this afternoon and drove him here, to this farmhouse, remote and isolated amid these thick woods and boundless hills.

He watched as his Papa helped a blonde-haired girl out of the vehicle, taking her by the hand as she stepped out, conscious of her high-heeled boots upon the slick, icy driveway. She was the last to exit. Papa then helped her up the stairs to the house. From across the road, the boy noticed something about the girl.

Something about her was unexplainable. He watched her with his wide oval eyes, shiny black marbles gleaming through the falling snow. He read her with his intrusive mind. The blonde girl had three eyes, but only two were visible. Interesting, she was not quite like the rest of them.

The boy pointed and spoke. His warped, mechanical tone went unheard amid the vast and vacant countryside. "That's him. That's my Papa. But who is *she*?"

The red-haired boy studied her equally, watching as the blonde girl entered the house. "*What* is she is a better question." The same type of voice droned from the other boy, yet his tone was deeper, more haunting in its timbre.

The black-haired boy turned to his counterpart. "She knows him well. She can lead us to him. We'll follow her as well. I want to find out why she has three eyes."

———

DAYLIGHT QUICKLY TURNED TO DUSK. DUSK RAPIDLY edged upon nightfall, which blanketed the fallen snow with a great blue shadow. Sidney dropped off Susan first, then Dylan, and then Leah. After Leah safely entered the house, Sidney drove away, anxious to get home to his computer and conduct some preliminary research. Earlier at the meeting, he didn't mention what was bugging him. Sidney had read several theories about the Black-Eyed Kids, or BEK, but he wanted to make certain that he had his facts straight about those theories before opening his mouth. The fact that Dylan dreamed of a young boy calling him "Papa" weighed on Sidney's mind.

Within ten minutes, Sidney arrived home. Removing his coat and gloves, he fixed himself a cup of hot-chocolate and sat down at his desktop. He typed in the keywords, "Black-Eyed Kids" into the search engine, and a plethora of hits appeared on the screen. Most of them were detailed eyewitness accounts. People reported encountering young pre-teens with black pits for eyes and strange voices. Nearly every witness described an instant, unexplainable fear that overwhelmed them in the presence of these odd children.

The BEK would try to convince eyewitnesses to let them into their homes or cars, always with some suspicious story of how they were lost and searching for their parents or needing a ride home. Witness after witness told how they immediately rejected the bizarre kids, citing that they didn't look at all like regular teenagers, but some type of being that seemed human but not quite human. Sidney read the words of a paranormal investigator who claimed it was obvious that the children couldn't gain admittance to a home or vehicle without being invited. This drew the investigator and several witnesses to ponder the possibility that these wayward youth were vampires. Having read this before, Sidney scoffed, silently dismissing the claim.

He read through many unsupported assertions that the children were demons, minions from Hell who assumed the bodies of innocent children. Since encountering demons some years ago in Cedar Manor, Sidney shrugged off this claim, knowing well that demons didn't need to go to extravagant lengths to bring about Hell on Earth. Then, as Sidney skimmed down the page of article listings, a headline from a magazine feature caught his eye. He heard his heart pounding in his ears as he read the words.

Black-Eyed Kids — Are They Alien-Human Hybrids?

After reading the entire article in less than five minutes, he closed his eyes tightly and then opened them again. He hadn't imagined that he'd read it, not now, and not before. The article and its words remained on the screen. He'd been hoping that he'd been wrong about reading it the first time. He'd even wished that once he searched for BEK info online that no such article existed. He would've been wrong about this possible theory existing, but he wasn't. The author of the piece was another paranormal investigator, one more reputable and well-known than the vampire theorist. A history of bestselling books adorned his resume.

Sidney moved his mouse and pointed the arrow at the PRINT option. He printed out enough copies to distribute at Saturday's meeting. It seemed much easier than sending it to everyone's phone. Besides, he didn't want Dylan to see this without his being present. He put one copy aside, specifically for Dylan. A reason existed as to why the black-eyed boy called Dylan "Papa" in the dream. Sidney silently prayed that he hadn't found it.

9

THE CHILDREN ARE WATCHING

THEY POSSESSED STEALTHY YET STRONG BODIES resilient to the earthly cold and ice and oblivious to the burning sun, bodies unlike those who inhabited this world. This was one of many gifts obtained through their genetic configuration. The guardians had explained much to them, calling them miraculous achievements, perfect combinations of what thrived above and what dwelled below. The guardians also explained how they were created and had even told them why, though they were never to discuss it. They were strictly forbidden to ever reveal the reason.

The guardians had granted them temporary permission to explore this world and research, and they were not the first to whom this opportunity was granted. Countless others roamed and investigated this world before them. Each new generation was awarded this privilege. Now, it was their turn. Like their older brethren, they remained resilient to the icy cold and unaffected by the searing heat, their bodies more than adaptable to the earthly atmosphere. They roamed, staunchly unafraid of the rough and often dangerous aspect of this society. Such instigators were no match for them, nor were those who, from the shadows, preyed upon children. Fear abounded in those who laid eyes on them, and fear is what the children wielded so aptly. But the black-eyed children had been warned not to show their anger, their strength, or their unearthly abilities. They'd also been warned not to interfere.

The female guardian, with the soft, soothing voice, who sang lullabies to them during their infancy, had given them final instructions. One of six guardian parents they'd ever known, her voice almost sang with serenity, yet her point remained absolute and unyielding. She spoke fluently with her mind.

"All of you have seen visions and dreamed of your biological parents, those who have helped to create you. This outcome was expected. You have seen them in your dreams. You know who they are. While they mean you no harm, they are unaware of your existence. That's why it remains essential that you do not contact them. It is not the time to reach out to them. Their world is not yet ready."

The black-haired boy had stood side by side with the others and listened. His red-haired counterpart stood to his left and asked a question telepathically as was the custom.

"Guardian Mother, our biological parents have been chosen from this small part of the world. Is there a reason for this?"

"There is a reason for everything," she responded in her lulling tone. *"But that reason is not to be revealed, not until such time as the earthly world is ready."*

The black-haired boy had always wondered why he and the others could communicate telepathically with the guardians, yet they couldn't read their minds. The children could read each other's minds, just not those of the guardian parents. He obliterated his thoughts and focused his mind, projecting an invasive push toward the Guardian Mother. He felt his attempts being blocked by a great gray wall. The Guardian Mother looked sharply at him, though her expression never wavered from one of tranquility and understanding.

"Remember my words, Young One," she advised. Her lips never moved. He felt like she reached in and touched his soul as her

black oval eyes bore down on him. *"You must watch and learn, not interfere, or you will become lost. And you must never, never do that which is strictly forbidden."*

He stood across the road from the Taylor farmhouse with his red-haired counterpart, remembering the Guardian Mother's words of admonition. But an overwhelming surplus of curiosity flourished within him. It always had. He'd always been the one more infused with enthusiasm, the one who possessed a greater willingness to learn and discover. Most often, the guardians had accepted it as healthy eagerness, but sometimes their watchful eyes lingered on him, their expressions denoting something unspoken, as if they were secretly apprehensive of him.

Then, enwrapped in the deep green sea of light, he and the others had descended through it from leagues above. When the green light evaporated, black-eyed children stood in a vast field, the world covered in a white blanket around them. They'd bent down, scooping up handfuls of the icy white powder that covered the ground and crunched beneath their clenching fingers. Earthly precipitation, it was the first of their research observations.

Now, he and the red-haired boy had stood for hours watching the Taylor farmhouse, waiting for their subjects to exit the premises. Turning their black eyes up to the sky, they observed how quickly it darkened during the earthly winter season. Nightfall approached. It would not be much longer. Suddenly, as if their silent thoughts had triggered it, yellow light beamed from the farmhouse's front porch, casting a golden glare over the snow-covered lawn.

They watched as the subjects exited the farmhouse. The heavy man with the odd-looking spectacles stepped out first, followed by the older blonde woman. Then, the man he called "Papa," and the girl with the strange third eye followed. Each of them climbed into the large white vehicle from different sides. Quickly, the vehicle fired up, its engine purring while front and back lights blinked and signaled its mechanical pulse. The vehicle eased backwards from the driveway, and then positioned itself in its desired direction, south. The boys could see the heavy man piloting the vehicle, the older blonde woman beside him, yet the other two passengers remained unseen. The vehicle's engine roared as it drove off down the road, a slight trail of exhaust billowing behind it.

They maintained their objective to follow them, especially the girl with the third eye. She could lead him to the father he'd met in his dreams. But catching up to them was not possible, not on foot. Yet he and his counterpart were not without options. Like the blonde girl who had caught their attention, the boys were also endowed with the gift of foresight. For them, it was a natural ability, but for the blonde girl to possess the same gift remained a mystery. Were there others like her? It would stand to reason. If so, then why did so few of them exist in a world full of those unable to see the future, those who remained unaware?

The black-haired boy stepped out from behind the wooded copse and onto the road, watching as the vehicle disappeared. He turned to his counterpart.

"Gaze with me," he said.

The black-haired boy raised his head slightly toward the burgeoning full moon, the light of which had turned the twilight scene into a soft blue winter land. The boy's black oval eyes opened wide and gazed into the night, projecting his sight through time and space, stealing quick glimpses of a certain future. They'd all done it before. It was like grasping the fabric of time and using it to climb slightly upward to peep at what had yet to be revealed. Thin sheets of falling snow reflected in his shiny black eyes, sleek like onyx. Just behind him, the red-haired boy followed his lead. Now they stood together in the road, using their minds to follow the vehicle's path through its nearest future.

The visions were quick and hazy, but the black-haired boy had always stood proudly proficient among those able to clearly interpret the resulting images. He saw the vehicle speeding through desolate winter roads. He saw it cruising through spiraling paths, all of which led to a gated community. "King's Haven," the sign read. There, the heavy man left off the older blonde woman. The man he called "Papa" stepped out from the vehicle and took her vacated seat in the front. The vehicle moved swiftly again, traveling roads that changed with every second that the vision progressed. Soon, he saw the sprawling domicile again, the one they'd watched, the one that belonged to Papa. He watched as Papa got out, and the young blonde woman took his front seat. The vehicle waited as Papa pressed a few buttons and stepped through a gate, disappearing in the darkness.

"Do you see what I see?" the black-haired boy asked. His counterpart nodded. "We must closely follow the vehicle with our minds from this point. We know where *he* lives. Now we must discover where to find the girl."

The red-haired boy stood closer to his counterpart. The vision belonged to both of them, and they watched it together now, as if it were a film displayed on a screen. They saw the white vehicle pulling away from the sprawling estate, its tires plowing through the brownish-slush of wintry roads. Down an immense hill, the vehicle traveled. The boys marked spots and signs in their minds: Morgan's Café, Grant Avenue, and a stoplight at the bottom of the hill. They observed the vehicle stopping before a round red traffic light. When the light switched to green, the vehicle drove over a long bridge, one cradled and supported on both sides by black iron railings. The bridge led to an equally long, two-lane street that unfolded for half a mile.

The boys observed another road, one that twisted and turned into a small valley filled with pine and spruce trees. They'd already learned of this world's botany and geology. They'd heard it all from those who'd come here before them. A smaller two-lane road led through a valley of trees, and the vehicle climbed up another hill and into a residential area, where quaint yet stylish cottages sat snugly and remotely. Streetlamps glared yellow and white, distorting the vision for mere seconds. Then, the moment they'd hoped to see with their minds presented itself.

The vehicle stopped in front of a cozy white cottage with light-blue shutters. A light glowed from inside. The blonde girl stepped out of the vehicle's passenger side and stood talking to the heavy man still seated behind the wheel. After a few moments, she shut the vehicle's door, turned, and walked to the front door. The vehicle waited. The heavy man sat watching her enter the house. The girl opened the front door and waved from the porch. The vehicle drove away as her front door closed.

The black-haired boy wrested himself away from the vision as a slight pain sliced through his head. He turned to his counterpart who had done the same.

"*That* is where she lives. We'll follow the same route as the vehicle did when it left my father's estate. Do you remember it as clearly as I do?"

The red-haired boy nodded, turning his head up to the sky again and gazing as if there were more to see. Then, he lowered his eyes to meet those of the black-haired boy.

"It will take us a while, hours as they call it," he said. "The sooner we walk the better."

"Let us walk then," the black-haired boy replied. "We'll be there before the night ends."

———

WITHIN NINETY MINUTES, THE BLACK-EYED BOYS STOOD outside Dylan Rasche's estate once again, watching and contemplating, attempting yet resisting. They stood silently waiting to espy any passing movement within the soft glow emanating from inside. Then, the red-haired boy broke the silence.

"Why not just approach him? We're here now." His haunting, mechanical tone echoed through the icy quiet.

Silence followed. The black-haired boy simply stared at the sprawling estate, his black eyes fixed, seeking to see something inside from outside. Finally, he responded.

"No. He is not ready. I feel his fear of me in the dreams.

Besides, it would ruin our chances of studying the girl. If we appeal to her more understanding feminine side, she may bridge the gap between him and me."

More silence.

"And if that doesn't happen?" The red-haired boy spoke, but also kept his eyes fixed on the immense domicile.

Silence continued.

"Then we continue with our agenda."

———

ONCE INSIDE HIS LONELY FORTRESS, DYLAN WENT straight to his office-study to catch up on recently neglected paperwork. He answered a few emails from his students, one from his publisher, and then the subject line of another email stood out in all caps.

I READ YOUR BOOK. WE NEED TO TALK

Dylan didn't recognize the sender, but early feedback usually didn't come with an adamant invitation to talk. He opened the email and read. The email's author introduced himself as a local attorney. Dylan thought of the possibility of legal action by someone connected to Eagle Rock Mountain or the secret facility. He continued reading, struck by the words that came next.

> *Prof. Rasche, I decided to write to you after finishing your book. I have also been abducted by the same craft you described, but my experience remains drastically different from yours. I can only describe my own experience as miraculous, one that may have saved my life. I would rather meet with you in person than reveal the extraordinary details here in an email. You are the first and only person I will reveal my story to, as I am not interested in public attention.*

Dylan stopped reading. Something distracted him from the email. The inexplicable feeling of being watched, as if unseen eyes hovered over his shoulder, made him turn around in his chair and focus his attention on the window of his study. The window faced directly out at the front gate. Something about the window seemed to silently beckon him. He stood up and walked over to it, his steps seemingly involuntary. He opened the blind and peeped out at the front gate.

There was nothing there, nothing except the slow spiraling snowfall.

———

SIDNEY LEFT LEAH AT HER DOORSTEP THREE HOURS ago. Like always, she'd convinced him she didn't need to be escorted into the house. She was a big girl. But when she got inside, she quickly flicked on all the lights, locked the door, and searched through every room in the house, making sure she was alone. Old habits die hard, especially when you were a young, single woman who lived alone. Deep down, she felt sure that her third eye would have shown her danger, if any existed. But she learned early not to depend upon her psychic ability. She could think back on many events in her life and her career as a paranormal investigator that she hadn't foreseen. Yet after the strange day it had been, she had no intention of drudging up the past because oddly enough, that's exactly what was about to happen.

So, other abductees with stories similar to Dylan's had come forward. Leah felt the slightest wave of déjà vu. It wasn't long ago that they predicted the emergence of other witnesses either threatened into silence, or abductees too fearful or embarrassed to speak out. That time had come, as Dylan's published account drew them out like ants after a rainfall. Tonight, she would remain neutral and allow the stories to tell themselves. Susan and Dylan swore by these emerging testimonies, but between her, Sidney, and Brett, they would easily spot any that came from attention getters or overzealous enthusiasts.

She felt the slight buzz of the one-too-many beers she'd had at Brett's house, but right now, it provided her with just the right amount of wooziness she needed to relax and eventually sleep. She'd had a quick shower after her brief paranoid inspection of the house and all its rooms. Now, she'd spent the last two hours on her couch, watching a movie about seven strangers who wind up at the same hotel, infamous for its mysterious past. The film had held her undivided attention, and now she couldn't get it out of her mind. She thought back on it, marveling at its mystery while mindlessly surfing through TV channels.

The abrupt and repetitive clang came from her dining-room clock, announcing the midnight hour. Leah felt almost too comfortable to rise from the couch and ready herself for bed, especially as the furnace heat transformed her quaint little cottage into a cozy haven against the freezing winter outside. She lounged a little longer, relishing the late hour's tranquil lull.

The twelfth clanging chime sounded, and now only the rambling pitch of a TV advertisement filled the room. She would get up from the couch, just as soon as she felt the needed burst of energy.

KNOCK, KNOCK, KNOCK

She jolted, startled by a sudden and rude rapping on her door. Three thuds pounded slowly, one right after the other, not rapidly like normal knocking. Nearly leaping up from the couch, her heart beat into a full and thriving pulse, rudely awakened from the snug softness she lounged in. She glanced over at the door. Who could it be at this hour? Sidney wouldn't return hours later without calling first. Her nearest neighbor was a quarter-mile down the road. And though she worried constantly about her father, she'd received a text from him, telling her that he was calling it a night and would catch up with her in the morning. Who could be outside her front door at this late hour?

KNOCK, KNOCK, KNOCK

This time, the rapping sounded harder, more forceful. She stood by the couch, contemplating whether or not to answer the door. If she glanced out the side window, whoever was there would most likely see her. The unknown visitor would keep knocking, seeing the light from the dim lamp she'd left on in the living room and the glow from the TV. Too late to turn them off, she felt trapped. Her nerves twitched as she stepped slowly toward the side window.

Leah gently lifted the light lacy curtain that covered the window. Her porch light was off, yet the moonlight illuminated enough for her to see two young boys standing outside her door. They wore mere hoodie-sweatshirts against the cold and hung their heads down low, making it impossible to see their faces. Young boys, she thought. From what little she could see, they looked no more than thirteen or fourteen. Could they be lost? What would bring them here to her door in the dead cold of a winter night? Something told her not to answer the knocking, but what if they needed help?

Leah let the curtain fall back into place. Then she drew her head back and closed her eyes, seeking out images through a sea of blackness. She saw whiteness descending in spirals, feet forging one after another through the night, making footprints in the fallen snow. They'd walked here. Strangely, she saw Dylan entering the gate of his estate, an image she witnessed earlier in real time. Then, the images abruptly stopped, cut off as if someone had flipped an off-switch in her mind.

The rapping boomed through the house with a persistent fervor. Creeping fear constricted her insides and weakened her knees. Her first thought was to call Sidney or Dylan, but she'd left her phone in her purse. She'd left her purse in the kitchen. Then, a strange sounding voice called from outside.

"We know you're in there. Please let us in."

Leah stepped to the left and positioned herself in front of the door. She closed her eyes again, this time attempting to gaze *through* the door, much like she had two years ago when she'd seen the Men in Black. Now, utilizing everything inside her, she gazed hard, but saw nothing. The insistent pounding continued with a slow, non-stop repetition. How odd it sounded, as if the boy was unaccustomed to knocking.

Now, Leah experienced a combination of both fear and anger. Who did these vagrants think they were pounding on her door and demanding to be let in after midnight? She flipped the porch light on and in the rashness of irritation, unlocked the door and whisked it open wide enough to see them, her anger and her fear seemingly locked in battle. The boys kept their heads down, their eyes focused on the porch floor.

"We need your help. Let us in."

Fear froze Leah in place. There was that voice again, warped and somehow mechanical, similar to the sound produced by electronic distortion. Haunting in its tone, this voice sounded more demanding, devoid of the initial eerie politeness of the first voice. This was the voice of one who controlled.

"Who are you? What's the problem?" Leah spoke quickly and sternly, a psychological trick to ensure that she wouldn't lose her nerve and give in to fear. Within the porch light, she noticed one boy's black hair jutting out from his red hoodie-sweatshirt. The other boy had reddish hair, and like his friend, he also wore a similar sweatshirt, a faded drab-gray in color and seemingly worn. Their apparel appeared more appropriate for October, rather than the frigid arctic blasts of January.

Neither boy responded. They kept their heads down in silence. The uneasiness Leah felt from the beginning had not subsided but rapidly intensified, watching these young, silent strangers. Her heart pounded. This moment didn't seem real. Within an instant, she went from feeling that anything *could* happen to feeling that something horrible was about to happen. Something was definitely not right about the two boys in front of her. She opened the screen door slightly, but only far enough for her to quickly slam it shut if she needed.

"Again, what do you want from me?" Leah spoke again, ready

to shut both doors and call the police if the boys' silence continued.

Slowly, the black-haired boy lifted his head. The red-haired boy did the same. Fear gripped her pounding heart. She felt her blood freeze. Big, black, oval eyes glared back at her. Pale, ashen faces snugly framed beneath their hoods. Leah's third eye reacted with an instant flash, and in that second, she saw inside their bodies—bloodless. Their bodies contained no human blood.

"Take me to my father." The black-haired boy's warped tone heightened the chill Leah already felt inside, one that equaled the January cold. The haunting voice had uttered a demand, one she didn't understand. The boy sounded obstinate, somehow convinced that she *owed* him.

Leah pulled the screen door shut and quickly slammed the front door. She fastened the dead bolt, and then linked the chain just inches above it.

"Leave now or I'm calling the police," Leah yelled through the door. "I know them well. It won't take them long to get here."

"Why do you have a third eye?" The voice of the other boy called out from the porch. The question hit her like a shockwave. She trembled, standing only inches from the door. They knew about her. They *knew* what she possessed. They hadn't known because they'd randomly heard it through the grapevine or read her memoir like most people. Those solid black eyes had sized her up when they'd gazed directly at her. They'd assessed her. She had drawn *their* attention.

Leah ran to the kitchen, snatched her purse from the back of a stool, and quickly retrieved her phone. She ran back to the side window and peered once again through the curtain. They were gone, both of them, in a matter of seconds.

Why had she seen the afterimage of Dylan walking through his front gate? Leah suddenly thought back on tonight's meeting. Witnesses came forward, claiming to have dreams of black-eyed children, roughly in their pre-teens. Dylan dreamed of a boy wearing a red hoodie, a boy who called him "Papa." Leah took a deep breath as she trembled slightly. Had the black-haired boy been referring to Dylan?

Maintaining her gaze through the window's curtain, she saw no one, but she would keep the porch light on all night. She remained hesitant about calling the police, especially if those boys were somehow connected to the current case unwinding before them, and especially if Dylan would be somehow affected. Sidney, she would call Sidney.

———

WHO WOULD BE CALLING HIM NOW, JUST SHORTLY after midnight? Sidney sat late into the night at his computer, finishing up a final outline of a speech he was to give next week. Leah's picture flashed on his phone's screen. Accepting the call, he skipped the usual and outdated, "hello."

"Let me guess, you left something behind in my van?"

"Sidney! They were just here, outside my house!" Sidney heard the fear rising in Leah's voice as she breathed hard between words.

"*Who* was just there?"

Sidney thought of the MIB, remembering how they'd stalked the team two years ago. He wasn't prepared for Leah's response.

"Those black-eyed kids, BEK, or whatever you call them. Two of them just knocked on my door, asking for my help." Leah's heavy breathing crashed like static through the phone. "They had black eyes, not normal eyes, just black pits, and pale faces." Using a flurry of words, Leah described the boys and their odd voices. "The black-haired boy demanded that I take him to his father."

Sidney felt his insides plummet. "Listen to me," he said. "Are they still outside?"

"I don't think so. I went for my phone and they were gone within seconds. They knew about me, Sidney. One of them asked why I had a third eye. These so-called children are watching."

"Keep the door locked, and don't answer it. I'm coming over."

"I'll watch for you. What do you think this all means?"

Sidney opened his mouth, and then hesitated. The strange boy on Leah's doorstep had mentioned his father. Leah was right. The children were watching, just like the Men in Black two years ago. Were they listening also?

"I'll tell you when I get there."

10

A STARTLING THEORY

Sidney didn't need to worry about waiting on the front porch in the frigid weather. On the other side of the door, Leah quickly unbolted the lock, and with a loud clack, unhooked the chain when she recognized him. She let him in, and then hastily shut and relocked the front door. Nervously, she turned and blocked the door with her body, backing herself firmly against it, as if the deadbolt and chain were not enough. Without saying a word, he handed her a copy of the article he printed out earlier. Sidney watched as her big blue eyes widened when she read the headline.

"What?" The word dragged from her lips in a whisper, the sound of soft-spoken surprise and blatant bewilderment.

"I didn't want to mention this earlier at the meeting. I'd read an article on this theory before, but it was so long ago I wanted to be sure. After arriving home from Brett's, I searched the internet." He paused before continuing. "I thought of Dylan's dream as I read this."

Leah cupped her right hand over her mouth in shock. She told him about envisioning Dylan walking through his front gate. "In my mind's eye, I saw exactly what I saw when we dropped Dylan off tonight. That moment was connected to those kids outside my door. In my vision, I saw them walking here. I think they followed us, Sid." Leah paused as unspoken conclusions lay buried between them. "The black-haired boy wanted me to take him to his father. You don't think—"

Sidney gasped with frustration. "I don't know what to think." He felt himself being swayed by the slightest stirring of apprehension, quickly becoming the weaker arm being pinned down in an arm-wrestling match. "I don't think we should get ahead of ourselves, not yet."

"Is that the real you talking or the fear we're both feeling right now?"

She knew him so well. "Leah, I can't help feeling the need to remain cautious. This theory is just that, a theory."

"An uncontested theory by one of the nation's top paranormal investigators," she rebutted. "The man specializes in UFO abductions."

"And he theorizes that these BEK are alien-human hybrids, the manufactured offspring of those who have been abducted. He maintains that through genetic and reproductive experimentation, the inhabitants of these strange crafts have merged human and alien DNA, creating hybrid offspring who live out their existences beyond our world. Yet he has no proof. And as investigators ourselves, we cannot rule out other theories that exist."

"Vampires? Seriously, Sidney?"

Sidney closed his eyes and shook his head. "That's not the theory I'm talking about." By now, they'd already eased away from the door and sat down on Leah's living room couch. Sidney pointed to the article. "There's another theory regarding those strange kids, one that could use attention from your own experience."

Leah held the copy of the article in front of her, speed-reading through the paragraphs.

"Demons." She turned her eyes away from the page and gazed

up into the air. Sidney watched as her brilliant mind thought backwards, encapsulating and then discerning a series of lifelong events within seconds, marveling at how she gazed with her third eye into somewhere he would never see. She lowered her head and shrugged. "I don't know, Sid. I felt an overwhelming sense of fear when I encountered those kids, but I can't really attribute it to anything demonic. The two boys had two different personalities, one stronger and more demanding, and the other seemed docile and even-toned. I think back on the demons we fought in Cedar Manor. They made no excuses for themselves. We knew they were demonic presences from the beginning. They were anything but ambiguous."

About this, Sidney knew she was right. He considered the same thing earlier. "The theory asserts that these demons have taken human form, whether by assuming the likenesses of the kids you saw tonight or possibly possession."

"And how long or successful would such a possession be, Sidney? Did we not learn anything from what happened to Susan nine months ago? And if the demon's objective is to deceive, then why not don the disguise of smaller, younger children and gain more sympathy? Why take the forms of pre-teen kids often misjudged by society? I'm not buying it. I remember what I felt when I faced those demons in Cedar Manor. I felt strangely righteous, ready to fight them, ready to vindicate myself. I felt no fear of them, only repulsion." Leah's misty eyes drifted away from the past and back toward Sidney. "I felt an instant fear around these kids, a fear of the unknown; as if they were something my human mind could never understand."

"Dylan detailed his dream of the boy in his book," Sidney said. "Even though he didn't quite understand the dream, he knew for sure it was connected to his abduction. One of the abductees experienced a similar dream and sought him out."

Leah laid the printout on her coffee table, sat back, and let out a long sigh. "So, now, the abductees who've contacted Dylan and Susan all claim to have dreamed of these black-eyed kids. The boy wanted me to take him to his father, which means, these children are seeking out their parents."

Sidney stared at her, hoping he wouldn't have to spell it out. Surely, she'd thought of the obvious. He waited seconds before countering.

"There's one problem with that theory. The Green Valley UFO incident was only a couple of years ago. You described these kids as pre-teen. Aren't they a little old to be the abductees' hybrid offspring?"

"How do we know what we're dealing with, Sidney? We have no clue as to what kind of biology they possess, or how they live, breathe, or age, for that matter. Aren't we witnessing Tahoe getting younger by the day? Come on, Sidney, we know far better by now than to rule out anything."

"Then, wouldn't that include vampires?" Sidney's comment lacked his usual smart-ass comical stab. He intended to prove a point to her that unless certain possibilities could be ruled out, all things must be considered.

Leah let out a long, exasperated sigh. "Sidney, *I saw inside them.* I'm not drawing any conclusions from it, but they were bloodless. *Their bodies contained no blood.*"

Sidney shrugged, silently feeling his usual smart-ass irony spring to life.

"Maybe it was feeding time."

Leah slapped her hands over her face. "UGH!" Sidney sniggered under his breath. Leah yanked her hands free. "God, I pray we soon realize what it is we're dealing with."

Sidney had always been the skeptic, the one who shied away from religion and all its claims. Nine months ago, he had somewhat of an epiphany, praying for the malevolent spirit to leave Susan's body, begging God to let her survive. His prayers had been answered. But now, his thoughts and emotions bounced back into a state of confusion.

"I wonder how much God actually has to do with this," he said.

"Come on, Sidney. You know the Bible. God created the universe and everything in it."

She had him on this one. Genesis was a book Sidney studied laboriously from as far back as grade school, thanks to his devout parents.

"One way or another, I have a feeling we're about to find out."

———

THEY'D WALKED FOR MILES ON FOOT, UNAFFECTED BY the biting bitter cold, undeterred by the lengthy distance they'd quickly put behind them. Their instincts served them well, eventually leading them off the roads and onto familiar terrain, wooded areas where hidden pathways led them to the field, the ground zero on which they'd first arrived. They trudged even deeper through the snow here in the field. Here, the snow was unattended to, allowed to cover the unending grassy terrain and amass into a great sea of white. The crunch beneath their feet sounded even louder here in the field. Here in the field, the four of them had gathered themselves and sent out telepathic messages, messages intercepted through dreams.

At the far end of the field, the boys walked along another pathway, one that winded down and led them to the base of Eagle Rock Mountain. It loomed high above them, a silent giant that stood forever, a magnanimous focal point the guardians once studied from afar. The mountain's base offered them yet another path, an incline that led to a cave. The cave sat high and far enough away from the world, the perfect abode to keep them all safely and remotely hidden. As the two boys approached the entrance, the smoke from a lighted fire inside swept out toward them.

Iona stepped out from the cave, her red hair hanging down the sides of her hoodie, her face a female match for her red-haired brother, Indrid. Indrid was his research partner and cohort in tonight's activity. Lingering behind Iona, the much fairer Medea stood silently, waiting to hear any news. The four of them remained clad in similar clothing, those of the so-called sweatshirt variety provided to them for their mission. Clothes that had been gathered from research activities here on Earthly ground, even possibly stolen from subjects through experiments the guardians had conducted. Medea was dressed no differently, though her blondish hair hung longer from her hoodie. As Iona's research partner, she often trailed behind her, lagging her long, slender form in a somewhat clumsy fashion. Iona stood awaiting the news, her expression eternally skeptical.

"Orion, what's happened?"

"The girl with the third eye, she rejected us," the black-haired boy responded.

"We could feel her fear. It surged from her in waves," Indrid added.

"And so did her ignorance." Orion spoke blatantly, seething with impatience and irritation.

"They are not ready for us," Iona said. "Indrid and I both saw it in our mother's dreams."

"And I did as well." Medea's voice echoed from the background. She took a few steps forward. "The dream of my father was quick. I knocked on the door. I saw my brother. But the door was slammed shut against me."

"They are too afraid, Orion." Indrid spoke with his usual calm and even tone. "They fear the unknown. Even she who is attracted to the unknown has an underlying fear she doesn't realize. They assume they are alone."

"Don't you see, Orion?" Iona's familiar insistence irked him. "We are part of them, and we are also part of the guardians, those who created us. This is why they will never accept us."

Orion felt his anger rising. His black eyes gleamed in the moonlight. Stoic, unreadable features formed into a menacing frown. "Then they will be forced to accept us."

———

THE DARK OF NIGHT LOOMED THICKER AND BLACKER ON Eagle Rock Mountain. Once the stationary lights around the mountain temporarily extinguished themselves, only the moonlight and the fallen snow cut dimly through the near pitch-blackness, casting a soft indigo glow in the dark. Green Valley slept, as did those who dwelled on the mountain. The soft, howling winter wind echoed across the mountain.

A bright green ray of light suddenly pierced the darkness and infringed upon the mountain's peaceful slumber. Hovering just above it was a gray rotating craft. Disc-shaped in appearance, it spun the great green light in all directions, searching and attempting to pinpoint those who had gone astray. The green light focused on the entrance of a cave many feet below. The craft lingered briefly, watching.

Then it was gone.

11

FRIDAY'S APPOINTMENT

JAMIE HAD BEEN COUNTING OFF THE DAYS UNTIL Friday, and finally, it arrived. Today was the day when she could let everything out; let someone else judge her dreams, if that's what they were. Today, she no longer had to keep them trapped inside her mind, recurring in vivid snippets at the oddest of moments. Today, she hoped to discover whether or not the dreams were real, or if she was, in fact, crazy. Either way, Jamie was prepared.

Arriving at University Hospital, she managed to quell the slightest stirring of her nerves. Don't be nervous now, she thought. The time had come to let it all out. No more would she be a prisoner to the dreams. It was time to fight, to be armored with knowledge and certainty, yet Jamie continued to tremble inside. Her frequent attempts to forge a hard, tough exterior often dissolved, melted away by the heat of her sparking nerves. She would hyperventilate, until her trembling heightened into a full-scale shaking fit.

Outside the door of Susan Logan's office, Jamie remembered giving permission for Dylan to be present. Dylan was who she'd reached out to, and if her dreams were real, they both shared a connection. Jamie felt as if she could use all the help she could get.

After three rapid knocks, a female voice from inside told her to come in. Jamie entered as the blonde woman behind the desk rose from her chair. A strikingly attractive older woman, she appeared much younger than her real age. Across from her desk sat Dylan Rasche.

"Jamie, I presume?" the woman asked. Jamie nodded. The woman extended her hand; Jamie shook it. "I'm Susan Logan. And of course, you already know Dylan." Dylan stood and greeted her. Susan pointed to a small area across the room. "Jamie, how about you sit in the middle of the couch over there? I think you'll be more comfortable. Dylan will sit at the end of the couch, and I will sit across from you."

Approaching the plush, tan-colored, leather couch, Jamie noticed the painting on the wall. A girl walking and holding an umbrella against the pouring rain, embroiled in a flurry of vivid and shimmering watery colors. The girl in the painting appeared to be so relaxed, so tranquil, striding through the heavy downpour that engulfed her—so unlike *her*.

She and Dylan sat where Susan suggested. Then Susan sat in the chair she purposely placed in front of the couch.

"Jamie, before we begin," she said. "I just want to clarify something. It's rare that a third party is given consent to observe the session of another, but since your issue pertains to Dylan, and he and the team are able to help you, I just want to reaffirm that you've given your consent for him to be here."

"Yes, I need Dylan to hear this," Jamie responded. "I need to connect with someone who may know what I'm going through. He's why I'm here in the first place."

"Good, then let us begin. First, Jamie, give us an introduction. Tell us about you."

"Well, I'm twenty-six. I'm unmarried, no children, and both of my parents are gone. I work full-time at the convenience store on Route 22, and I live alone. Well, except for my cat, Misty."

Susan smiled. "Tell me, Jamie. Is there someone in your life, right now? Are you seeing anyone?"

"Yes, my boyfriend, Sam, but he doesn't know about any of this. I haven't told him."

"Haven't told him what, Jamie?" Susan probed.

"About my dreams," Jamie sighed, releasing what felt like an exhaust trail of pent-up tension. "If that's what they are. He knows that I sometimes have nightmares, but I haven't gone into the details with him."

"The dreams are what we'll segue into now. We'll return to the prior subject in a few moments if that's okay." Jamie nodded. "So, Jamie, you've told me a little already about your dreams. I'd like you to go into detail now, not just for our benefit, but your own as well. Tell us about your dreams."

"They began shortly after my mother died two years ago. I question whether or not they're dreams because, unlike most dreams, I remember every moment, every detail almost perfectly. These are not the type of dreams that fade shortly after waking, the kind that eventually disappear. They remain. Sometimes a dream will go further than the last one. Then, I wake in my bed."

Jamie told them about seeing herself rise out of bed, watching in frozen horror as her body floated upward, away from her house, and into the night sky. She described a disc-shaped, metallic object, gray in color, and a blinding green light that emanated from it. She turned to Dylan.

"I knew exactly what you meant in your book, Dylan. The blinding white lights that moved above me, the cold hard metal against my back, it was a gurney I was being transported upon." Dylan closed his eyes and nodded. Jamie turned back to Susan. "They took me to a room, a sterile room, almost immaculate." She paused and sighed again.

"Take your time, Jamie," Susan coached. "This is a story of which we are well-familiar."

Jamie turned her eyes up toward the ceiling in thought, and then back again.

"I can see them, but not quite. A sort of shadowy veil distorts their likenesses, but I can see enough of them. They're frail, gaunt, with large heads. I can see their dark eyes, eyes like big black medallions, eyes that aren't human. These strange beings are not really malicious, just silently intimidating. What they're doing to me is beyond my control. I can't stop them. I'm helpless."

Susan lowered her voice to a comforting, soothing tone. "What are they doing to you, Jamie?"

Jamie took a deep breath. "They clamp my legs into these stirrup-like contraptions on the sides of the gurney. One of them holds up a needle. Soon, it pierces my naval. Then, then—" Jamie sighed again. Another gush of pent-up tension made her initiate her breathing exercises. Susan studied her, seemingly keen on what Jamie hadn't yet revealed.

"Go on, Jamie. It's okay." Dylan spoke to comfort her. "No one is going to harm you."

"They invaded me. *I know* they have." Jamie described the pressure inside her as one of the odd beings used some type of object to enter her. "Before I woke, I saw a face, a woman's face peeping through a window in the door. Then she was gone. I woke in my bed, like always, as if I'd only been dreaming." She glanced at Dylan, and then back at Susan. "But I don't think I was."

A silent pause ensued. Not only was it enough for Jamie to hear the hum of the ceiling lights above her, but it literally confirmed her worst nightmares and the thousand dreadful fears that followed later.

"Jamie, you described these beings as 'not really malicious.'" Susan broke the silence. "Tell us more about that."

Jamie thought for less than a moment. "They spoke with their minds. I remember feeling this unexplainable assurance. It was coming from them. Then, a female figure's voice entered my mind." Jamie described the female figure's soft, soothing tone of voice, as well as her long, lanky fingers that stroked and caressed her. "She instilled a sudden tranquility, one that induced acceptance, and then release. Soon after, I awoke in bed."

"You said you see yourself floating upward toward the UFO," Dylan interjected. "That's what we'll call it, Jamie, because technically that's what it is." He continued. "Before you wake, do you ever see yourself floating in the opposite direction, say back toward your house?"

Jamie considered this, and then shook her head.

"I'm wondering about the woman you saw," Susan said. "Can you describe her at all?"

Jamie shrugged. "I only caught a glimpse of her in the length of a few seconds. She had auburn hair and a fair complexion. And then, she was gone."

Jamie had never seen the woman before in her life. She continued to describe as many minor details as she could recall, specifically the tiled room, the strong sense of profound sterilization, and the seemingly immaculate environment.

"Was that the last dream you had, Jamie?"

For mere moments in time, the details of the last dream had slipped Jamie's mind. Susan's question sent a jolt through her, one that caused a visible reaction, a quick expression of shock that only Susan and Dylan would see. Jamie glanced at both of them, suddenly realizing the extent of their knowledge was more than she ever imagined.

"Tell us about the last dream, Jamie," Susan probed. "I get the feeling that obviously, the last dream is what brought you here today. Something was different about the last dream, Jamie. What was it?"

The trembling started up inside her, like the response from a quick key turn in an ignition. Keeping her eyes focused on Susan, the trembling quickly stopped. The dreams are what brought her here. It was time to reveal them. She fought the trembling and beat it down, but for how long she could never be sure. But now was long enough. She took another deep breath.

"I saw my mother in the last dream. She was frightened, more so than I'd ever seen in life. She was touching my stomach. I looked down, and I was pregnant."

Jamie fixed her eyes on the gold broche pinned to the lapel of

Susan's jacket, using it as a psychological lifeline to pull her through this difficult narrative. Susan sat forward.

"Go on," she prompted.

"She told me to let them take it, that I didn't want it. She said I couldn't keep it, and that they would come and take it from me. She said I wouldn't want it." Jamie told how her mother was religiously pro-life, and such a statement was contrary to the person she'd been. "She would never have said such a thing. This last dream convinced me of how perverse these dreams are."

"Allow me to ask," Susan began. "Are you pregnant, Jamie?"

Jamie felt her eyebrows arch together, the smirk of incredulity spreading across her face.

"No." She shook her head. "I'm not."

"Alright, Jamie," Susan nodded. "Now, let's turn the conversation back toward you." Susan asked how long she'd been dating Sam.

"A little over a year," she responded.

Susan nodded, and then zeroed in on her, eye to eye. The crack of a grin on Susan's face told Jamie that here was a clever woman, a worthy psychiatrist well-schooled in coaxing out the answer she wanted. There would be no hiding anything from her, even if Jamie wanted to.

"Do you not trust Sam enough to tell him about these dreams?"

Jamie relented. Susan would get her answer one way or another. "No, I do trust him. I just don't want to scare him away. Let's face it, I'm a basket case."

Susan continued to nod, all the while knowing what Jamie's answer would be, but relishing her achievement of getting Jamie to say it aloud.

"What makes you a basket case, Jamie? Is it the dreams, your mother's death," Susan paused, "or something before that?"

A flurry of images invaded Jamie's mind, incited somehow by the sound of Susan's voice and her provocative questions. Like a slideshow, the recollections were vivid and abrupt. Jamie remembered how Mother looked, wasting away and dying in her bed. She remembered holding Mother's hand, squeezing hard, as if doing so would allow her to hold onto her forever. Numbly, bitterly, she stared at Mother's closed casket, unwilling to accept. She recalled the panic attacks in high school, long before she understood what they were. She saw their faces once again, teachers and fellow students alike. Their disdainful stares sized her down, depreciating her as if she were some odd specimen unlike the rest of them. She saw her father, pointing and yelling at her mother just before he walked out the front door forever. She saw herself as a child, standing along the side of the road and clutching her mother's leg. Something terrible had happened.

She felt herself trembling. Jamie gasped, heaving heavily for a breath she'd forgotten to take.

"Breathe, Jamie. Breathe." Jamie sat, struck by Susan's words. Ironic, as if Susan had already known. Jamie's breathing slowed as the images in her mind faded. "Jamie, tell us what just happened."

She shook her head. "I don't know. I saw things in my mind. Some I remember and some I don't." Jamie stumbled in speech, her words rushing out in confusion.

"Let's revisit it next time, Jamie," Susan interrupted. "I want you to take a few days and think about the images you just saw in your mind. We'll discuss these images next time."

Jamie took another deep breath, the trembling now replaced by a sudden calmness. She felt slightly embarrassed, but Susan and Dylan aimed reassuring smiles at her.

"So, these dreams," Jamie asked. "What do you think they are?"

Susan laced her fingers together in front of her. "Well, Jamie, I'm not going to lie to you. I believe you. As I said, I'm also a para-psychologist, and what I'm hearing from you fits the profile of alien abduction. I believe you are an abductee who has been repeatedly abducted from the safety of your bed. In short, Jamie, I don't believe you're just dreaming."

Jamie's eyes lingered on Susan for just a moment, before shifting to Dylan, and back again.

"So, all of this is real?"

Susan paused. "Jamie, from what I've heard, you're an abductee just like Dylan and countless undeclared others here in Green Valley. I think you're another victim of what Green Valley has deemed, the 'phantom in the sky.'"

Jamie felt the stun of Susan's words, the finality of unwanted confirmation, like the smothering grip of a thick unseen force surrounding her. So, she'd been right all along; the dreams were real. This was reality—unthinkable.

"If I'm right," Susan continued. "And I do believe I am, Jamie. By definition, you're a 'sleep abductee.' Sleep abductees are predominantly women, reportedly taken from the safety of their own beds. Yet they wake in their beds from vivid dreams of being abducted, dreams that don't fade so easily. Obviously, cases like these are even harder to prove than those of regular abductees. No one knows why women are targeted specifically, but most of them report being experimented upon much in the same way you describe.

"For the sake of our investigation, Jamie, you are a Class two abductee. Class one abductees are those abducted from the ground in the out and open, those who have missing time and lost memories, like Dylan. The team has scheduled a meeting for tomorrow at two o'clock in 208 of Levin Hall. Other abductees who've recently come forward have agreed to participate. I'm hoping you can make it, Jamie."

Jamie worked until three on Saturdays. Tina, her co-worker, would cover for her if she left early around 2:30. "I'll be there, but I'll be a little late." She explained the situation. "I'll definitely make it by three."

Susan nodded. "Your story is a unique one, Jamie. I'm really hoping you'll share it. This will become much easier when you surround yourself with others in the same situation. It's crucial for you to interact. In fact, I may start an abductee group-therapy project, if this situation brings out more abductees who were once reluctant to tell their stories."

Jamie reassured her that she would arrive as soon as possible.

Susan glanced at her internet tablet, which sat snuggly on her lap. "So, next Friday, same time?" Jamie agreed. "Great. Next week, we'll discuss the sudden images you recalled today. I know it's hard not to worry, Jamie, but trust that there are others like you, the girl you saw through the window for one. Continue to calm yourself, Jamie. Try not to panic."

Jamie felt a sense of relief that the session was over, but the image of herself as a child, grasping Mother's leg appeared over and over again in her mind. The lost and suddenly recovered image badgered her mind like a random stranger banging on a locked door. Jamie stood and thanked them both.

Susan handed Jamie her card. "Feel free to call me, anytime, day or night."

"The same goes for me," Dylan said. He offered to listen, if she ever wanted to talk about her experience from one abductee to another. She thanked them again and left.

Jamie's legs wobbled as she walked slowly to the elevator. Reality suddenly ripped away from her, and she felt an inner stirring of fear. Slightly different now, it became a fear of the unknown, a fear she couldn't see except in what seemed like dreams, a fear she was helpless to stop. The fear made her feel numb right now, but silently it lingered inside her, threatening to heighten into a full-scale eruption.

She recalled Susan's and Dylan's words about how she was not alone. She'd calmed herself inside Susan's office, and outside of her inner fears, she now felt a sense of subdued angst. But as the elevator's doors opened, Jamie's stomach turned from the slightest wave of nausea.

———

As Jamie left Susan's office, Susan shut the door behind her. Turning to face Dylan, she formed a steeple with her hands clasped together and held them in front of her face, a habit she often displayed while in deep thought.

"Is it ethical of me to ask what you're thinking?" Dylan quipped.

"I think Jamie is someone we need to watch closely." Susan lowered her hands as she spoke.

"Why is that?"

"She's fragile, more fragile than she leads on. Did you notice how she knew to breathe properly when something was affecting her?" Dylan nodded. "That is someone with a history of panic attacks. Her breathing exercise has been learned. I'm also afraid there's something in her past, something she doesn't remember. I probed her in a certain way so that images were provoked in her mind. She remembered something unexpectedly. I've seen it happen before, and it happened to Jamie only moments ago, here in my office."

"So, you think this lost memory has something to do with what's happening now?"

Susan closed her eyes and shrugged. "I don't know, Dylan. I know that something in her life has led Jamie to be a 'basket case,' as she called it. It could be a separate issue, but I can tell it has something to do with her mother. I think her sleep abductions will coincide with her past issues and eventually culminate into a mental fiasco. I sincerely hope she makes it to the meeting tomorrow. She needs emotional support. As I said, Dylan, we need to watch Jamie closely. I don't think she's mentally prepared for what's happening to her."

12

BLINDSIDED

"ANOTHER ONE HAS COME FORWARD." CLOSING THE door behind him, Dylan informed Susan of the latest development. They were the first to arrive in room 208, shortly before Saturday's meeting was to begin. Phone in hand, Dylan retrieved Troy Adler's email. "I'm forwarding you an email I received the other night, after I got home from Brett's."

Prompted by the ding of her message alert, Susan checked her phone. Dylan watched as she read Troy's email.

"Miraculous?" She glanced up at him from her phone. "That's an interesting choice of words."

"He claims that 'they' removed a benign brain tumor from him."

Susan's jaw dropped. "You've got to be kidding me."

"I waited before telling you because I wanted to meet him first. I did that after Jamie's appointment yesterday. His name is Troy Adler, and he's a local attorney. He claims that after his abduction, the tumor was no longer there. He's even offered me permission to access his medical records as proof of what he's saying. Obviously, his doctor was even more baffled than he was."

"Who was the doctor?"

"A neurologist named Brighton."

"Yes, I've heard of him. Go on."

"Oddly, Troy bears a connection. He was the lawyer who represented Ursula when she tried to sue over her radiation exposure. In addition to knowing Ursula, he'd seen my story in the media, but at the time, thought nothing of it. Now, he's had his own experience, and it's a recent one. He bought my book as soon as he read of its release. He'll be here today to tell us his story."

"If his story turns out to be true, it will shed light on a whole new perspective, one we've never imagined before, which makes this entire business even more perplexing."

Overlapping Susan's words was the hissing sound of room 208's heavy door opening, and a familiar voice interrupting.

"Perplexing doesn't begin to cover it," Sidney announced. He stood in the doorway alongside Leah. Brett and Tahoe lingered just behind them.

"Good, you're all here, and early I see," Susan said.

"We're early for a reason," Leah said. "Something happened last night, something we need to discuss immediately."

————

"I WAS PAID A VISIT LAST NIGHT." LEAH'S TONE OF warning prepared them for the bottom line. "The Black-Eyed Kids showed up on my doorstep."

Susan gasped. Brett and Tahoe quickly sat themselves at the long conference table, their attentions fully focused on Leah, but Leah's eyes remained fixed on Dylan, whose complexion waned to a ghostly gray from the shock of her revelation. The seriousness of her gaze prompted the words from his mouth.

"What did they want?" he asked.

Sidney stepped forward, leafing through a manila folder he'd brought with him. He slid a sheet of paper from the folder and handed it to Dylan. It was a copy of the article promoting the theory of BEK being alien-human hybrid offspring. "I wasn't there, but apparently the boy with the red hoodie was looking for his father." Dylan glanced at the paper as Sidney continued. *"This* is what I remained hesitant to speak about at our last meeting. I'd read this article before, but I wanted to be sure before I opened my big mouth. Dylan, we all know of the investigator who wrote this. You, of all people, are familiar with his reputation."

Nervously, Dylan exhaled, and then took his usual seat at the end of the long conference table. Silence filled the room as Dylan continued to read. Sidney passed out copies of the article to Susan, Brett, and Tahoe.

"It was shortly after midnight." Leah removed her gloves and coat as she spoke. Stashing her gloves inside her coat pocket, she then slung her coat over an empty chair behind her, and then sat. "I know because I'd just finished watching a movie, and shortly after, my clock chimed midnight. Moments later, I heard this weird knocking at my door. It sounded like this." Leah demonstrated, striking her closed fist off of the table. "It was one knock after another—*boom,* a pause, *boom,* another pause, and *boom.* It wasn't normal knocking, you know, a continuous rapping in succession."

She described seeing the two boys standing on her porch when she gazed out the window. "I heard them speak. One had a more controlled, even tone, and the other was more insistent, more dominating in his demeanor. He was the black-haired boy, the one who insisted I let them both in. He practically ordered me to take him to his father."

Dylan listened while skimming the article he held in front of him. He stopped, lifted his head, until his gaze met hers. She didn't know what to say to him. He knew about this matter more intimately than she did.

"Leah, can you describe this black-haired boy's appearance?" Dylan asked.

"You already did, Dylan, in your book." Through the ensuing pause, Leah could almost hear a collective breath taken by everyone in the room. "His description is the same, down to the very last detail." Leah then described the more docile-toned boy:

red hair, gray hoodie, drab, grungy clothing, same as his counterpart. "They both had the same eyes, like big, black shiny marbles. And while their voices differed in tone, they both spoke with an eerie, almost mechanical distortion, one that chilled me to the bone."

"Do you think it's possible that their voices were just that, some kind of mechanical trick?" Susan asked in an effort to eliminate all possibilities.

"No, I don't," Leah said. "I think that's how they spoke. They elicited some type of fear from me. A wave of dread washed over me at the door. Some inner instinct told me not to let them in. I don't know what they were, but they weren't completely human. I know that. But as I explained to Sidney, while I felt fear around them, I'm not convinced they were demonic in nature."

"She called me as soon as it happened," Sidney interjected. "I drove right over but saw no one. I stayed for a while, and before I left, I checked all around outside the house—nothing."

Leah told how she ran to the kitchen for her phone, and when she got back to the front door, they were gone. "They disappeared in less than a minute. But what they said before they left is what freaked me out. It's why I ran for my phone to call Sid. They asked me why I had a third eye. They knew about me. Moments earlier, at the door, I tried to gaze and see what I could. The visions I saw were cut off, as if intercepted. I know it was one of them. But from what I saw they followed us, most likely from Brett's house. They walked for miles to Dylan's, and then to my house. They know *where* we are."

"Then something is happening here," Susan concluded. "Two of our guests today have been dreaming about these strange kids. They'll be describing these dreams for us, as well as the incidents that brought them here today. As all of this begins to add up, I wonder if there have been any recent UFO sightings in this area. If this theory about the BEK is true, then it's safe to speculate that these strange craft are not far behind them. That's something we should look into."

"If these kids followed you all from my house, then they were watching it that night." Brett's observation met with no rebuttal.

"If they *are* alien beings, I wonder to what extent they were observing us," Tahoe pointed out. "Could they have been telepathically eavesdropping on us, and if so, what are their plans?"

"To find their parents." Dylan's voice remained low but loud enough to get everyone's attention. His eyes remained fixed on the article. Then he let the sheet of paper fall to the table. He sat silently, staring at nothing.

"Dylan," Susan asked. "Are you alright?"

———

SPEECHLESS, DYLAN SAT LOST IN HIS THOUGHTS. A thousand different things he wanted to say began to bury themselves within. He didn't want to talk. He didn't want to say anything. A sting of bitterness taunted him, realizing the denial he'd lingered in. He'd dismissed the dream, pretending to not understand, when clearly the boy had called him "Papa." Deep inside, he'd known what they'd done to him, yet part of him remained reluctant to fully admit it from the beginning. Then, everything he'd overlooked seemed to come back and bite him in the ass. He sat silently, steaming.

"Last night in my study I had the strangest feeling," he said, "like someone was watching me. I couldn't take my eyes away from the window. I walked over and peeped through the curtain, but no one was there."

"Sidney and I suspect it was them," Leah said. "From there, they made their way to my house. That's what I saw in my vision."

"That's quite a trek in the icy cold night," Susan suggested.

"Yes, it is," Leah admitted. "But I saw them. They're not like us. They're not human." Dylan shot her a glance. "They're only part human." Leah detailed the vision she'd had at the door, a fast flash depicting seemingly sterile bodies devoid of blood.

"Then their bodies are capable of sustaining what ours

cannot," Tahoe concluded. "This could be a vital point to remember."

"If this proves to be true, that these kids are the offspring of abductees, this doesn't change a thing about your life, Dylan." Susan spoke past the others and directly at him. "We are still facing the unknown, one way or another. We've traveled this route before. All we have of the mysterious 'phantom in the sky' are myriad photos taken the day of Leah's Commencement. We have our memories of that day. Dylan, you have yours. But will we ever have proof the rest of the world will finally deem as 'concrete?' Hopefully in your lifetime, but I doubt that will happen in mine."

Dylan listened to her words, but the unforgettable dream played out again in his mind. It had now become the most vivid dream he'd ever had, and it haunted him again with cinematic recollection. The boy with the black bangs jutting from beneath a red hood walked toward him from across a field. Then the boy stopped, lifted his head, and Dylan saw those eyes, those black oval eyes.

"*Papa,*" the boy said again, in Dylan's mind, where the boy's stoic face remained frozen in a picture-perfect glare. The eyes were not like Dylan's, but from the nose down a faint trace of similarity was there and suddenly gone. Dylan stood and stepped away from the table, anything to erase what was going on inside his mind as it strangely competed with his breaking heart.

"My son," Dylan half whispered through his weakened voice. But spoken aloud, the sound of those two words was a loud confirmation of the ominous possibility he'd silently pondered all along. His own flesh and blood created not by his choice, now seemingly stalked him, first through dreams and now through inches of snow as real as the ground itself. He turned to Susan, pleading for an explanation through his anger, bitterness, and confusion. "How could I have ignored this? How could I have dismissed what the boy called me?"

"Don't you see, Dylan?" she responded. "You did your job as a paranormal investigator, objectively, as is required of you. You remained cautious and even skeptical, as is protocol. You did your job by the book, and now you're angry because you were blind-sided. Dylan, no matter what that boy called you in the dream, there was no way for you to conclude *this*." Susan held up her copy of the article. "It would have been irresponsible of you as an inves-tigator to jump to any conclusions based upon a dream, and you know that."

"If I may," Brett interrupted. "Right now, Dylan, we need to look at the bigger picture here. They watched my house and may have spied on us in some way. They've visited Leah and fixed their curiosities on her. It looks like these kids have now turned their attentions toward all of us. We need to remain alert and aware at all times now. Obviously, we have no clue as to the extent of their capabilities. They could be watching us now, and they could be extremely dangerous."

"You're right." In the midst of the conversation, Dylan and the others had not even heard the hiss of the heavy door opening. Heads turned toward the voice that abruptly interjected. Brad Byers stood in the doorway, arms akimbo and listening for what had to have been almost a minute. "Those kids are not human. The dreams are real. They're coming for us, all of us."

13

VOICES FINALLY HEARD

"EVERYONE, THIS IS BRAD BYERS." STEPPING FORWARD to greet him, Susan introduced the young man standing in the doorway. "Welcome, Brad. You're the first guest to arrive."

"I saw Nadine in the parking lot. She must be on her way up. Look, I'm sorry to have barged in like that. I've been anxious to get here."

"That's understandable." Susan already knew about Brad's dream. She'd instructed him to call her immediately. But since not all were present yet, she asked him to hold off on the details for the group discussion. "Brad, allow me to introduce you to the rest of the team."

A knock on the door interrupted greetings and small talk. Dylan opened the door, and Nadine modestly entered, her curiosity peaked by the surplus of technology surrounding her, the vast bay of apparatus where the investigators were said to decipher the sights and sounds of ghosts and poltergeists and other oddities through audio recordings and video footage. Before her were no amateurs; they were experienced and now somewhat famous investigators renowned not only for their work but for their results. It's why she was here. They knew more about this "phantom in the sky" than she did.

"And this is Nadine Parks," Dylan introduced her to the others. They stood casually speaking in a small circle, awaiting the arrival of another. Nadine and Brad took turns divulging simple facts about themselves, who they were, their occupations, and their family. Both were lifelong residents of Green Valley.

Susan checked her watch, two minutes to two. A third knock sounded at the door. This time, Dylan admitted a tall man in his early forties, with dark-brown hair and a slightly olive complexion.

"Thanks for coming, Troy." Dylan shook his hand, and then introduced Troy Adler. "Like all of you, Troy has a story to tell. I'll let him tell it, but you'll soon discover that Troy's experience can be labeled as nothing short of miraculous."

Susan introduced herself and then the others. "Dylan has filled me in on the details, and as a doctor, I am more than anxious to hear your story, Troy. We have one more participant who will be here today. She will be a little late, but we're hoping she'll arrive within the hour. With that said," she turned to Dylan. "Dylan, let the meeting begin."

———

NADINE REMEMBERED HOW ADAMANT SHE'D BEEN TO BE first in line at Dylan's book signing. Now, being the first to tell her story to the entire team, the jitters made her breathe deeply. She'd kept quiet back then, back when Green Valley erupted in the UFO controversy. So, it was now or never. Speak, or forever live with the memories and the strange dreams that coincided with them.

"Like Dylan," she began. "I was also abducted by what the local news called 'the phantom in the sky.' I didn't remember at first either." Nadine recounted the night she left work at One-Eyed Jack's, and how the radio went haywire during her drive home. She described the blinding green light, and then pulling over to the side of the road. "Soon, I realized I was far from Green Valley, nearly twenty miles, and an hour and a half had mysteriously passed. When I was listening to the radio on my way home, I was traveling Farmington Road just behind Eagle Rock Mountain. How I later ended up so far away, and where the time went, I had no clue."

Nadine and the others had consented to giving videotaped testimony for the archives. She paused and silently observed Brett manipulating what looked like a television news camera and slowly stepping away when he had it positioned correctly. Then she continued.

"Two reasons for my initial silence were my little boy and my aging mother at home. After seeing your press conference, Dr. Logan, I thought it best to keep my mouth shut, especially if those men were involved. Besides, at the time, I couldn't remember much of anything. I wouldn't have known what to tell you. Later, the dreams began. The first of which brought the entire experience back to me, as if I were living it over again. But I remembered. I remembered everything."

Turning her attention to Dylan, Nadine continued. "Dylan, I also recall the white lights and the cold gurney. The same happened to me." She paused for a brief second, collecting herself before her voice cracked. She couldn't let her emotions explode here and now. The last thing she wanted was to sound over emotional. "I remember seeing people but *not* seeing them, as if some shadowy veil hindered them, rendering them to be translucent figures within the light. But then one of them made sure I saw him. He stuck his face right up to mine. I saw deep dark ovals for eyes, a gaunt body, and a misshapen head. I felt frozen in terror, but the fear was quick, soon gone and forgotten, as if my emotions were somehow being remotely controlled."

She told them about the sterile room, and how they'd injected her with some sort of tranquilizer. She described the feelings of peacefulness, abandon, and the sensation of floating. She stopped talking and looked around her. Her natural instinct reminded her that six men sat in the room and only two other women. Yet three of these men had been abducted as well. Dylan had been violated as equally as she had. Still, she focused her gaze on Susan and Leah before revealing the next part of her story. She started by describing the stirrup-like contraptions. Then Nadine paused, turning her head downward and staring at the table. She lifted her head back up and refocused.

"That's when they entered me. They violated me with some type of instrument. I was unable to resist. Some force, the same magnetic force Dylan mentioned in his book, kept me pinned to the gurney. Then, I saw myself floating back to my car. The dream had brought it all back to me, as if I was supposed to remember. I didn't want to remember. I would rather have gone through my life never knowing what happened because little did I know, that first incident was only the beginning.

"Three months after the first dream, the one that made me remember, I had another. But it was no dream. It was real. The next time there was a needle, one that descended from above and entered me through my navel. That never happened the first time. The first time, there was no needle. So I knew it wasn't a dream. It was really happening." Nadine felt her face reddening and the sting of sudden watery eyes. She spoke fast. "Then they invaded me again with um," she wiped at her eyes, "some type of injector. But I awoke in my bed. I didn't know how that was possible, but there I was, in my own bed, in my own room."

She mentioned her clock's digital display reading 3:04 a.m., the same time she found herself along I-70. But she feared the next part of her story would be met with the most doubt. The details she was about to divulge were incredulous, even to her, but they had to believe her. If God was her only witness, she spoke the truth.

"About six weeks later, I felt ill and went to the doctor. He told me I was pregnant, but what I didn't tell the doctor was that it wasn't possible. I hadn't been with anyone in over a year. The only way it was possible was—"

She paused, suddenly unable to finish. A slight pain ached in her throat. Susan reached over and clasped her hand in support.

"Through your abduction," Susan finished the sentence for her.

Nadine nodded as an unavoidable tear rolled down her cheek, one she instantly regretted. She wiped it away, cleared her throat, and continued.

"I was six weeks along, the exact amount of time since my second abduction. Then, they abducted me a third time, again from my sleep. I tried to fight them, but I was subdued and then sedated. I woke up on the gurney, cold and alone in a similar, familiar tiled room. I got up from the gurney and wandered out of the room."

Nadine described the alien surroundings, the giant metal beams that protruded up from a lower ground, the metallic framework that made a maze throughout the vast unknown, and the strange feel of the floor her feet had rapidly pounded.

"Eventually," she continued. "I found another room, just like the one I was kept in. I peeked through a square window in the door. Inside the room lay a young woman prepped on a gurney, just as I was, with her legs clamped in the stirrups. She looked at me, pleadingly. I attempted to help her, but I felt their hands on me, yanking me away."

Nadine noticed Susan swiftly turn her head toward Dylan. His eyes met hers amid the silent pause. Nadine wondered what part of her story had triggered Susan's sudden reaction.

"Again, I awoke in my bed."

"I don't mean to interrupt you, Nadine," Susan sounded calm, her attention now redirected back toward Nadine. "Can you describe the young woman you saw in the other room?"

Nadine recalled her, ten or more years younger, with shoulder-length brown hair and the look of absolute fear on her face. Nadine watched as Susan's expression remained unchanged.

"I just wanted that on record," Susan said. "Please, continue."

Now beyond her fear and hurt, her grief open-ended and ongoing, Nadine felt a flash of anger. She used it now to get her point across. She glanced at each of them, one by one.

"Those bastards took my baby." A collective unleashing of gasps and sighs surrounded her. Her own bewilderment took hold, and she gasped along with them. "They took my baby." A bursting dam of inevitable tears gushed forth, tears she could no longer control.

Nadine described the sonogram results as Susan handed her a tissue. She wiped her eyes.

"My first blood test showed I was pregnant. I felt something inside me, just the same as I had when I was expecting my son Todd. They removed the fetus from my body on the third abduction. I know it. But I have absolutely no proof outside of that first blood test, which can easily be chalked up to a false positive. That's what I told my mother it was. I never told a living soul about any of this until today.

"Time passed. I thought it was all over. I decided to try and block it from my mind forever. Then, I dreamed of those kids with the black eyes, eyes like those of the being who stuck his face up close to mine." Nadine detailed the setting of the dream, a field, like the one Dylan had written about. "The dream was so real, yet I couldn't feel the cold around me. I saw one of them walking toward me. Then, there were two." She described the girl and the boy, recalling their reddish hair and the sleek grayness of their flesh. "Fear gripped me as soon as I saw their eyes. They glared at me, and then they both called me, 'Mother.'" She paused and took a deep breath. "God forgive me. I never wanted to admit it to myself, but for a split second in the dream, I saw my face in theirs. But I don't see how it could be possible. If I'd had twins, they wouldn't be that old. They would be babies right now."

Nadine's voice cracked as she felt the pain of heartbreak in her throat once again.

"What's worse is that the fear that came from them was overwhelming. I didn't know what to think. I could almost feel their conflicting emotions. Curiosity, anger, something bittersweet emanated from them. I *feared* them. I felt like they wanted to hurt me." She paused, letting them all absorb the numerous details she tried to recall as clearly as possible. "Then I awoke in bed yet again."

Brad, who sat to her left, had been watching her intently throughout the entire story. Like everyone else, including Troy who sat to her right, he hung on her every word. Yet Nadine couldn't help but realize that Brad's peaked interest was because her story mirrored his own. He sighed and closed his eyes.

"Oh, no," he said, hanging his head slightly.

"What's the matter?" Nadine asked.

Opening his eyes, he rested his hand over the lower part of his face and displayed a troubled expression. "Everything you said is exactly what I was afraid of."

———

Brad began with his fishing excursion, and how the peaceful night was suddenly interrupted by the sound of rushing water and a strange force that parted the river into halves. He described the bright green light that descended from the sky and the gray metallic craft hovering above the river. "It appeared like it was coming closer to me. Then I found myself standing yards away from my original position. I also experienced missing time.

"I knew something had happened to me. I felt strange, dazed maybe. Reality seemed unreal, you know what I mean?" His question was met with unanimous nods. "When I got home, my wife Sheila knew something was wrong just by looking at me. I remember dashing off to my son's room and checking on him. I remember feeling like I was no longer in control, as if I were now powerless to protect myself and my family.

"About a year passed before I also had a dream that brought everything back. It was like an awakening." He sneered. "A rude awakening, if you will." He noticed Nadine nodding her head in agreement. "I saw myself being sucked up into that thing, the UFO. I could see the riverbank below me, but it was like I was paralyzed."

Brad's story echoed Dylan's and Nadine's, down to the white lights, the cold gurney, and the suctioning force that secured him to it. He described the shadowy figures having large, deformed heads and inhuman eyes.

"I recalled trying to fight them, squirming beneath the suctioning wrap that enveloped me. They injected me with some type of tranquilizer. A female spoke to me, but she spoke inside my mind, telling me to calm myself and that everything would be all right."

Nadine grasped his wrist. "Yes! I remember her."

Brad returned the gesture, covering her hand with his. "They experimented on me too." He turned his gaze toward Dylan. "As I've already told Dylan, everything he wrote about happened to me."

He described the robotic arm that came down upon him, the feeling of quick pain, ecstasy, and then abandonment. Then he saw himself floating back down toward the riverbank.

"I told Sheila everything. We did an internet search. The night I went fishing was a day after the mass UFO incident that took place right here at the university. That's when I read up on all the past headlines and saw the notice about Dylan's book."

"So," Dylan cut in. "Given the time frame Brad describes, he was abducted around the same time as myself. The same goes for Nadine. This proves we were part of some type of agenda implemented by these beings we described." A silent pause no one wanted to break ensued. The agenda Dylan spoke of remained loud and clear, almost thundering within the silence. Dylan nodded to Brad, signaling him to continue.

Brad had already described his first dream of the girl to Susan and Dylan. Now he recounted it for Nadine, Troy, and the rest of the team. "Recently, I dreamed of her again. In the dream, I was playing ball with my son in the house, until he dashed away and answered a knock at the door. The girl with the black eyes stood on my doorstep, beckoning Adam, telling him that she was 'his sister.' He ran to her. I couldn't stop him. Then, I awoke.

"That's why I was so anxious to get here today. When she stood in the doorway in my dream, I felt paralyzed with fear, even in my sleep. When I woke, I thought my heart would explode. This last dream was a message, maybe even a warning that if she can't get my attention, then she's coming for my son." Brad gazed at each of them. *"I'm not* going to let that happen."

———

FOR NEARLY THIRTY MINUTES, TROY SAT AND LISTENED in both horror and bewilderment. His was not the same type of story. He felt somewhat guilty even telling it. Troy recalled the same strange beings Brad and Nadine described, their identities cloaked in a shadowy veil, their misshapen heads and lithe bodies unmistakable. Black eyes like onyx ovals penetrated the same seemingly translucent veil meant to disguise them. Brad and Nadine spoke of the same beings, yet Troy felt himself choking on the gratitude he felt toward them.

"As I've already explained, my story is vastly different," Troy began. "My abduction didn't occur at the same time as the rest of you. Mine was more recent, but with equally unexplainable results."

Troy described his reaction at being diagnosed with a benign brain tumor.

"I was both devastated and slightly relieved. It wasn't malignant but at the same time, no one wants a brain tumor. Even worse was that at that moment, all the doctor could do was continue to watch and monitor its progress. I threw myself into my work. I stayed really late at my office one night. That was the night it happened."

He'd dropped his keys in the street, and then bent down to pick them up. An explosion of green light surrounded him.

"The next thing I knew, I was standing next to my car in the parking garage. But I'd never made it to the garage. I was still standing in the street when I saw this intense green light. It was 10:30 when I left my office, yet the time on my phone said 12:16." He told them about walking out of the garage and noticing the sky had turned darker. "There was nothing wrong with my phone. My watch displayed the same time. Like all of you, I was missing almost two hours."

Troy paused, pondering how to explain the next part of his story to those who had darker experiences.

"A month later, I also dreamed of what happened to me." He glanced at each of them. "I saw the disc-shaped craft. I too was being sucked up into it." Troy's details of being inside the craft echoed those of the others. "What I recalled was being lulled by this overwhelming warm heat that calmed me. Then I saw myself standing next to my car in the garage.

"Knowing what happened to Ursula Masters a couple of years ago, I decided to look back into the details of *everything* that happened back then. I bought Dylan's book and delved deeper into his story. I had to because when I went back to my doctor, my brain tumor was gone." More gasps filled the room. Troy couldn't help but notice the looks of awe from Nadine and Brad. "'Spontaneous Remission,' my doctor called it. I said nothing. I knew why it was gone. Those beings, whoever they are, removed a tumor from my brain."

Troy took a moment to let his words sink in.

"I'd also like to mention that Ursula Masters suffered the effects of radiation exposure after witnessing this craft. That didn't happen to any of us. We were abducted, she wasn't. After having the dream, I thought about the intense heat I felt on the gurney. I suffered no effects of radiation exposure, but I'm sure that the heat I felt was the tool they used to perform some kind of miraculous surgery on me. When I researched other abduction stories online, I discovered that the suppression of tumors is widely reported.

"I have to admit, I was never one hundred percent convinced of any of this. As a lawyer, I continually look for some logical explanation, but now, I'm afraid there isn't one. It's become clear to me beyond a reasonable doubt that these beings are experimenting on humans in many different ways. The question is, why?"

Troy noticed how Tahoe and Leah leaned in closer, keenly listening and assimilating his every word. Brett's face held a look of incredulity only deterred by his occasional glimpse of the rolling camera's feedback. Sidney also listened intently, taking notes frequently as Troy spoke. Dylan had already heard his story and spoke after Troy's final pause.

"You're absolutely right, Troy. So many across the world already know this, and we here in Green Valley have been seemingly targeted by the so-called 'phantom in the sky.' We knew back then there would be others like me. We knew you all would come forward and you have, but I'm not convinced it's limited to just us. I'm sure there are many others out there. We want to thank the three of you for sharing your stories with us."

"That's right," Susan interjected. "As I said earlier, your voices are finally heard. And as I've already told the team, we may never reach the end of this mystery, but together we can try. We can at least get through it together and hopefully add some missing piece to the puzzle along the way." She paused. "Troy, with your consent, I'd like to examine your medical records and submit copies of them to our archives."

Troy agreed. Susan glanced at her watch. It was almost two-thirty.

"Our next guest should arrive any minute now. You'll all find her story equally compelling, and I must warn you, just as frightening."

14

THE GIRL IN THE WINDOW

JAMIE FELT THE QUICK THRILL OF LEAVING WORK EARLY today, a relief slightly overshadowed by the thought of telling her story over again to strangers. But she'd agreed to do so. The underlying fear she felt yesterday seemed at bay, yet ready to overwhelm her at any given moment. Maybe Susan was right, maybe sharing with other people who understood would help her through it. That *is* why she contacted Dylan in the first place, wasn't it?

All night she'd tossed and turned in bed, thinking about the images that popped into her mind yesterday in Susan's office. It was as if Susan's questions had opened up her mind and caused it to trace back to the onset of her panic attacks. She remembered having them in high school. Then, the earlier images of her and her mother standing along the side of the road, the random memory of a helpless younger woman with a little girl clutching her leg wouldn't go away. The more they played out in her mind, the more she seemed to remember, yet she still couldn't pinpoint the reason for the latter occurrence. What happened back then? Had she been too young to understand? Why had she forgotten such an event for so many years? None of it made any sense, but Jamie trusted Susan to help her identify these memories. At her next appointment, Jamie would ask Susan to hypnotize her into recalling these fleeting glimpses that were hastily snatched away before she could make any sense of them.

Jamie turned North onto University Road, and soon, the GVU campus sprawled out before her. She gazed to her left, over at Commencement Field and the sky above, imagining how the infamous disc-shaped craft had looked when it lingered there almost two years ago. Inside Levin Hall, her feet shuffled up the stairs, creating an echo through the stairwell on her way to the second floor. Soon, she knocked on the door of room 208.

———

NADINE SAT CLOSEST TO THE DOOR WHEN A BRISK knocking sounded loud and clear. Susan was the first to react.

"That's Jamie now. Come on in!" she called out.

Slowly, the door opened. When Nadine saw her walk through the doorway, her heart nearly stopped. It was her, the girl in the other sterile room, the girl she'd seen through the window during her sleep abduction. Nadine felt a wave of heat. A breaking sweat washed over her face. She rose from her seat at the table and took a step toward the girl. No doubt, it was her. She had the same shoulder-length brown hair and the same eyes.

"I don't believe it," Nadine said. "It's you."

Nadine could see as the girl's eyes widened that she recognized her.

"My God," Jamie exclaimed. "I can't believe this." Jamie glanced at the rest of the team as she began to tremble slightly.

Nadine glanced back at the others. "This is her, the girl I saw through the window."

Susan rose from her seat. "I suspected as much. When you told us that part of your story, Nadine, your description of the girl matched Jamie perfectly. Jamie had told us a similar story only a day before." Susan walked around the table and stood near the both of them. Then, she introduced them both by name.

Nadine reached out both hands to Jamie, who took them in hers, tears welling in each other's eyes.

"I was so afraid for you," Nadine said, choking back a flood of tears.

"Likewise. I wasn't sure what happened to you. I certainly never thought I'd ever see you again."

"But you have." Nadine let go of Jamie's hands and wiped at the tears in her eyes. "And there's so much I need to tell you, so much you need to know."

"Agreed," Susan interrupted. "But first, I want everyone to hear Jamie's story. Then you can fill in the blanks for her."

Jamie took the empty seat at the long conference table, one that was meant for her. She told everyone her story from beginning to end and most of everything she told Dylan and Susan yesterday. Her story echoed Nadine's, down to the details of the disc-shaped craft, the examinations and of course, being invaded. For now, Nadine kept quiet and let Jamie tell her story. Nadine had known all along that the girl she'd seen in the window had been there for the exact same reason as her. Nadine's heart sank when Jamie detailed the dreams of her mother and her mother's warning about a baby.

Jamie shrugged. "But I'm not pregnant."

Oh God, she will be, Nadine thought. *She will be.*

Jamie finished telling her story, and then Sidney cut into the conversation.

"Jamie, you've been deemed a Class Two abductee. Dylan, Brad, and Troy are Class One abductees. Nadine is also considered to be a Class One abductee because she was originally abducted from her car. I find this to be interesting that you don't fit the profile of a Class One, but I have a more pertinent question. Have you had any dreams of these Black-Eyed Kids?"

Jamie shook her head. "No, I haven't."

No, because she's not with child yet. Nadine kept her thoughts silent.

"I just want to point out that Dylan, Brad, and Nadine all dreamed of these kids. Jamie and Troy have not." Sidney spoke to get his words on the record. Drawing contrasts and connections was always a main factor in their work.

"And something else I'd like to mention," Brett interjected. "Jamie, Nadine, and Brad's abductions began at the same time as Dylan's. Their abductions have continued to present day, including the dreams of the BEK. Troy is the only person whose abduction occurred recently. His description of the disc-shaped craft and green light matches everyone else's. This brings up Susan's earlier suggestion."

A pause filled the room. Tahoe took the liberty of breaking the silence. "It means Green Valley is still being visited by this 'phantom in the sky.'"

Murmurs of awe and discontent threatened to carry the conversation off course.

"I would have to agree," Leah chimed in. "I've seen those kids outside my door." Leah revealed her story again, this time for the abductees. "The one with the black hair claimed that Dylan is his father. If this is true, then it's clear what's going on here. Whoever these beings are, they are merging their DNA and ours, possibly creating these strange hybrid children."

Murmurs of surprise persisted, but Nadine knew Leah was right. *They all* knew she was right.

Leah continued. "As I've already discussed with Sidney, who are we to say how quickly these hybrid children age? We can't know that. If the theory is correct, they possess only one-half of human DNA." Leah paused, and when she resumed, her tone turned dire. "The other half belongs to something else. These kids are here, and so is whoever brought them here."

"I want to check out our social media page, which I haven't done in a while," Brett offered. "I want to see if we have any reports of new sightings in the area."

"That's an excellent idea, Brett," Susan said. "And while you do that, let's all take a ten-minute recess, collect ourselves, and then meet back here."

Everyone rose from their seats. Chairs scooted back, legs stretched, and a small line formed for the door. Nadine touched Jamie's shoulder, and then whispered in her ear.

"Walk with me to the lounge area. There's something you need to know."

Once they reached the end of the hallway and turned left, they sat next to each other on plush, orange leather chairs in the small student lounge. Then Nadine told Jamie everything.

———

THAT FAMILIAR STORM OF FEAR AND TENSION gathered and erupted inside her once again, as Nadine's words shook her to the core of her being.

"They took my baby." Nadine clasped Jamie's hands once again, hands that now shook within her grasp. "That's a part of my story you need to know. I was pregnant one day, and then not the next. Now, I'm dreaming of these Black-Eyed Kids, twins to be exact, who call me 'Mother.' What you need to do now is stay mindful and alert. I'm going to be here for you, every step of the way."

Nadine's face faded in and out, as Mother's image appeared in Jamie's mind, pleading once again.

"You can't keep it, Jamie. You don't want it!"

Jamie breathed harder and faster as she saw images and reminders, and buried fears resurrected inside her. In her mind, she saw the needle and the strange injector with which they'd invaded her. Her pulse raced. Her heart pounded in a rapid, ascending percussion.

Breathe, Jamie. Breathe, she told herself. She pulled her hands away from Nadine's and took a deep breath, struggling to control her respiration.

Nadine, realizing Jamie's panic, reacted, grasping Jamie's shoulders. "I'm sorry," she said. "Honey, I don't mean to scare you." She hugged her. "We don't know what's going to happen. None of us do. But we're all in this together. Just remember that. If you need me for any reason, I'm here for you."

Jamie remembered the wave of nausea she'd felt yesterday after leaving Susan's office, yet she hadn't felt it today. Probably just her nerves, she thought, as she began to breathe normally.

Probably just her nerves.

15

WITNESSES IN THE NIGHT

THE LAST TIME BRETT MONITORED THE SOCIETY'S social media page, he noticed nothing except requests to join the page and claims of Bigfoot sightings in the area and statewide. No surprise there. Sightings of the infamous biped abounded throughout the Green Valley area since 1973. Green Valley had been famous for being a number one hotspot for such paranormal phenomena long before any of them were born. Now, Brett felt the sting of self-chastisement for not checking the page earlier, but he and the team had been so wrapped up in what was happening with Tahoe that it slipped his mind. Little did he know that a local conversation was erupting right here on the society's page, and the team had yet to respond.

He scrolled down to the earliest posts and comments, going back at least a few days. The discussion began with a post from Debbie K, of Green Valley. Debbie had posted on the society's page the day after Leah's visit from the BEK. As Brett read her post, it became clear to him that Susan's earlier hunch was startlingly accurate. Debbie K wrote:

"Have there been any current reports of UFOs atop Eagle Rock Mountain? Last night, my bf and I were traveling northbound around the

mountain when this bright green light surrounded us. I had to pull over because it blinded us, but Greg (my bf) was able to see something move quickly out of sight just before the green light vanished. I'm wondering if this UFO business is starting up again because we definitely witnessed something in the sky."

Debbie's post garnered a few comments. Brett read through them, paying attention to the more serious ones. Brian D, also of Green Valley, responded.

Yes, I saw the green light also, though I may have been farther away from it. I was on my way home from my late shift. The light came from the mountain, and as I got closer to it, something shot quickly through the sky and disappeared, taking the green light with it. I sped up but saw nothing after.

A flurry of various responses ensued. Brett read through their sudden surprise, noticed their wowed reactions, and then stumbled upon, expectedly, a naysayer. John G. wrote—

Bullshit. It was bullshit then. It's bullshit now, all of it.

And then Bobbie R. fired back, referring to the past incident at Commencement Field.

"How is it bullshit, Mister? How do hundreds of people witness the same damn thing in broad daylight, at an event in which many were almost trampled to death? Were they all hallucinating? Really? And they all saw the same thing? Go back to bed!"

John G. failed to respond.

The next post came from Bill B., originally from Erie, but temporarily staying in Green Valley because of a business enterprise. Bill posted his words along with a picture.

"I was out late that night. On my way home, I drove past Eagle Rock Mountain. The green light in the sky rotated, projected itself in all directions like a lighthouse beacon. I pulled over and got out of my car. I saw that thing, massive and rotating like the light, it was grayish and disc-shaped. I wasn't fast enough with my phone to catch a video, but I managed to take this still shot just before it disappeared."

Brett zoomed in on the picture. Somewhat blurry, it appeared to be taken by a shaky hand. Brett could see the green light but only a small slice of a silvery-gray, metallic object within it. He estimated that not only was a shaky hand involved, but a quick movement of the subject had obviously contributed to the picture's shabby quality. But something was definitely there.

Coming to the more recent posts, Brett noticed an item posted by Shannon S. of Sewickley. Shannon had been in Green Valley visiting her sister. They'd both been out for the evening when they saw the green light and something in the sky, just above Eagle Rock Mountain. Shannon wrote—

My sister and I saw this bright green light all around us. It grew brighter and brighter until I had no choice but to pull over. We were at the base of Eagle Rock Mountain, not far from Farmington Road. I got out and took this video. The disc-shaped craft emitting the green light lingered for a few moments. Then it was gone in a flash. This video was taken at night, but you can see how the craft looks exactly like what appeared in the newspapers a couple of years ago during the Commencement Field incident.

Brett examined the video and immediately regarded it as one of the best UFO footages he'd seen so far, especially taken at night. Shannon's video was clear enough that he could see the violet tinge of midnight sky behind the object. He could even point out the crags descending from the mountain top. The craft was rotating, just as Bill B. described it. The rotation emitted scorching green bursts of light through the video, blinding out the object for a second at a time. Yet Brett could see it clearly, gray, metallic, and disc-shaped, simply turning and not making a sound. Shannon was right; it appeared exactly as it had in Commencement Field. Then, the craft soared at an unimaginable speed and suddenly vanished, as if it were never there, leaving only the craggy mountain top as the video's subject. Here was undeniable proof.

Shannon's video received forty-seven comments, fifty-six reactions, and was shared twenty-three times. Posted only a day and half ago, Brett guessed the video would soon reach trending status. He skimmed through the comments, finding a combination of surprise, curiosity, and skepticism, all of which were expected.

Brett viewed the video again, which he noted ran a total of thirteen seconds.

So, Susan's theory was right, which made Leah's theory probably and terrifyingly accurate. If these Black-Eyed Kids were hybrid human-alien beings, then they were brought here by the infamous "phantom in the sky." That's why UFO sightings resumed. These strange children were being watched, and so were they. Those who manned the disc-shaped craft were watching over their creations, the haunting children who roamed the wild winter in search of their earthly parents. Brett's mind projected an image so dark he felt his blood turn cold. The various implications of this unimaginable scenario dropped a dark curtain over his mind, creating an almost apocalyptic depression. He sat back, closed his eyes, and sighed.

Those who'd left the room were returning. It was time to play back Shannon S's video, another piece toward what this puzzle's frightening finish could be. It had taken him only minutes to program his laptop to project images onto the giant screen, absorbing most of the room's western wall. Brett felt a heightening wave of curiosity swelling around him. The eyes of those who began taking their seats lingered long and hard on him. As he fidgeted with his laptop, he noticed Susan stepping slowly toward him.

"What's going on, Brett?" she asked.

"You were right," he said. "It looks like we have a returning visitor." Thick silence filled the room as the society's social media page appeared on the giant screen. "Quite a commotion has begun, and much of it is taking place on our page. Let me start with the most recent post to the page. Brett introduced Shannon's video. "This was taken by a Sewickley woman. Our 'phantom in the sky' has reared its ugly head again in the dark of night, while the rest of the world slept, and when none of us were looking."

Brett clicked on a white arrow and the video began. Watching the video on the giant screen made the rotating gray-metallic object with its spinning bursts of green light much easier to discern. Within seconds, Brett heard gasps and cries of shock, the sounds of nightmares and strange dreams suddenly realized. Fear, awe, and confusion combined as everyone watched how the UFO had vanished in an unimaginable flash.

"That's it, the same craft I see over and over in my dreams." Jamie enforced her adamant declaration by pointing at the screen.

"I'm sure of it," Nadine said.

"We're all sure of it," Brad added.

"Seeing that green light rotate on the screen was almost like it was happening again." Troy's sentiment was instantly echoed by the others, their heads nodding in agreement.

"I remember that thing like I'd seen it only yesterday," Susan said.

Through a dead silence, unspoken fear reverberated.

Brett coasted the cursor down to Bill B's blurry photo. "This was taken by a man staying in Green Valley on business. He stopped his car not far from Shannon's location. We can see this because the angle of the craft is slightly eastward this time. I would guess he was about a quarter mile away from her. This picture is not the greatest, but it clearly shows the same UFO as in the video. Then there are the eyewitness testimonies."

He arrived at Debbie K's post and the various responses. All of them placed the craft above Eagle Rock Mountain.

"I wonder why it's appearing near the mountain again." Susan's bewilderment did not go unnoticed. "The government shut down the secret facility after I exposed it. After the mayhem, the government occupied the mountain for six months or so, but they're gone now. There isn't anything there except the observatory and the gift shop. What is the continuing attraction?"

"It has something to do with those kids," Leah exclaimed. "I know it does."

Sidney turned his head toward her. "You think they're hiding there on the mountain?"

"They have to be somewhere, Sidney," she said. "Where could they possibly stay without drawing attention to themselves?"

"That's an interesting theory." Susan spoke before Sidney could answer the question. "I never doubt your intuition or visions, Leah, but if it's true, how do we go about solving this mystery? Do we wait for further contact, or do we go to the mountain and seek them out? If these kids are as dangerous as many fear, the latter may not be a good idea."

"I don't want any of you to do that." Dylan issued an abrupt command from the top end of the long conference table, down to the bottom. "It's me they've sought out. I'm the main person they're looking for. If they're watching, as we believe, then they know who we are and what we do. I'll draw them out on my own. I don't want any of you risking your safety." Dylan glanced at Nadine and Brad. "Especially you two."

Brett noticed Tahoe sitting with his eyes closed, a habit that often occurred when Tahoe envisioned. Then, as if Tahoe had caught Brett's thoughts, he opened his eyes and spoke.

"There won't be any need to draw them out," he pronounced. "They will make themselves known." Tahoe glanced ominously at all who sat around the table, allowing a solemn pause to settle in. "It is inevitable."

16

LEGEND OF THE STAR PEOPLE

AN AWKWARD SILENCE SETTLED BETWEEN THEM DURING the first five minutes of the ride home. From the corner of his eye, Brett noticed that something disturbed Tahoe who sat in the passenger side, lost in a sea of troubling thoughts.

"You saw something while we were there, didn't you?" Breaking the maddening silence, Brett's eyes darted back and forth from the road to Tahoe.

Tahoe drew a big unhindered breath and released it with a sigh. "Am I that obvious?" he chuckled, gazing out through the windshield at the rapidly darkening horizon. "I saw those children in my mind. Their faces somewhat human, their eyes sheer blackness. Their feet will continue to trample snow in haste and anger. I envisioned them in a field. The field is near the mountain. I didn't see beyond that, but I meant what I said. They *will* make themselves known. But questions remain. What are their intentions? How far will they go to achieve their goals? I do not know. But I know they were attracted to Leah because of her third eye. She was right when she claimed that her visions at the door suddenly ceased, as if they were being controlled. That's exactly what happened. These kids have the same ability, only to a far greater extent. They possess a gift far more advanced than Leah's or mine. They know how to wield it to their advantage and manipulate it in those who possess it to a far lesser extent." He turned his head and glanced at Brett. "They invaded Leah's mind and stole her thoughts and visions."

Brett drove the car, stunned by Tahoe's words. "They're squatting up on Eagle Rock—amazing."

"And that's not all," Tahoe continued. "In that nearby field is where they will come face to face with the others." Tahoe wriggled from an icy chill, the body's reaction to a sudden sense of fear. "I'm sure of this."

"So why not mention it at the meeting?" Brett quickly caught the dire look on Tahoe's face, one that sunk his features into a frown.

Tahoe paused before answering. "Fear." Slowly, his eyelids closed. "Unexplainable fear."

———

TAHOE FELT THE CHIEF INSIDE HIM, TWO SOULS coinciding and intermingling within one body, one that rapidly descended in age. Unexpressed emotions fought for clarity. Unspoken words stifled within him. Tahoe's heart beat more vigorously. Thriving, younger life flushed his face and cheeks a crimson hue.

Once again, night came early and draped the rural backdrop in total darkness. Unrelenting icy cold stung the skin and chilled the bones. But inside the farmhouse, toasty warmth swept out from the hearth, creating a peaceful calm in the quiet night. For Tahoe, the blistering cold was a drastic switch from the blazing desert sun that wrinkled his skin over time, but it was a change he welcomed. Those wrinkles had vanished, and his once aging leathery skin had tightened; although, neither of these advantages were a result of the weather. Tahoe's newfound vitality discovered the cold to be invigorating. He inhaled fresh, crisp wintery air into his rejuvenated lungs and marveled at the massive white blanketing of snow. The snow clung to the treetops, creating breathtakingly beautiful scenery he'd never experienced before. Beholding such beauty made him feel as if life was starting over again. And secretly he knew it was, at least from a certain point in time.

But gazing out at the world from the living room window did nothing to order his thoughts or give him a clear answer on how to curtail the edginess he felt right now. Recently, he'd been communicating with the chief through dreams, at least when the chief decided it was time. Now, there was no longer any need. Tahoe knew well that both he and the chief inhabited this body now, just like he and Brett cohabitated under one roof. Tahoe no longer needed to seek out the chief through dreams. All that was needed was a brief interlude of quiet meditation, a sharp focus, and Tahoe would then lapse into a trance somewhat like the dream state only sharper, clearer, and more precise.

As the day's pulse died away into the steady stream of night, Tahoe decided to meditate before bedtime. He rose from the chair, bid Brett an early goodnight, and ascended the stairs to his bedroom. On his bed, he situated himself in a position he hadn't been able to achieve in decades, with his legs crossed underneath him in a manner once known as "Indian style." He remembered how sitting this way had caused his legs great arthritic pain when he became older. It seemed like another life because it was hardly noticeable now.

Tahoe closed his eyes and extended both arms outward on each side. He opened his hands and exposed his palms, feeling the slightest tickling of air as unseen energy coursed through them. Then Tahoe let his head fall backward as his third eye gazed into another realm. A wave of serenity washed over him. He felt himself plunging into it, sinking deeper and deeper until he became lulled almost to sleep, but not quite. Colors flashed before him: red, orange, yellow, green, blue, and violet. He remembered them well from his dreams of the chief.

He felt himself being lifted upward, as if his soul had been summoned out of his body. Then, he saw the familiar sky with the same endless plethora of colors. Just below it, he stood in the vast eternal desert where he'd met the chief in his dreams. This time, the colors were sharper and more breathtaking, seemingly boundless throughout a vast eternity. Tahoe marveled at the preciseness of the colors he could identify and stood aghast at the ones he'd never seen on Earth before. They thrilled him with their indescribable beauty.

The desert appeared the same, now fluidly vivid and less dreamlike. The vast stretch of sand, slightly orange in color, matched that of the great monumental rocks that stood fixedly in the distance. Tahoe could even feel a slight sting as tiny grains of sand blew around him. He focused on something shimmering in front of him, something that grew brighter until it erupted into a flame. Tahoe watched as the flame danced and then intensified into a full, thriving pyre. He felt an inner tugging inside, like something being pulled from him. Then, the fire was gone, extinguished by the presence that stood stoically in its place.

The chief stood before him, arms akimbo and feet firmly planted. The feathers of his great white and red headdress billowed softly in the warm desert breeze. This time, Tahoe studied every light line, every soft wrinkle of the chief's face in an attempt to ascertain his age. An impossible task now, death and eternity had erased all signs of earthly aging.

The chief gazed into Tahoe's eyes, a slight smile spreading across his face. "If it is time you search for, Ulisiatsutsa, you will not find it here." The chief turned his gaze up to the great colorful sky, his eyes searching the boundless ceiling encompassing his ethereal realm. "Time does not exist here. There is only eternity. All times and ages are one."

Tahoe gently lifted his hands so the chief could see the backs of them. Then, he lightly swept the sides of his face with his fingers, demonstrating.

"Time seems to have left me."

"It is my gift to you, great-grandson. You and I are one now. It is my eternal semblance that dwells on you, my soul that thrives within you alongside your own. For you, Ulisiatsutsa, time has reversed and will eventually stand still."

Tahoe felt his heart beating, his ears burning. "You mean—" His voice trailed off. He would allow the great chief to answer the question and respond to his amazement.

The chief closed his eyes and nodded. "You are a soul sharer now, Ulisiatsutsa."

Tahoe's mind marveled at the thought of time standing still. "For how long?" He watched as the chief erupted in laughter.

"For as long as you remain alive, and then one day, you will join me here."

The chief turned and waved his hand across eternity behind him, a boundless desert fresh with thriving plumes of unknown purple flowers, flourishing pea-green cacti, and a warm sun pulsating in the picturesque sky. The balmy desert breeze carried the musky scent of desert spice as it calmed and caressed Tahoe, his long hair billowing behind him. Tahoe experienced a feeling of grand exaltation, a natural high elicited by the prospect of endless time. A temporary feeling it would be until the future day the chief had just prophesied. He gazed out into the vast eternity, literally seeing forever, and it soothed him.

"Come, walk with me, Ulisiatsutsa." The chief pointed with his outstretched hand toward the desert. "Our time together is short. Your receding years are not the only reason I find you here. There is much to tell in such a short duration for the answers you seek."

Tahoe moved alongside the chief, but he wasn't so much walking as he was floating. Yet he said nothing, as the feeling of flotation seemed normal in this instant and in this timeless place. The great monumental rocks in the distant background loomed even closer now. The chief was right, there was much to tell, and instantly, a natural instinct told Tahoe where to begin.

"I have moved away from the desert." Tahoe gazed into the desert landscape before him. "Of course, I cannot go back. I enjoy Green Valley, and what anchors me even more solidly to this place where the shadows once followed me is the realization that something is strange about it, something unique, as if this routinely quiet little town is a portal for the unworldly."

The chief nodded. "Your perception serves you well."

"So, it's true? But how and why?"

"Only time and eternity can answer those questions. They are not for me to explain. But the great green light that beams over Green Valley belongs to otherworldly visitors, a fact of which many are aware."

The chief lifted his hand up to the sky as a great green ray beamed down from above. The green light grew brighter until a gray metallic object suddenly appeared just above it. Tahoe watched the object form into a rotating, disc-shaped craft that controlled the green light and began spinning it in different directions.

"Your grandfather, my son, once told you about a legend. Remember the Legend of the Star People? They were no legend, my great-grandson, they were so."

Mesmerized by the rotating object, Tahoe remembered one of the many legends his grandfather had told him. Star People, beings who once inhabited the Earth and who would one day return. Previously, he'd thought of the old legend, but said nothing to the rest of the team. In his adulthood, he learned about how various Native-American tribes told the same story about these beings yet called them by different names.

The chief read his mind. "Different names for the same beings, Ulisiatsutsa. They visited our people many years ago. They came from the stars in crafts such as this." Tahoe witnessed the elaborate sky suddenly darken and fill with a vast network of stars. The chief pointed to the lingering craft that still projected the rotating green light. "They announced themselves as the original inhabitants of Earth and promised to return one day. That day is hastily arriving."

Continuing to watch the craft, Tahoe made an observation.

"The green light is moving like a searchlight. What are they looking for?"

"Not what, Ulisiatsutsa, but whom. They are searching for their children."

Leah was right. Tahoe had suspected as much. Still, he felt the stun that came from this revelation even in this realm of eternal oblivion.

The chief continued. "With your third eye, you have glimpsed the black-eyed children trudging through the snow. They have been allowed to roam throughout their ancestral home, but for how long remains to be seen."

"These children appear to be menacing," Tahoe explained. "They elicit fear from those they encounter."

"The children are adhering to their own misguided agenda," the chief advised. "The end result cannot be predicted. They have been warned by their elders not to interfere, nor should they engage in one specific task, one that is mysterious and strictly forbidden to them, otherwise things will drastically change." The chief lifted his arms up to the vast sky. Tahoe watched as the gray metallic craft quickly vanished and was instantly replaced by planets and moons that appeared within the vast network of twinkling stars. "Should the true revelation of the Black-Eyed Children be made known, the course and the fate of the universe will be irreparably altered."

Tahoe felt stricken by the chief's words, warning him of something futilely out of his control. No longer were they dealing with menacing shadows or a malevolent spirit, or a house filled with immovable demons. Green Valley was once again facing the otherworldly, something far greater than human minds could comprehend.

"What is it the children are forbidden to do?" Tahoe felt the pressing of time. He asked the question quickly, knowing that the chief's answer might not only be soured in ambiguity, but tainted by the fog upon his rudely awakening.

"In a way, they hold something in common with you,

Ulisiatsutsa." The chief lowered his eyes from the sky and gazed intently at his great-grandson. "They are dual beings."

"Dual beings? What does that mean?"

Just as the words left Tahoe's lips, he felt himself drifting farther and farther away from the chief. Tahoe could no longer see the fine lines of his ancestor's face. The chief stood too far in the distance now, so far that he appeared smaller. Ethereal time was slipping away, but there was so much more to say.

Tahoe became distracted by a shrill buzzing sound, the noise building in a massive wave of volume. Turning his eyes away from the chief for just an instant, Tahoe saw the burgeoning swarm. Cicadas, by the thousands, swarmed toward him. They enveloped him where he stood and created a whirlpool around him. Tahoe felt the sting from the slight pitter-patter of their tiny wings.

The chief called out to him. "Welcome the cicadas, great-grandson! Embrace them! It is for you that they swarm. It is you to whom they are attracted."

Tahoe felt the cicadas tickling his arms, legs, back, and forehead. They tussled through the tresses of his hair. A few of them flew off his hand when he lifted it and called out to the chief.

"What about Green Valley? I want to know."

"Time will reveal all, regardless of the moment. Remember, Ulisiatsutsa, the Star People are watching, and so are their children!"

Tahoe awoke, lying with his back flat down on the bed and his arms outstretched. He'd been in a sitting position when he began the psychic journey. He remembered the sensation of drifting or floating. Turning his head, he glanced at the digital clock display on his nightstand—shortly after midnight. He rose up from the bed and walked into the bathroom, catching a glimpse of himself in the mirror just above the sink. An undeniable truth stared back at him from the mirror. His facial lines had grown finer. His skin felt tighter and smoother as he gently caressed his face with his fingers. Tahoe appeared even younger than he did this morning.

17

THE LOST MEMORY

JAMIE LAY DREAMING AGAIN, BUT THIS TIME, HER dreams brought her back to the past. Her unconscious mind revealed a scene that had already happened; she'd lived it before. Her father stood at the door, yelling at her mother, pointing his finger with damning condemnation.

"Crazy bitch," he spat. *"I'm done. This ends now."*

"Go to Hell and don't come back." Her mother screamed. *"You worthless bastard! Go ahead, leave! You won't see* her *again—that you can be sure of."*

And Jamie didn't. This was the last memory she had of her father, standing in the door, looking at her, contemplating. His black hair slicked back, and his six-foot-three frame nearly busted through his shirt and jeans. He glanced away from her, and then glared once again at her mother. Then he slammed the door behind him.

Jamie lived the moment over again in her dream, while scattered sunken fragments floated to the forefront of her mind. This occurrence had been triggered by Susan's subliminal provocation of her past memories, a fact of which Jamie remained only semi-aware. Her father exiting her life had been one thing, but the memory that came next had been long buried and forgotten.

She'd been riding in the car with Mother. The familiar road unwound toward the base of the great mountain. She knew the mountain, Eagle Rock. Something happened to the car. Mother pulled off to the side of the road. Then, Jamie dreamed of standing alongside the berm of the road, clutching Mother's leg, seemingly afraid of the floating gray object in the sky. It wasn't a plane or anything her young eyes had witnessed before. Mother stared straight up at the object, transfixed, her expression unflinching. As Jamie continued to watch the object, the summer sunlight blinded her, blotting out the image and then the memory—until now.

Jolting and nearly jumping out of bed, Jamie wrapped her arms around her upper body in a protective embrace against the night-time chill. Then, she quickly paced back and forth, attempting to ensure herself of the here and now. Discerning between reality and non-reality was something she no longer felt capable of achieving. Nothing seemed real anymore except the dreams and the images that invaded her mind in the day and even worse, at night.

She'd gone to Susan for help, but after waking only moments ago, the feeling of having opened Pandora's Box pervaded her. As dawn lightened a new day, she stumbled through the dimness and switched on her desk lamp. She retrieved a pad and pen from her desk drawer and began scribbling notes. Everything she recalled about the dream became documented with one or two-word phrases she would later elaborate on.

During her session with Susan, latent images had suddenly flashed in her mind. Jamie had recalled the memory of her and Mother standing alongside the road. She'd mentioned remembering something to Susan and Dylan but hadn't gone into detail. She'd been too distracted and unsure as to whether or not the memory was real. Now she was convinced. Her pen filled the page with little things she now recalled such as the bright sun and the thriving greenness that flourished the trees. She remembered the strange noise the car began to make. The memory was real.

Barely 6:00 a.m., too early to call Susan. Even the sun had not yet fully risen. She would wait a few hours and call her. This could not wait. If she waited until Friday, the vividness of the dream and its details would be mired, smudged by the reality of time passing.

Jamie felt a greasy spill wash over her stomach. She turned, ran to the bathroom, and hurled into the toilet.

———

FEELING LIKE HER NORMAL SELF BY 11:00 A.M., JAMIE decided it was time to call Susan. Her abduction dreams were never diluted by the passing of time after awakening. Last night's dream of long forgotten memories was no different. Her abductions were real, and so was her past. With the notepad she scribbled on earlier in front of her, she dialed Susan's number.

Susan answered on the third ring. "This is Dr. Logan."

"Susan, this is Jamie. I remembered something. I hate to bother you on a Sunday but—" Suddenly overwhelmed, Jamie struggled to catch her breath, a fact that hadn't gone unnoticed by Susan even in a phone call.

"Take your time, Jamie. You're not a bother. That's why I'm here."

"The other day in our session, you triggered something in my mind, an old memory."

"I thought as much, Jamie. Relax. Tell me what you recall."

Once Jamie got her breathing under control, she took a deep breath and exhaled. "It came to me in a dream last night, a childhood memory, one I'd long forgotten. The dream brought it all back to me, but what I recall are fragments, bits and pieces. I woke and quickly wrote what I remembered."

Jamie described the memory of her father, the moment when he walked out of her life. Susan asked a question, accurately assuming that the memory depicted the last time she saw him.

"But that memory was always there. I knew it in my heart, if nothing else." Jamie continued. "It's the memory it segued into that seemed like—I don't know—like I was living it a second time." Jamie described the car ride toward the base of Eagle Rock. Mother had been driving, and she was a little girl in the front seat. "Something happened to the car. We were stranded along the side of the road. I saw the UFO in my dream. Mother stared at it, mesmerized. I remember being afraid, but that's all I can remember. Then, I woke. I know the memory is real." Jamie's tone turned adamant. "I saw that thing before, as a child. Obviously, I was so young that it became buried over time."

"Or you blocked it out, forever," Susan concluded.

"Susan, I want you to hypnotize me, like you did to Dylan. I'm remembering for a reason. I need to get to the bottom of it."

Jamie listened to the dead pause on the other end of the line.

"Well, Jamie," Susan responded. "I must warn you that hypnosis is not a guarantee of anything. It may not even work. Some people can be hypnotized, and some can't. Then, there's the possibility that I put you under and you can't reach the details of that memory. You *were* very young at the time, Jamie. As I said, there are no guarantees—"

"I have to do this, Susan. I don't care what the cost may be. It can't wait until next Friday's appointment."

Jamie waited as another pause became a sea between them.

"Are you free tomorrow?"

"Yes, I'm not working tomorrow."

"I'll see you in my office, this time, tomorrow. And Jamie, try to stay calm. If anything else recurs in your memory, write it down. We'll explore it tomorrow."

Jamie thanked Susan and ended the call. Tomorrow would be a day of discovery, one that would provide her with a long-awaited explanation.

————

Enjoying her coffee in her dining room, Susan was not in the least bit surprised after ending the call with Jamie.

In her office the other day, it was obvious that Jamie remembered something. Susan had told her to wait, to let whatever it was flourish in her mind. They would discuss it at the next session. But memories resurfaced on their own schedule. That's the way the subconscious mind worked.

She couldn't help but feel a slight inner tugging, something telling her that Jamie may not be the right candidate for hypnosis. If Jamie suffered frequent panic attacks, hypnosis could possibly do more harm than good. Susan suddenly regretted triggering old memories in Jamie's mind. She felt dismayed that Jamie's forgotten memories steeped as far back as early childhood. Susan didn't want to do anything to worsen Jamie's situation, yet she sounded determined on the phone. Jamie wanted to remember because it had something to do with the UFO mystery that plagued Green Valley for years, possibly decades.

On the other hand, could unlocking this past memory help Jamie come to terms with what was happening to her? That was also a possibility. Susan feared she hadn't learned enough about Jamie to judge whether or not she'd be a proper candidate for hypnosis, but if Jamie continued to struggle with memories that refused to unravel, her mind could reel and send her panic attacks into a whirlwind. Was it possible that Jamie's abduction dreams had merged with her memories of the past? Susan thought it only slightly possible and readied herself for a darker revelation, one that told of a prior abduction long ago that Jamie had blocked from her mind.

Susan couldn't refuse Jamie now. She'd come to her and Dylan for help with this issue in the first place. All Susan could do now is warn Jamie about how this mystery might play a much larger part in her life than she'd originally assumed. If this was the case, Susan was not surprised. She glanced at her appointment schedule on her laptop in front of her. The eleven o'clock space had already been free. She typed Jamie's name into the empty space. Tomorrow would reveal all.

———

JAMIE AWOKE EARLY THE NEXT MORNING, ANXIOUS AND unable to fall back to sleep. She'd hoped to sleep in for just a few hours, but no such luck. Sleep evaded her. Her ongoing nausea rolled in and out like a wave, causing her a queasy stomach that settled as quickly as it worsened. She hoped she wasn't coming down with something. Her doctor and Susan both worked out of University Hospital. Jamie would check in with him after leaving Susan's office later today. Maybe it was just the stomach flu, but an inner inkling told her to find out. Right now, she couldn't think of anything other than the last dream.

She hadn't told Susan she called off work in order to be at her office, only that she wasn't working. Jamie didn't want to waste time. If this forgotten memory was real, she needed to know now. Late yesterday afternoon, she phoned Dylan and told him about the dream and her newly scheduled session with Susan.

"I want her to hypnotize me, like she did to you," she told him.

Dylan reminded her of how Susan's first attempt at hypnosis on him hadn't worked. He warned her not to get her hopes up.

"That's the thing about hypnosis, Jamie. Susan and I don't know if the memories were buried too deeply, or if I just couldn't face what was too traumatic to recall. But if this is what you want, I support you, and yes, I will be there for you."

Dylan assured her he would clear his schedule in order to be at Susan's office at eleven, and he'd kept his word. Minutes before the hour hand struck eleven, Jamie spotted Dylan outside Susan's office door. Together, they entered after a quick knock. Expecting only the two of them, Susan sat behind her desk, perusing her laptop screen as she waited.

"Right on time," Susan greeted them. She swirled around in her seat and removed her glasses as she glanced at Jamie. "It sounds like someone's had a breakthrough. This was expected, Jamie." She turned her gaze toward Dylan. "And Dylan, thank you for being here to support Jamie. As another abductee, your presence here is crucial."

Like last time, they retreated to the cozy corner at the far end of Susan's office and were seated just as they were: Jamie on one end of the plush couch, Dylan at the far end, and Susan on the chair directly across from Jamie. After settling in, Susan attempted to ascertain how Jamie felt with a few quick questions.

"I'm fine, really," Jamie assured her. "I just want to know if this memory of my mother and me is real or not."

"Jamie, you mentioned the memory of your father walking out on you and your mother. Do you think this a real memory?

"Yes, I remember it happening, but haven't thought back on it in a long time. It just seems like I'd forgotten it. My life happened."

"Okay," Susan probed. "In your dream, did you dream of your father first?"

"Yes." Jamie had explained it all on the phone, but now Susan was making a point Jamie clearly couldn't see.

"And this elusive memory of your mother came second, a memory in which you were an even younger child. Am I right?" Jamie nodded. "Then, Jamie, you're dreaming of time in reverse. I believe my original assumption was right, that the memory is real and something you blocked as a child. The memory of your father is more real to you because you were older, and you recall it more precisely. It's also a somewhat hurtful memory, so it solidifies itself as genuine in your mind. It's also possible this memory of your father didn't completely leave you because you were too old to permanently block it."

Susan leaned in toward her, as if doing so would make her point more direct. "It's this memory of your mother we have to examine. But Jamie, Dylan and I have already warned you. Hypnosis may not resolve the issue, and if it does, the memory you recall could be a traumatic one. This is entirely up to you."

Jamie sat resolved. This was the reason she called off work and came here today. Nothing was going to stop her. Her mind was made up.

She nodded unwaveringly. "Let's do this now."

"Alright then, Jamie," Susan sat back in her chair. "First, I want you to sit back and relax. This is the most crucial part. Sit back, calm yourself, and relax." Jamie complied. "Now, close your eyes, and listen to the sound of my voice. Clear your mind of everything."

Jamie listened as Susan's voice subsided into a soft, soothing purr. She felt the plush of the couch cradling her head as she drifted back, and the foot of its reclining end ejected outward, lifting her feet slightly off the floor. Susan's voice, like a gentle symphony, continued.

"I want you to picture a place in your mind, somewhere you've been before or somewhere you'd like to go. It should be not only a place that makes you feel safe, but somewhere that makes you comfortable, a scene that soothes your mind. Picture it and go there."

Jamie envisioned a sandy-white beach and crystal clear aqua-colored waves that caressingly crashed upon it. She could almost feel herself lying on her back, her toes dug snugly into the fine white sand. She relished the scene in her mind and indulged in it. The waves, not far from her feet, soothed her. Softly, Susan's voice could be heard over the sloshing waves.

"Have you found a place, Jamie?"

"Yes," she responded.

"Tell me where you are." Jamie described the scene, her words uttered in monotone. "Good," Susan continued. "Now I want you to immerse yourself in your surroundings. I'm going to count backwards from five. When I reach one, you'll be asleep, understand?"

Had she just said "yes?" She wasn't sure. Feeling too relaxed to respond, Jamie simply nodded. The familiar voice began counting backwards.

"Five, four—"

Jamie felt herself drifting. Sleep was descending upon her like a curtain.

"Three, two—"

The curtain of sleep draped over the scene she felt so relaxed in.

"One."

Jamie fell asleep, and only the familiar soothing voice could be heard.

"Can you hear me, Jamie?"

"Yes."

"What do you see?"

Jamie saw only the dim, flickering light of a distant memory.

"I want you to watch that light, Jamie," Susan instructed. "Watch it as it enlarges."

Jamie watched as the light grew brighter and developed into a picture, which turned into a moving scene in her mind. Once again, she saw her mother and father shouting briskly back and forth.

"I'll ask you once again, Jamie. What do you see?"

"My parents, they're fighting again." A hint of distress broke through Jamie's monotone. "I'm standing there watching them. It's like they don't even care. They hate each other so badly. I feel like it's my fault, like they're fighting about me."

"No, Jamie, they're not." Susan's tone turned forceful. "The discord between them has nothing to do with you. Your mother is demanding. Your father is distant. You are a child who has not caused this. Jamie, this is the last time you see your father. You know this. I want you to move past it. Breathe, Jamie, and leave it in the past."

Jamie inhaled deeply, her chest rising and falling as the image in her mind faded. Again, Susan's voice slipped into its soft caress.

"Jamie, there's another memory from your past, one you dreamed of afterward. I want you to find it, Jamie, and then tell me where you are and what you see."

Instantly, Jamie envisioned herself in the front seat of the car, her mother, much younger than she normally recalled, drove down the spiraling slope of the mountain.

"I'm in the car with Mother," she said. "We're nearing the base of Eagle Rock."

"Good. Now, something happens along the main road. Remember it, Jamie."

At the mountain's base, Jamie watched the recollection. Mother waited for a car on the left before making a right turn back onto the highway. After turning, Mother drove until a loud noise screeched and dragged from underneath the car. Jamie could still hear the clunk and clatter colliding below her seat. Then Mother swore.

"Shit! Not here, of all places."

Mother coasted the car alongside the road and stopped.

"Just one second, Sweetie. Don't worry. Everything will be alright."

Jamie's concern grew when Mother stepped out of the car, the oncoming highway vehicles whizzing dangerously past her. Surely, she wouldn't leave her here. No. Mother walked around to the front of the car and opened the passenger door. She took Jamie by the hand and led her out. They walked a few paces to the trunk of the car when Mother loosened the tight, sweaty grip of her large hand.

"You stay right there, Jamie." Mother kept her upraised finger pointed at her as she turned and strutted a few feet away from her, toward something that lay strewn halfway along the berm and uncomfortably close to the highway.

Unconsciously, Jamie's adult mind recognized an oddly-shaped hunk of metal. Cars raced past. Horns honked as Mother stepped closer to the edge of the busy highway. Mother grabbed the object with both hands and dashed quickly back to where Jamie stood. She opened the trunk, laid the object inside, and slammed the door shut.

Mother clasped her hand tightly around hers once again as they walked to the front of the car. Jamie clearly recalled the bright sun, the screeching cicadas, and even the rustling of foliage from the light summer breeze that blew at the mountain's base.

"You keep hold of my hand, Jamie," Mother advised. *"If I have to step forward, you stay right in this spot and don't move."*

Three more cars fled past them. Each time, Mother raised her arm and tried to wave them down. Stranded, in need of help, but each driver ignored her plea. They stood waiting for the next car. Mother made an arch with her hand and bridged it above her eyes, glancing backward down the highway and seeing nothing. A sudden lapse in traffic provoked Mother's frustration.

"Damn it! You've got to be kidding me!"

Another car whizzed past. The male driver didn't even bother to glace at the side of the road.

"Asshole," Mother muttered under her breath.

Then, looming overcast clouds from the distance slid steadily above them, shading the daylight with sudden drabness. Déjà-vu struck Jamie as a bright green light beamed down from above, engulfing them in its radiant glare and seemingly policing them. Something was happening. Mother squeezed her hand as both of their heads turned up to the sky, their eyes mesmerized by the great unmoving disc that hovered above. Jamie knew it wasn't an airplane or a helicopter. She glanced at Mother, whose eyes widened behind a frozen mask of fear. Jamie had never seen Mother so afraid. She and Daddy weren't afraid of anything.

"It's hovering above us, in the sky. It came out of nowhere."

"What's in the sky, Jamie?" Susan softly probed.

"Something neither of us has ever seen before." Jamie's poignant description had not failed so far. She continued to depict the lost memory through her sleepy monotone unhindered. "It's gray, maybe silver in color, disc-shaped. It's watching us. I can feel it. Mother knows it too." Jamie wriggled in her reclining position. "It's shining a light down on us, a blinding green light. Mother is squeezing my hand even harder. I feel weightless, like I'm flying because the ground is now beneath me. Then there's gray all around us. We're pulled apart by hands that quickly grip us, strange hands. Mother screams as she's pulled in one direction, and I'm whisked away in another."

Jamie breathed deeply, letting the air fill her lungs until she slowly exhaled.

"You're doing fine, Jamie," Susan said. "What happens next?"

"*Mommy!*" Jamie screamed.

"*Jamie, my baby! Who are you? Where are you taking her?*"

Mother's screams continued, lessening into an echo that died away just as Jamie realized she'd been relocated by means she didn't understand. Another sense of déjà-vu as Jamie sat in a tiled room, recalling the strange yet soft hands that stroked her head soothingly.

"*Everything will be alright.*" A calm and equally soft female voice reassured her. "*No one will hurt you.*"

Jamie felt the female's hands press upon her shoulders and gently push her down on a table. She could see the strange woman and her counterpart who stood at the foot of the table, yet she couldn't distinguish them. As a child, she had assumed her vision was blurred, but the child failed to see the shadowy translucent veil shielding these beings that the adult would later recognize. Jamie now saw misshapen heads, not distortions she had once ignored and forgotten.

The silent male counterpart stepped forward. Using his lanky fingers, he pried Jamie's right eyelid wide open. Then he shined a light so bright in her eye, a pain flashed through her skull. He scanned with the light in and around her eye, and once she winced from the pain, he repeated his actions on her left eye. Retrieving a pointed object from his pocket, he pressed a button and a thin blue ray of light ejected from it. He used it to measure the length of her body, her legs, her arms, and the circumference of her head.

Then, as did the woman, he ran his fingers through her hair, examining every fine strand and studying them down to the roots. His fingers traced the shape of her hairline and her face, gently pressing upon her skull in the process. The next thing Jamie knew the hands turned her until she lay face down. The same fingers coursed the trail of her spine, counting her vertebrae. They examined her down to her feet, tallying her toes and testing her pedal reflexes, but Jamie said nothing, feeling a sense of calm. Her worry for Mother had lessened to curiosity. The unknown woman's words resounded in her mind.

Then she felt herself moving again, experiencing that familiar vision of rectangular lights passing above her. The lights merged and became a brilliant bright-green shaft she glided through. She spotted Mother within the green light.

"Jamie!" Mother screamed.

The next thing Jamie knew, she and Mother stood alongside the road near the trunk of the car. Dusk now settled into a pink sunset spreading across the horizon. Mother clutched her to her waist, seemingly dazed and still staring beyond the highway when something approached from the distance.

"Mother and I are standing alongside the road. There's a pickup truck coming towards us. Mother's waving him down."

The recollection was suddenly interrupted. Jamie's breathing intensified as the strange, alien female figure appeared in her mind. Her large black eyes peered back at her through distance and time. The veil that once seemingly shaded her alien presence had now vanished. She waved her lanky index finger and shook her misshapen head. Jamie gasped.

"Jamie, what's wrong?" Susan's soothing tone turned serious.

"Oh, no," Jamie lamented. "I wasn't *supposed* to remember."

"Jamie, focus on the sound of my voice. Let it lead you. When I count to five, you're going to wake up and remember."

This time, Susan counted forward. "One."

A sudden haze overshadowed the memory in Jamie's mind.

"Two."

The memory faded into darkness.

"Three."

Jamie felt herself floating.

"Four."

Her eyes flickered.

"Five."

Jamie opened her eyes and glanced around her. Susan sat across from her, Dylan, at the far end of the reclining couch. The same faceless girl stood oblivious to the rain in Susan's office painting. A fast-flashing thought made Jamie wonder why she envied her.

"How do you feel, Jamie?"

Jamie's eyes narrowed in recollection. "I remember it now." She sat up, pushing the end of the recliner inward with her feet. "Mother and I were taken as we stood alongside the road." A cry escaped Jamie. Her jaw dropped as tried to get the words out. "They abducted me long ago when I was a child." She glanced at Susan and placed her hand over chest. "They did to Mother what they did to—"

"Jamie, listen to me," Susan intervened, holding her hands out in front of her in an attempt to calm her patient. "That moment is far in the past. Your mother is gone now, Jamie, passed on from something completely unrelated. You don't actually know what happened to your mother then. You didn't see it. The good thing is that from your recollection, you weren't violated as a child. You precisely described a thorough physical examination. This seems to be a ritual with these beings."

Susan continued. "Jamie, I provoked your subconscious last time because I suspected some memory lay buried in your past, one that, in the back of your mind, is responsible for your sense of fear and panic. I thought it likely had something to do with your sleep abductions. You were deemed a Class Two abductee by the team, but since Class Two abductees are rare, I wasn't convinced."

"What Susan is saying," Dylan interjected, "is that you were the only abductee who came to us that wasn't abducted from the ground and out in the open, yet the fact that you were somehow connected to these beings and this mystery remained undeniable. As it turns out, you *were* abducted from the ground, but it was something you blocked from your mind in childhood. You are therefore a Class One abductee."

Jamie felt a surge of overwhelming doubt. "No, I don't think that's what happened." She described the image of the woman waving her lanky finger at her just before she woke. "They erased it from my memory. I wasn't supposed to remember."

"This is interesting, Jamie," Susan said. "Memory loss after abduction is extremely common, but why do you think you weren't supposed to remember?"

Jamie's mind searched for an explanation. Susan was right, she hadn't witnessed what happened to Mother back then. And she herself wasn't harmed as a child. She guessed it was for the same reason that the shadowy veil hung over those who had taken her. She shook her head.

"I don't know," she said.

"And I've never discovered the answer to that question either," Dylan agreed.

Susan nodded. "The mystery continues, but we're making progress. As I've often said, we may never fully have the answers, but we *can* move forward. We *can* live without fear."

Susan asked again how she felt. Jamie conveyed the feeling of weight being lifted from her mind, but the fear inside her remained. She failed to express how her sense of fear felt like it was widening, especially as a new wave of nausea washed over her stomach.

"You should feel proud of yourself for what happened today, Jamie," Dylan added. "You had the strength and determination to come in here and undergo the hypnosis. You stood your ground, and unlike me, you remembered. The fact that you did is a positive sign."

Susan agreed and reiterated her instruction to write down any further memories. She reminded Jamie that she and Dylan were available any time, day or night.

"I'll see you again this Friday, at our usual time," Susan reminded her.

"Don't forget our group meeting on Saturday," Dylan advised.

Jamie agreed and thanked them as they walked her to the door.

Secretly, something inside told Jamie that by the weekend, the mystery surrounding them would take a radical turn.

———

DYLAN WATCHED AS SUSAN CLOSED THE DOOR BEHIND Jamie. Deep in thought, she turned around, her eyes cast to the floor.

"What are you thinking?" he asked.

"Well, I accurately assumed that something lay buried in Jamie's past, but what perturbs me is the image she saw just before waking. This strange woman admonished her for remembering. I felt a chill when Jamie claimed she wasn't supposed to remember. She said this under hypnosis, and while she was awake. The fear is still great in Jamie. I saw it on her face. She's underplaying the extent of what she really feels. She's hiding something. I can't help but be worried about her."

"Are you suggesting some repercussion awaits Jamie because she remembered?"

Susan turned around again and stared at the door, her hands forming that familiar steeple she held in front of her lips every time she became engrossed in deep thought.

"God, I hope not. I seriously hope not."

18

BLACK-EYED BABY

JAMIE LEFT SUSAN'S OFFICE AND RODE THE FIFTH-floor elevator down to the second floor. After switching her phone back on, she noticed five missed calls, two from Sam plus a text message he left her shortly after calling the second time.

Where are you? We need to talk.

Sam called her three times yesterday; each time, she ignored his calls. She couldn't talk to him, not now, and certainly not after what just happened in Susan's office. Her mind reeled in multiple directions, producing thoughts that strengthened her fears. She'd become the basket case she never wanted Sam to encounter. Now was not the time to have to avoid his questions or to make dinner plans that ended in an early evening. She was on her way to yet another appointment, and when it was over, she would phone Sam. Now, she didn't want to think. She wanted to just move.

Dr. Webb's office was on the second floor. She was about to find out what exactly was going on physically inside her. What was causing her consistent nausea? Was it the constant apprehension she felt? Was it her nerves or was it something else? She recalled the dream of being pregnant and Mother standing before her, pleading with her not to keep it. She remembered Nadine's words of admonition.

"They took my baby."

She rid the thought from her mind as Dr. Webb's receptionist logged her in for her appointment. While Jamie sat in the waiting room, she revisited the memory that not twenty minutes ago had been unlocked from her mind. No longer did bits and pieces sporadically and briefly resurface. Jamie remembered it all now, every moment as though it were yesterday. All this time, Jamie believed the dreams of the bright green light and the sleek gray craft were exclusive to her. Now, the image of her and Mother enwrapped in that same green light replayed over and over.

She'd been abducted by these beings as a child, nearly a quarter of a century ago. What was it that they wanted from her? Why did they keep coming back? Jamie also wondered why Mother had never mentioned the incident. Had she also blocked it from her own mind?

"Jamie?" The nurse's voice startled her. It was time for the doctor to see her. She stood and walked through a side door into a hallway lined with observation rooms. As always, the nurse measured her height and weight. Jamie gained four pounds since her last visit six months ago. Nothing about this day pointed her in the direction she'd hoped to be in. Moment by moment, her worst fears seemed to be edging closer and closer toward reality.

Dr. Webb arrived within minutes and closed the door behind him. He asked the usual questions, and then Jamie described her nausea. He probed as to when it began and how long it lasted each time.

"Anything else bothering you?" he asked.

"No," Jamie denied. "Other than a flip-flopping stomach, I'm fine." No need to mention her constant nervous condition. She wanted out of here as soon as possible. Besides, she was working with Susan on the matter.

"All right," he said. "We'll get to the bottom of it."

Within minutes, a nurse entered the room and drew her blood into two separate vials. She told Jamie the doctor's office would phone when the results were in. Jamie thanked her, checked out, and anxiously drove home.

She arrived home in time to fix herself a quick lunch. Then, she spent the rest of her free day doing anything to distract her mind from today's session, everything from cleaning the kitchen to flipping through the TV stations. She could no longer think about the lost memory, or she would drive herself mad. Jamie jumped slightly when her phone rang. Glancing at the screen, she recognized Dr. Webb's office number. She hadn't expected a call back so soon, only four and a half hours later. She waited just a second as her hands slightly trembled before answering.

"Jamie, it's Dr. Webb." She recognized his voice. "You can relax, there's nothing wrong you." He paused. "You're pregnant."

His words repeated over and over in her mind. She envisioned Mother again, just like the dream, warning her to let "them" have it. Nadine's fearful prediction was upon her, a reality so real no fighting could deny it. Only one question went through her mind, one of which she already knew the answer.

"How far along am I?"

"Approximately three months."

She cringed at how cheerful his voice sounded in this moment, utterly oblivious of the circumstances. But his words were undeniable. Reality had presented itself, whether her mind accepted it or not. Deep inside, she knew. She hadn't received her monthly bloody visitor in quite some time. Three months ago, they invaded her. But then again, this baby could belong to Sam. It was *possible*. They'd been together only days prior. It *was* possible, wasn't it? What if this unborn entity inside her had nothing to do with her abductions?

"I see," Jamie uttered the only words she could muster.

"I take it this pregnancy was unexpected?" he asked. Dr. Webb didn't wait for an answer. "It happens, Jamie, don't worry. The good news is that you'll live."

He laughed. Jamie felt a chill tickle her spine.

Dr. Webb mentioned another appointment in three weeks, citing that he would schedule her for a separate appointment with a trusted obstetrician. He spoke, but Jamie heard only words, yet his point was taken, nonetheless. She wanted off the phone as soon as possible.

"My office will phone you when the next appointments are scheduled, alright?"

Jamie agreed and thanked him, ending the call and staring blankly at her living room wall. Pregnant, she thought, yet some part of her deep down inside had already known all along. She needed to tell someone. Sam? No, not yet. She thought of calling Susan but remembered Nadine's words to her in the university lounge.

"We are all in this together. If you need me for any reason, I'm always here for you."

Phone still in hand, she attempted to dial Nadine when the phone rang. Sam's name appeared on the screen. She couldn't avoid him anymore. It was time. Jamie pressed the answer button and greeted him, and then heard a slight pause.

"Wow, you finally answered my call," he said. His voice didn't boast of his usual jovial self. Now, he sounded irritated, impatient.

"I'm sorry," Jamie's tone inadvertently came off as defensive. He had no idea what she'd been going through, but admittedly, that was her fault. "I've had a rough few days. I have something to tell you."

He sighed. "Yeah, I have something to tell you, too."

Jamie knew well that her news was bigger than whatever he had to tell her, but she needed to hear what he was going to say next. She was carrying his child.

He sighed again. "Jamie, I don't know. I don't know what to say. You haven't been answering my calls lately. I haven't heard from you in almost a week. When we're together, it's like you don't want to be there. I drive you home, and then I don't hear from you."

"Sam," she interrupted. "I've been going through some really trying issues lately—things that go way back to my childhood." She paused. "Lately, they've been coming to light, and I haven't been sure how to handle them. But I have been seeing someone about it. I just—"

"See, Jamie, that's what I mean, you don't sound like you're able to be in a relationship right now. I've been looking for something more."

Jamie heard herself placating through a litany of weak excuses, some that didn't make sense even to her. She felt her lips about to form the words *I'm pregnant with your child*, but then, something stopped her. He continued as her attempt at words died away.

"I've been seeing Heather again. She wants us to pick up where we left off. I'm sorry, Jamie, but I think it's best if I explore this with her. I've wanted to at least to talk to you about all this, but you never answer my calls or my texts. I'm just not sure what to do anymore as far as we're concerned. Again, I'm sorry, Jamie."

"I see." Heartbreak, anger, and unexpected relief exploded inside her.

"You said you had something to tell me?" His tone was unassuming. Jamie could've blown his world away with just a few words. Then she thought of everything she'd been through, especially today. The lost memory replayed in her mind. Sam couldn't help her. Outside of maybe Dylan and Susan, no one could. She remained silent.

"No, it was nothing," she said.

"Come on, Jamie. Don't do this. Talk to me."

"I hope you and Heather will be happy."

Sam sighed again. "And I hope you get to the root of whatever's eating away at you, Jamie. I really mean that. I wish you well."

"Thanks," she said. Stunned, she ended the call.

The term "basket case" assaulted her. She closed her eyes and ran her fingers through her hair, her nails scraping her scalp. What just happened had been inevitable. If this was Sam's baby and not some fetal implantation placed inside her, she would have been better off without him. And if it wasn't—she turned her thoughts away from that possibility. She dialed Nadine as she'd originally intended. No answer.

She didn't want to bother Susan or Dylan again today. She would wait and call them later, maybe tomorrow. Jamie's eyes searched around her small living room, seeing everything and nothing at the same time. Another being lived inside her, yet she never felt so alone.

———

HAVING READIED HERSELF FOR BED, JAMIE COULDN'T wait to close her eyes, fall asleep, and leave the day's shocking revelations behind. She would face today's dilemmas again tomorrow with a clearer head when they became yesterday's news. Jamie closed her eyes and fell fast asleep.

Then she dreamed once again.

She stood in an unfamiliar field, recognizing the here and now and the icy snowy assault of winter. Snowcapped crags of rock stood out to her. Ice-covered brush froze solid until the spring sunshine would soon set it free. Jamie stood facing a cave, the entrance of which appeared impenetrable by the blackness inside. Then, something moved within that blackness, a streak of red that came closer and closer. Someone was emerging from the cave.

Jamie heard a baby wailing. An adolescent figure wearing a red hoodie came forward, cradling a bundle in his arms. The baby's cries grew louder and echoed. The hooded boy carried the baby, and steadily he approached Jamie. She tried to see the boy's face, but she couldn't. He hung his head too low, and the width of his hood draped his face like that of a praying monk's. But Jamie's attention to his unseen face was distracted when he held the bundled baby out to her.

"Take him, he's your son." Jamie heard the boy's strange voice, not out loud but in her mind.

Jamie glanced down at the stirring creature within the swaddling before she noticed its eyes. Large black ovals looked up at her. She saw darkness in two small pools, black like the entrance to the cave. Even the baby's wailing voice sounded somewhat different now, like that of the boy's. Jamie distinctly heard the unnatural mechanical whine of something different from mankind.

She turned her head up to the boy. Now she saw his face. He had the same eyes. The face appeared wan and thinner than most. She couldn't see through the blackness of those eyes. Fear swept her from inside, freezing her in place like the once billowing brush beside her. She backed away from the boy.

"I don't want him! I DON'T WANT HIM!" She heard her own voice echoing. *"GET AWAY FROM ME!"*

"They will come for you soon, Jamie," the boy warned.

Jamie awoke screaming.

19

THE TIME HAS COME

IONA RECALLED THE BRIGHT GREEN LIGHT THAT SWEPT the mountain top the other night. She'd seen it clearly from inside the cave; they all had. The same light that brought them here had sought to take them back. The guardian parents were searching, hoping to retrieve them, but Iona's intent to flee from the hidden safety of the cave and flag them down had been quickly subdued. Orion had read her thoughts.

"Don't." He'd stood in front of her, blocking her path to exit the cave's entrance. "It's not time yet, Iona. We have not completed our mission."

But by the thorough intensity of the green light as it searched the mountain, Iona knew differently.

"They want us to return, Orion. We were told not to interfere."

"They don't understand the extent of what we've learned so far, Iona." He referred to the girl with the third eye. "We're obligated to discover all we can, especially about people like her."

At first, she'd been against Orion's wayward plan, but now her reluctance somewhat lessened into skepticism.

"I'm afraid of the repercussions if we don't return."

He silenced her. "You let me deal with that. I'm the leader of this mission. I will face the responsibility."

Normally, she was the one intent on sticking to the rules, but since seeing her mother in the dreams, she couldn't help but wonder about her. She and Indrid had a brother here. So did Medea. Iona wanted to learn more about her mother. She wanted to catch a glimpse of her other than in dreams. Orion had made the point that if they returned now, none of that would ever be possible. They would never lay eyes on their Earthly parents again. It was now or never. If they could break through to their emotions, make them acknowledge them, they could be the ones to change things forever.

Now, another night had come. On the mountain top, an endless sea of stars spread above them, seemingly close enough to touch. Iona stood within the small circle, listening as Orion dictated his plan to the three of them. She remained skeptical but hopeful that he would somehow prove to be right.

"We *will* make them come to us," he said. "If we can't communicate with them, we must start with the children. It's the only way."

Indrid listened intently with his head hung low, his eyes staring at the frozen ground beneath him. Medea's wide-eyed expression as she hung on Orion's every word irrefutably displayed the extent of their leader's influence. It almost sickened Iona. If Orion's plan failed, the end result could spell disaster for the four of them, and Iona remained unafraid to call him on it even though she secretly prayed for his plan to work. She stood the farthest away from him, far enough to make her stance apparent. Orion walked over to her and laid his hands against the top of her shoulders.

"Don't worry. They will not leave us. I will make this work. I will show them. We're running out of time."

"I'm still afraid, Orion. Why do you think we haven't heard their words in our minds?"

"Distance," he maintained, but Iona recognized his weak excuse meant to extinguish his own denial.

"I don't believe that," she countered.

"The time has come for action, Iona. You're either with us or you're not."

She felt powerless against him in this moment. Neither Medea, nor Indrid, would look her in the face. She glanced up at the stars, and then closed her big black eyes against them. Orion turned away from her and continued.

"We will all walk together. Our journey will be a long one, but not too long. You're all aware of the assignment and the path we will take to our destinations." He glanced at each of them and noticed Iona slowly stepping forward. Then he finished his instructions. "As I've said, the time has come. Let's be on our way. The night awaits us."

———

THE STRANGEST SENSE OF DÉJÀ VU SWEPT DYLAN.

He'd pulled another late night work binge in his office-study, sitting at the computer grading student assignments and attending to loose ends regarding his book's release. Just like the other night, the feeling of being watched suddenly overwhelmed him. A quick chill caused an inadvertent quiver as he felt the glare of invisible eyes. Like before, he turned around in his chair and stared at the window facing out to the front gate. Again, he felt drawn to the window, positive that someone lurked outside, someone who was looking in. He sprang from the chair and dashed to the window.

He raised the window blinds and, after swiping at the frost, gazed out into the freezing night. Several shadows darted quickly past the gate so fast he failed to catch them. Someone was out there; he knew it. Dylan grabbed his phone and ran out into the front hallway, hastening to put on his shoes. He didn't bother to lace them. He didn't waste time searching for his coat to shield him from the icy wind outside. He opened the front door and fled into the freezing cold that bit into his skin.

He ran across the stone walkway to the front gate, nearly slipping on a sheet of ice beneath his shoes. He made it to the front gate and clung to the iron railing, turning his head as far as he could to see left and right. No one lurked outside the gate. No shadows moved under the arc lights. But just outside the gate he saw them, plainly set in the snow blanketing the ground—footprints and several of them.

A box containing the gate's control panel was set behind one of the stone posts. Dylan opened it and keyed in his pass code, which then unlocked the front gate. The gate's door screeched slightly as he pulled it open and stepped out onto the sidewalk. Two sets of footprints, average in size, lay freshly in the snow. One set faced the gate's door, as though whoever they'd belonged to stood directly there, staring at the front of the house. The other set of prints were marked right beside the other, as though two people had stood together.

Dylan captured a few shots with his phone's camera, and then traced the steps backward and then forward. Other footprints lay up ahead beyond the gate's door. At some point, the footprints merged together into a snowy mess, making it impossible to tell how many existed beyond the initial two. After closing the gate door and relocking it, he hastened back to the house as the icy wind threatened to steal his breath.

Back inside, he retrieved the pictures from his phone and examined them. There was no doubt in his mind as to who the footprints belonged to, the BEK, he was sure of it. Since the last meeting, Dylan had been devising a plan to draw them out. He'd made it clear he wasn't about to let the others endanger themselves by seeking out these sinister kids. Most of this debacle had to do with him. As selfish of a thought it was, it remained true. The time had come, Dylan thought, and he would need Leah to help him.

Knowing well she'd be awake at this hour, he called her without a single hesitation. Leah answered on the second ring.

"What's going on?" Slightly suspicious, trepidation crept through her voice.

"They were outside the gate again, watching me only minutes ago," he informed her. "Have you or do you see anything?"

Dylan meant both literally and with her mind's eye. A pause ensued.

"No, I don't. The only person here is Sidney. He's been staying on the couch, staking out in case they return. Tonight's been quiet."

"It's possible your house is their next stop. I'm on my way over."

"Did you see them?" Leah asked.

"No, but I could feel them watching me." Dylan told her about the quick passing shadows outside the gate and the footprints he photographed. "I need you to look at these pictures. Tell me what you think."

She agreed. Within minutes, Dylan was in his car and speeding away via the back roads. He arrived at Leah's cottage in a little over ten minutes and parked behind Sidney's van. Exiting the car, Dylan's eyes roved all around him, searching for signs of anyone lingering outside. All seemed quiet here, except for the slight whistle of the icy wind. The packed snow lay frozen into a powdery crystalline mass of white, seemingly soft-blue under the full moonlight. The smell of fresh burning hickory wafted through the cold air as its smoke pumped from Leah's chimney. Rock salt crunched beneath his shoes on the sidewalk, allowing him to tread quickly to the front door. The porch light turned on as he approached. Then Sidney opened the door and let him in.

Leah stood in the background behind Sidney. Dylan heard Sid quickly locking the door behind him. Dylan retrieved his phone from his inner coat pocket.

"Look at these." He pulled the photos up on the screen, handed the phone to Leah, and removed his coat. "I took those over a half-hour ago."

Sidney moved to Leah's side so they both could examine the

pictures. Dylan watched as Leah enlarged the pictures, and she and Sid examined them from different angles. Then, she closed her eyes for a moment.

"Yes, it was them. I see more than one of them standing outside your gate," she said.

Dylan crossed over to the fireplace and briefly let the flames warm the cold from his body, while Leah and Sidney continued to study the photos. After rubbing his hands together over the fireplace, he turned back to them. "I'm going to draw them out tonight, Leah. That's where you come in."

Leah handed the phone to Sidney. "I see," she said, turning to Dylan. "So, you need me to *lure* them out, right, the girl with the third eye?"

"There's no other way, Leah," he said. "Unless we sit and wait for them to come back for us, but as Brad said, they *will* be back for us. Tahoe said as much himself at the meeting. We can continue to live with this eerie apprehension they've instilled in us, or we can confront them. I planned on going about this alone, but realized I can't do it without you. After all, you're the one who foresaw them being up on the mountain. You're the one who can locate them."

"Wait a minute," Sidney said, situating himself on the living room loveseat. "I realize this directly affects you, Dylan, but surely, you as chief investigator understand that we're all in this together, are we not?"

"I meant what I said at the last meeting, Sid. I'm not about to let anyone else risk their lives over this. It's up to me to seek them out."

"I can respect that," Sidney countered. "But did you realize anything from this picture?" Sidney held up Dylan's phone, the screen displaying one of the pictures Dylan took. "This mess of distorted footprints should have told you right away that you have no idea how many of these kids were lingering outside your window. From what Nadine and Brad told us of their dreams, we can count at least four of them. That makes you and Leah outnumbered. We still know nothing about these kids. It's way too dangerous to go it alone without the team, Dylan. We thought you learned that after your solo trip to Eagle Rock Mountain."

"The more people involved, the greater the responsibility, and the greater the danger." Dylan's voice rose slightly as the conversation heated, yet Sidney remained calm.

"Going it alone is what got you into this mess in the first place."

Dylan paced in his attempts to spit his point out. He stopped, breathed deeply, and then sat down. Sidney was right; he knew it. But he still couldn't shake the vibe that others would be harmed all because of him. After a pause, he turned his attention back toward Leah.

"I wanted to take you because you psychically saw them being atop the mountain," he explained. "You're the best chance of locating them, and yes, your presence may draw them out. But I will *not* let anything happen to you or anyone else for that matter."

"I can't let you do this." Sidney rose from the chair, determined and perching all of his weight adamantly into a standstill. "Going it alone is a direct violation of the society's code. The case would be left with no documented or established proof of anything that could occur, including your death. Need I remind you that last time you went, that's exactly what we thought happened? So, either we all go or no one goes to Eagle Rock Mountain."

"Sidney's right," Leah decided. "I'm the one who saw them, right on my front porch. I'm telling you both, these kids possess capabilities far beyond our understanding. Believe me when I tell you they stopped my third eye from gazing any further than they wanted me to see. They knew who I was from the moment they saw me. Fear exudes from them. I felt almost paralyzed by it. I don't know if they wield it intentionally, or if it's our natural human reaction to their unexplained existences, but I can definitely tell you the fear is real, and it's there for a reason."

Dylan sighed. "I'm worried that all of us being there might deter them from coming out of hiding."

"Nothing will deter them," Leah insisted. "They're not afraid. *We* are afraid, and my natural instinct tells me it's for a good reason."

Dylan realized that whether on top of the mountain with Leah or here in her living room, he was outnumbered either way. His case for a single-handed approach had lost the argument. He turned and faced them.

"Fine, call the rest of the team," he said. "But we need to move fast. I have a feeling that something is about to happen."

———

"The time has come, Ulisiatsutsa." THE CHIEF'S VOICE thundered.

Asleep, Tahoe stirred on the living room loveseat. He'd drifting off while watching the eleven o'clock news. Now, he inexplicably found himself facing the chief in another dream. But rather than a dream, this was a quick and dire warning.

"The Black-Eyed Children have gathered and are on the move." The chief spoke with a grave tone. His face formed a somber expression; his ebony eyes widened. *"You must be there. You must remember my words and warn the children of that which is forbidden. It may be the only way to stop them."*

Tahoe felt disoriented, even in the dream state. *That which is forbidden,* he wondered.

"Ulisiatsutsa, waken!"

He rudely awakened, feeling a desperate sense of urgency. The eleven o'clock news was winding down with a brutal weather forecast. The now familiar weatherman pointed to the projected screen behind him. Tahoe watched the screen as a white wave rolled over western Pennsylvania. The forecast was yet another warning.

"As you can see, the windy arctic blast continues, as this area of low pressure from the northeast seeps over Pennsylvania and the Ohio Valley region.

Unfortunately, this icy barrage will remain for at least another twenty-four hours before we see any hint of things warming up."

Tahoe pressed the mute button on the remote when the weatherman signaled back to the female anchor. Just then, Brett entered the living room from the kitchen. Tahoe noticed the seriousness of his expression as he walked toward him on the couch with his phone in hand.

"I just got a call from Sidney," he said. "Those weird kids stalked Dylan again tonight. Sid, Leah, and Dylan have decided to search for them tonight up on Eagle Rock. They want us to be there."

"I'm aware of this. I've had another dream of the chief." Tahoe explained the chief's warning. "If these children, these vehement offspring go forth with their agenda, if they ignore the warnings bestowed upon them, there will be consequences for all."

"Sid mentioned that Dylan planned to go up to the mountain alone with Leah."

"A stupid contemplation." Tahoe stood briskly from the couch.

"Yeah, well, Sid put a stop to it, which means we all have to be there. Whatever happens is going down tonight."

"I'm afraid it already is. The time is now. We must hurry."

———

"IF YOU DECIDE TO SIT THIS ONE OUT, SUSAN, IT'S MORE than understandable. It's late, and it's freezing outside. Believe me, we've got this handled."

On the phone, Brett's attempt to placate her failed.

"I might be getting old, Brett, but I'm not that old. I'm still a parapsychologist, remember? As the director of the society, it's impertinent that I be there. I was afraid Dylan would attempt to go rogue on this. Thankfully, he went to Leah's first."

"I'm taking the Range Rover up there," Brett explained. "Tahoe and I will pick you up in about twenty minutes."

Susan agreed and ended the call. She took a deep breath and sighed. She *was* getting a little old for sudden expositions late at night during a frigid winter blast that kept the rest of this small part of the world frozen inside. But Susan would never let the team know that. She couldn't. They would begin to coddle her and dote on her like they did nine months ago. No, she couldn't make their past concerns for her become a permanent spotlight. It would interfere with the work at hand, whatever the case may be.

Sit this one out? Never. It was she who broke the story to the world about the Eagle Rock conspiracy. She'd faced down the Men in Black and exposed them at a great risk to her life. Now, as a parapsychologist, she felt a duty to lay eyes on these strange kids. She had to meet them face to face and discover if what was written about them was true. Do they really wield some unexplainable level of fear and transfer it to others around them? According to Leah, they did, but it was essential that Susan find out for herself and hopefully study it. Susan's instinct told her she'd already faced worse in her explorations, especially over the past two years in which she experienced the unimaginable—several times. What could possibly stop her now? Fear had become less and less of a factor for her.

After dressing appropriately for tonight's excursion, she stood gazing out of her living room's picture window, waiting for Brett and Tahoe and wondering if tonight would turn deadly. She certainly hoped not. Tonight's events could hold many different possibilities and outcomes. Tahoe had predicted that these kids would make their presences known. Silently, Susan prayed for reasonable and respectful communication, but a dark vibe that twisted and turned inside her insisted otherwise.

20

COME, PLAY WITH US

ADAM WAS DREAMING OF THE GIRL AGAIN, THE GIRL who called herself his sister. He dreamt of her last night but never told Mommy or Daddy. He'd felt afraid, way too afraid to tell them. Maybe it was because of her black eyes that didn't seem like eyes at all. In the first dream, he'd backed away from her because of how her eyes looked, and her voice had sounded strange like she talked in slow motion.

"Hello, Adam." She saw him take a step backward. Then her voice changed. It sounded normal, like everyone else's. *"I'm your sister."*

When he heard her friendly tone of voice, he felt sorry about her eyes. Something must have happened to her. If she was his sister, why hadn't Mommy and Daddy told him about her? Was she a surprise? Did she live somewhere else?

He'd been in the front yard in the first dream, playing in the snow when she ran toward him and purposefully threw her legs out from under her, plunging herself into the snow and landing face up. She'd come to play with him.

"Look, Adam!"

She began making snow angels, her arms and legs stretching

farther and wider than anyone he'd ever seen before. The snow angels she made were bigger and wider than anyone else's. Then she bounded up on her knees and scooped up a pile of snow in her hands. She held her hands out in front of him. She smiled, and then blew the snow up into the air where it seemed to dance and collect without falling to the ground. He laughed as snow flurries from the wayward funnel she created fell and tickled his face.

"I'll be back, Adam," she said, *"and we'll play again."* Then she stood up, turned, and was quickly gone.

But she kept her promise. He was dreaming again when suddenly, she walked toward him in the yard. Her gray hoodie stretched almost to her knees, and the hood hung down over her face. He wondered why she wasn't wearing a heavier coat, but older kids sometimes didn't. She waved as she came closer. Then she lifted her hood.

"I told you I'd be back, Adam." He smiled at her, and as he did, she showed him a trick. *"Look at my eyes, Adam."* Adam watched as she raised her hands and used them to cover her big black eyes. When she removed her hands from her face, her eyes were bright, shiny, and blue, like crystals. She had normal eyes like everyone else. Adam stood in the snow, fascinated by her.

"Are you really my sister?"

She nodded. He asked her why Mommy and Daddy never mentioned her. Then, he asked her name.

"They wanted me to meet you first, Adam. I'm your sister, Medea." She kneeled in front of him and took his small hands in hers. He noticed her hands, how small and lean they were. *"How would you like to come for a little walk with me, Adam? I have some friends with me, and we're all going to play in the snow together. Come, play with us."*

Adam peeped over her shoulder but saw no one. He glanced back at the front door and then back at her.

"I'm not allowed to leave the front yard."

"But you can if you're with me, Adam. Daddy said it was okay since I'm your sister."

Adam turned and faced the front door again. It was closed. In the dream, Mommy and Daddy's faces failed to peep through the windows while keeping a constant watch on him. He wasn't afraid of Medea, not since she showed him her real eyes. But he didn't want to worry Mommy and Daddy.

"We'll be back before they ever know we're gone. I promise. We're going to make a really big snowman. Will you show us how?"

Funny, he thought. She was an older kid but didn't know how to build a snowman. But in this moment, he felt important, as if they needed him. Fervently, he nodded his head.

"Great. Here's what you have to do, Adam." Still kneeling, she gently clutched the sides of his arms in order to make him understand. *"You have to wake up, and then put on your snowsuit, coat, and gloves. Mommy and Daddy are asleep on the couch, so you don't want to wake them. Then I want you to unlock the front door and open it. You know how to do that, right?"*

He nodded again. He watched Mommy and Daddy do it all the time.

She continued. *"Remember, be very quiet. Don't wake Mommy and Daddy, okay?"*

Adam's excitement grew, and he felt himself nodding even faster.

"Now, Adam, wake up!"

Adam woke in his bed. The dream felt real, so real he had to find out for sure. He got out of bed but then had to use the bathroom. When he finished, he tiptoed out to the living room, and sure enough, Mommy and Daddy were asleep on the couch. They'd curled up together and nodded off watching a movie. The TV remained on, casting a dim glow through the darkened room.

Adam hurried back to his bedroom and put on his snowsuit and boots. Then, he crept back out to the living room, careful not to plod too heavily on the hardwood floor. He opened the living room closet and quietly removed his coat and put it on. Inside the pocket were his gloves. Once he slipped them over his hands, he tried to unlock the front door. His hands couldn't unbolt the lock at the top. His gloves were too thick.

Daddy stirred on the couch and let out a slight grumble. Adam nearly jumped, then stood very still. He watched as Daddy shifted on the couch and fell back to sleep. Relieved, Adam turned back to the door and removed his right glove. He unbolted the top lock and then the bottom and quietly pulled the door open. He turned and walked backwards out the door, keeping his eyes on them. His little heart fluttered at the thought of being caught.

Adam stepped outside and closed the door behind him. He took a few steps into the front yard and saw her walking down the sidewalk and toward him, her face hidden by the gray hood. She stood before him and held out her hand.

"You made it," she whispered.

He nodded. Her eyes were blue, maybe not as blue as in the dream, but still blue. He let her take his hand and lead him up the sidewalk and out onto the street. As they walked, Adam noticed the other kids just up ahead. He counted three of them. One was another girl, and two boys all wearing hoods like her. Adam couldn't clearly see their faces; they all looked at the ground rather than ahead.

Medea began to walk so quickly that Adam's small legs nearly sprinted to catch up with her.

"Are we all going to build a snowman?"

"Yes, Adam we will."

When they arrived where the three others were gathered, they formed a slow-moving circle around him.

"I have him," Medea said.

Hooded heads turned upwards. Adam gazed up at their faces. Their eyes were black, all of them. Adam quickly turned toward Medea, his sister. Her eyes had gone back the way they were, back to black. Suddenly, Adam was afraid.

———

THE SOUND OF SOMETHING OR SOMEONE OUTSIDE caused Todd Parks to stir and wake. He'd drifted off on one of the living room couches; Grandma had fallen asleep on the other. Mom's rule was that he be in bed by 10:00 p.m., school night or not. A far cry from the original 9:00, but he'd made the case that he wasn't a baby anymore; he was all of ten years now. She'd relented after Grandma sided with him. Then, since Mom worked at the bar most often until two in the morning, Grandma would let him stay up and watch TV with her until at least 11:00, sometimes 11:30. Tonight was one of those nights when Grandma fell fast asleep, and he would sneak off to bed before Mom came home, but tonight, he'd fallen asleep as well.

Until a sound from outside rudely awakened him. What he hadn't told either Mom or Grandma was that by staying up and watching TV, he sometimes avoided the strange dreams he'd been having. Twice he'd dreamed of a boy and a girl with pale faces and big black eyes like ink blots. In the first dream, they invited him to walk with them, and he did. That's when the girl explained that they were his sister and brother. It didn't make sense. Todd didn't see how that could be, but at the same time, after they told him who they were his initial feeling of fear had turned to skepticism.

The second time he dreamed of them they watched him from across the street. He walked closer toward them, and the girl who claimed to be sister, Iona, spoke.

"We're not here to hurt you, Todd," she said. "We only want to get to know you." Feeling less afraid, he moved closer toward them, but then he suddenly woke. The dreams were not night-mares, but they were all too real, enough that he couldn't forget them. They were odd dreams, and he remained embarrassed to speak of them. So, he kept the dreams to himself.

Now, from the couch, he spotted shadows moving across the curtained window. He glanced at the time on the TV's digital display. It was way too early for Mom to be home. Besides, she would be alone. More than one shadow moved outside.

Todd sat up on the couch and gently tugged the curtain aside from the window. Peeping through the slight crack he'd made with his finger, he saw them, hooded and looming just outside the front porch. Iona and Indrid, his "siblings," appeared just as they had in the dreams, but this was no dream. They were real and standing not far from the window he now snuck a peek through. Todd closed his eyes, shook his head, and then looked again. He wasn't dreaming. He was wide awake. His strange dreams had suddenly turned into reality.

Iona caught sight of the crack made by the slightly moving curtain. Todd could have retreated, but he hadn't felt the need. He brushed the curtain aside even farther and watched as Iona snaked her head toward the window and then waved at him. Indrid turned and gazed at the window. Then, Iona beckoned with a fetching motion of her finger.

"Grab your coat and come outside." Her voice spoke inside Todd's mind, just like in the dreams. He'd seen something about that once on TV, something called "telepathy." How cool would it be if she could show him how to do such a thing? Something distracted him from this thought, something that tugged inside of him, something that wondered what could they possibly want at this hour?

He glanced back over at the opposite couch, casting a quick eye on Grandma as she snored, her chest heaving up and down. Soon, her snoring segued into a silent, peaceful slumber. Todd tiptoed over to the living room closet, where he donned his snow boots and coat. Then he crept back to the living room window.

Quietly, he pulled the curtain aside and then stood between it and the window. Indrid and Iona were still there, looming outside the window, waiting for him, fidgeting in the cold. Still marveling at how real they were, he felt anxiousness, curiosity, and, most of all, an instinctive eagerness to hang out with the older kids. He motioned to them with his hand. He pointed to himself, then backwards with his finger, and then out again to them. They nodded.

He continued to tiptoe with creeping stealth through the living room, round the corner, and into his bedroom. He closed the door behind him and quickly crossed the room to the window. Using his desk chair, he unlatched the window, opened it, and jumped a mere foot and a half to the snowy ground. Then he ran around the house to the front porch.

They were waiting for him, having turned full face toward his direction as he rounded the corner of the house. Todd's boots crunched the snow underfoot as he hastened toward them. Approaching them, he wondered why they hung their heads low. Was it because of their eyes? If so, why? Todd suspected their oval black eyes were a trick of some kind, something that wowed the younger kids and kept them in awe.

"We've been waiting for you," Indrid said.

Todd stopped and froze in his tracks. Something about Indrid's voice sounded different from in the dreams. His voice sounded warped, almost robotic, like a machine. Suddenly Todd stood still, silently adhering to an inner notion not to move. He felt wary of them in this moment, unlike in the dreams. Iona smiled and trudged through the snow toward him. He didn't move; he let her approach him.

She crouched down in front of him. Todd watched as her eyes suddenly changed. They were no longer black, but a regular shade of green. She took his gloved hands in hers.

"How long we've been waiting to meet you, brother."

Todd heard how her voice began in the same robotic manner as Indrid's, and then quickly changed into a normal speaking tone. She laughed, and he laughed with her. Todd yearned to see more of their tricks. Indrid stepped closer and placed his hand on Todd's shoulder.

"Come with us, Todd," he said. His voice sounded normal now but low and even toned. "Come, play with us."

"We're going tubing on the mountain. Come, have fun."

"Tonight? But my mom could be home at any time, and My Grandma's asleep." Conflicted, Todd felt the regret of saying no and the fear of leaving on his own so late at night. "I don't want her to wake while I'm gone. She'd be scared."

"She won't wake before you get back, I promise," Iona assured him. "We won't be gone long. We already spoke with your mom. She said it was okay."

"She did?" Doubt swept Todd like the cold wind, but the hopefulness he felt was overwhelming.

"Yes," Indrid said. "We're siblings, remember? We're her children too, you know."

"But—"

"We have friends with us," Iona interrupted him. She pointed to the street. "There they are. They're anxious to meet our brother."

Todd looked out into the street and noticed three kids, a boy about Indrid's age and a girl, both of them wearing fall hoods in the biting cold. The girl was holding the hand of a small boy, who was dressed well against the cold and keeping close to her.

"I promise, we won't be long," Iona stressed. "We'll be back before you know it."

Todd said nothing as he glanced back at the house and then back out into the street where the other kids waited. His reluctance having lessened, Todd agreed, and then Iona led him out into the street to meet the others. As they approached, Todd noticed the other boy and girl with their hoods hung over their low hanging heads. When they looked up at him, their eyes were black pits, their faces expressionless. He glanced at the little boy, whose blue eyes seemed to plead with him. Todd noticed the look of silent terror on the boy's face. Now, he felt uneasy, but it was too late. Indrid's hand clamped down strongly on his shoulder as he led him away from the house and up the street. Between the cold and the sudden fear, Todd felt frozen and walked blindly alongside them.

21

TAKEN

ANOTHER NIGHT ENDED WITH AN EARLY LAST CALL AT One-Eyed Jack's. The frigid cold had shuttered many regular customers inside their homes, leaving the bar and grill deserted in ghost-town fashion. The televised forecasts of another brutal ice storm played repeatedly on the local news, and Nadine was ordered to close the bar early and go home for her own safety. She locked up and left after the last two customers, and then shivered for minutes in the car before the heater did its job.

Through her windshield, winter's forthcoming onslaught progressed. The screech and squawk of her window wipers washed away the oncoming sleet as it pelted down in its beginning stages. She drove cautiously on the slowly slickening roads, mindful to avoid black and icy spots hidden by the darkness. The drive home usually took fifteen minutes, but tonight it was more like twenty or more by the time she arrived on her street.

Thankful to be home, she pulled in front of her house and parked the car. Gathering up her purse and a bag of food she'd brought home from the bar, she glanced for a quick second through her windshield. Up ahead, she spotted figures walking up the street, kids by the looks of it. Then, she sat up closer to the windshield. Something caught her eye. At least three of the figures wore mere hooded sweatshirts in the bitter cold, but it wasn't just that. The hoodies appeared just like those worn by the twins in her dream.

No, couldn't be, she thought. It was just her imagination. But as the figures moved, she spotted a child wearing a coat much like the one she'd bought Todd and of the same forest-green color. Coincidence was her first thought, but that didn't stop her body from moving quickly to open the car door and get out. She stood in the street, her eyes searching up ahead to where she'd seen the figures. But they were no longer there.

Nadine looked around her. She saw no one now, only the wrath of winter as it hastened. She shook her head and moved quickly down her sidewalk, anxious to get inside and escape the cold. From outside, she saw the glow from the television in the living room. Quickly, she opened the door and entered.

The house remained warm, and the television's dim soft glow in the darkness made for a strangely comfortable setting. Nadine caught a police chase scene as she glanced at the screen. On the couch, her Mom had fallen fast asleep, like always, watching old reruns until nearly dawn. Nadine checked on her. She seemed out cold, a blanket clutched up around her, her chest heaving up and down in infant-like slumber. Nadine was glad to see that Todd was not sitting up and awake with Grandma in the living room, discovering old TV shows he would ask a thousand fervent questions about later.

Walking into her home brought a dormant sensation back to her. She had to go to the bathroom; she couldn't hold it any longer. Nadine hurried, dropping her purse on the floor and hanging her coat in the closet. Something seemed different about the closet, but her mind didn't have time to think on it. She made it to the bathroom, and after five quick minutes, she walked back out. She would take a quick shower, but first, she would check on Todd.

Nadine opened the door of Todd's room, and through the darkness what she didn't see made her flip the light switch and flood the room with light. What she beheld was no trick of the darkness. No sleeping shape slumbered in the bed. Todd's bed remained perfectly made, just as it was early today. Her heart pounded. Where was he?

She turned and ran through the hallway, quickly glancing into her own bedroom and her mother's. Todd wouldn't be in either of those rooms, and he wasn't. She flung open the door that led down into the basement, but her eyes met only darkness. The light was off.

"Todd!" she yelled. "Todd?"

She ran back to the living room and then the kitchen, reassuring herself that her son was not in either room. It wasn't a large house. Todd wasn't here.

"Mom?" Nadine's voice startled her sleeping mother awake. The older woman sat up, dazed and incoherent. "Mom, where's Todd?" Nadine could hear the panic in her own voice, as it slowly edged upon frenzy.

Through half-lidded eyes, her mother glanced around the room. "He was here when I dozed off. He's not in his room?"

Frustrated, Nadine suddenly remembered a boy wearing a similar jacket walking up the street with the other kids. She snatched her coat back out of the closet and searched with both hands and eyes. Todd's coat was gone. It was him she'd seen walking up the street. Those kids *were* the twins; they had to be.

"I'll be back," she said to her mother, yanking her purse up from the floor. "I'm going to find him. If he comes back, keep him here."

"Where could he have gone at this hour?"

Nadine didn't take the time to answer her. She heard her call out her name just before she slammed the door shut. Nadine ran to her car, almost slipping on the sidewalk. Once inside, she restarted the car, took her phone from her purse, and called Dylan.

He answered quickly, his tone sounding harried and less than emphatic.

"Dylan, it's Nadine. Todd is gone. They've taken him. I'm sure of it."

"Okay, Nadine. Stay calm and tell me what happened."

She couldn't stay calm. Her foot plunged on the gas pedal. Her eyes scanned the road, left and right as she told him everything from the moment she got out of the car and walked through the front door.

"I saw them at the top of the road. It looked like them, but I did nothing. He's gone. He was with them. I know it."

"Where are you now, Nadine?"

"I'm in my car, searching for them. They couldn't have gotten too far."

"Listen to me, Nadine." Dylan sounded somewhat louder, and the sudden serious tone of his voice did nothing to comfort her. "Stay calm and be careful, especially if you find them. If you find them, I want you to call me right back. Right now, Leah, Sidney, and I are on our way to Eagle Rock Mountain. We're going to seek them out. If you don't find them, I want you to drive to the mountain. When you get close to the base of the mountain, I want you to call me back. We'll meet. If they have Todd, Eagle Rock is where they're going. Do you understand?"

Nadine felt like she was losing her breath. "Yes, I understand. I'm at the top of the road, Dylan. They're nowhere in sight. I just saw them, minutes ago."

She heard herself crying. Anxiety sparked inside her.

"Keep watch in case you see them, Nadine," Dylan reminded her. "Call me back if you do. If not, call me when you get to the mountain. We'll find you."

Nadine agreed as the tears began streaming down her face. She ended the call and drove on, seeing nothing but the icy snow as it barreled toward her windshield. Then her phone rang again. She assumed it was Dylan calling her back, but when she glanced at the screen, it read, *Jamie.*

She spoke to the phone without answering the call. "Jamie? Now? I can't talk right now, Jamie. My son has been kidnapped."

Being in no shape to help Jamie, she ignored the call and set her phone down on the seat beside her. She scanned the road even more closely now, straining her eyes and struggling to see through a burgeoning white storm.

———

BRAD FOUND HIMSELF TRUDGING THROUGH THE SNOW, yet he couldn't feel the cold around him. The moon cast a blue shadow on the perfect whiteness that lay everywhere. Adam walked only a few feet in front of him, his hand clutching that of an older girl. Brad couldn't see their faces, but he knew his son. He recognized his coat and gloves, and he also recognized the girl from behind. He could see others walking with them, yet he failed to see their faces. Every time he tried, his attention was redirected to the girl who guided Adam forward on the snowy, slushy road. He moved to catch up with them but when he did, they moved also, gaining a few faster steps ahead and prevented him from catching up.

Suddenly, a burst of restless anger propelled him forward. He grabbed his son's hand, and after a brief tug of war with the faceless girl, he turned the boy around to face him.

"Daddy, I'm going to make a giant snowman," Adam said.

"STOP!" Brad yelled, but his voice sounded as if it went nowhere. He spoke mainly at the girl and her unseen accomplices, but only the girl turned around and faced him. It was her, the girl he'd seen in the dream, the girl at the door who called herself Adam's sister. Her eyes once again were black inkwells, but Brad recognized her face, rounded with a narrow forehead, just like his own. She was *his* child, a child conceived through an unearthly experiment. The dream he lingered in now would not allow him to deny it.

"Come with us to the mountain," she said to him. He stood staring at her face, unable to move. *"Come with us, Daddy. Come."*

Brad lost his grip on Adam's hand. He lunged forward but

couldn't catch up. They moved faster and faster, far out of his reach. Then his legs felt paralyzed.

Brad shook himself awake on the couch. His arm was crooked around Sheila's neck, just the way they'd fallen asleep. His rapid movement stirred her into waking.

"What's wrong?" she asked, with a sleepy, scratchy tone.

He leapt up from the couch and rubbed his hands over his eyes. "Nothing, I'm just dreaming again."

But Brad was not satisfied with his own answer. It was too real, just like all the other dreams. He didn't disperse any details to her. He strode down the hallway to Adam's room and flung the door open. When he turned on the light, his heart sunk in his chest.

Adam was gone. His bed was mussed, slept in, but now no small body slept soundly inside. Brad had tucked him in only a few hours ago. He wasn't in the bathroom. Brad passed it in the hallway. Where was his son?

"Adam!" Brad's voice echoed and bounced off of the walls in the hallway. He screamed for his son like he never had before. Sheila came running in from the living room.

"What's wrong? What's happened?" She dashed past him and into Adam's room, seeing what her husband had only a moment before. "Where is he?" Her voice became the sound of frantic hysteria. She grabbed Brad by the arm and turned him around, clutching desperately to the sides of his shoulders. "Brad, what's going on? Where's our son?"

"They took him." He broke away from her. "Where's my phone?"

Through the clearing haze of sleep, Brad suddenly recalled leaving his phone on the coffee table in the living room. He moved fast, with Sheila moving faster behind him.

"They who? Who are you talking about?"

"The girl from the dream, her and the Black-Eyed Kids, they took him."

"How do you know this?"

"I know. I just saw them in a dream. She told me to go to Eagle Rock." Brad fumbled with his phone. "I'm calling Dylan Rasche."

"Dylan?" Sheila screeched, "No, Brad, call 911."

"Dylan knows *where* to find them. I'm going after our son. I have to do this myself." Brad forced both arms into his coat sleeves and quickly dialed Dylan.

Sheila began yelling, her frantic tone ascending in panic. "He's out there in the cold. He's just a five-year-old boy! Brad, call the police!"

"Calm down, Sheila," he retorted. "Besides, what should I tell them? They'll never believe the truth."

Dylan answered, hearing the last snippet of shouting voices. He repeated his first hello even louder through the phone. Brad placed the call on speakerphone so Sheila could hear.

"Dylan, it's Brad. My son is gone. He's been taken." Brad told him about the dream of the girl just before he woke on the couch. "I looked in his room, and he's gone. He's not in the house. Look, Leah said those kids were hiding out on the mountain, right?"

"Yes, listen, Brad," Dylan began. "Todd Parks has been abducted by them as well. I just got off the phone with Nadine. Sid, Leah, and the rest of the team are on our way to Eagle Rock right now. Nadine is on her way to meet us there. I want you to come, too. We need both the kids' parents with us and all of us are going to face these kids down tonight. Get in your car, drive to the mountain, and call me when you're close. I will tell you what to do then."

"Got it," Brad ended the call. He quickly put his gloves on as Sheila persisted.

"I'm going too," she said.

"No, you're not."

"You heard what he said—"

"No, Sheila, you need to stay here in case they come back. Besides, I don't want to have to worry about you too. Keep your phone by your side. I will call you. I promise." Reluctantly, she relented. He kissed her quickly on the cheek. "Now, I've got to go get our son."

"Please, Brad, be careful." Sheila began crying, but Brad was out the door before she finished the sentence.

———

AFTER HANGING UP WITH NADINE AND RELATING THE details of the call to Sidney and Leah, Dylan ended a second phone call and turned back to them both. Sidney drove the van, while Leah sat in the backseat behind them. Sidney stole a quick glance away from the now slickening roads and looked at him. Leah leaned forward from the backseat.

"That was Brad," Dylan reported, even though Sid and Leah had already deduced as much. "They've taken Adam also."

Leah gasped.

"Looks like you were right," Sidney conceded. "They've found a way to draw us out."

"They worked like thieves in the night," Dylan continued. "Luring both kids out of the house while Nadine was at work and Brad and Sheila had fallen fast asleep on the couch."

"Scoundrels," Leah snapped, "stealing children out of their homes in the cold night."

"The frigid night," Sidney corrected her, shuddered from the cold, and turned the van's heat up even higher.

While talking to Brad, Dylan had heard his call waiting alert telling him that another call was coming through. But Brad's call was important, and as Dylan honed on his every word, he hadn't bothered to check who was calling him. Surely, Nadine hadn't made it to Eagle Rock that fast. Now, as Dylan checked to see who called, the van slid on the icy road, causing Sidney to swerve and narrowly miss the tree line on the roadside. Dylan's phone slipped out of his hand and onto the floor. He retrieved it as Sidney steadied the van and slowly resumed driving. The brief mayhem caused Dylan to forget about the interrupting call he hadn't taken.

"Just drive slower, Sid," he said. "There's no sense in having an accident on the way there."

Sidney said nothing. He took Dylan's advice and loosened his foot on the gas pedal. The heat filled the van in what would be temporary relief. Unnoticed, an alert flashed on Dylan's phone's screen. It read simply: *Missed Call: Jamie.*

22

ALLISON PRESCOTT

As the hospital's electronic double doors automatically glided open, Allison Prescott stepped through the opening gap and out into the freezing cold. Thankfully, her minivan was parked only a few yards away. She loathed working the late shift, though it became easier as the night progressed. Once patients were asleep, her job as a nurse became easier and the time went by faster. Leaving work at 11:00 pm was one thing, but in the winter, the frigid cold of night made her bones and muscles ache. At sixty-three, the late shift began to drain her. But such was life, and she was thankful to reach her mini-van within two minutes. The cold bit into her skin, and the walk made her breathe heavier.

Finally, in the driver's seat, she unwound and let the heat blow full-steam through the vehicle. She sat for a moment, catching her breath and letting the workday's events fall away from her. She'd spent the last forty years being a nurse, and she loved it, but she equally adored the prospect of retiring in two years. No more late-night shifts, no more unbearably nasty patients, and best of all, no more watching people die. She'd be free to spend time with her grandchildren, travel as much as she wanted, and who knows, maybe she'd start painting again. Concerned by how quickly the sleet now pummeled the road in front of her, she backed out of her parking space and pulled away.

The city streets were slickening as the sleet and snow came down faster and faster. She sensed an icy sheen even beneath the brand new snow tires her husband had put on before winter. Frank was always conscientious of such things, tending to his wife's safety was one of them. She was grateful. But Frank would explode if he ever knew the risks she took when driving home, like the one she was about to take.

Driving through the city streets took her the long way back home. But after three blocks through the main drag, she usually bypassed the city, taking a turnoff that led her to a back road, one that ran past Eagle Rock Mountain and got her home ten minutes earlier. By the looks of things, Green Valley Municipal still hadn't come out to shovel and salt the roads, and Allison guessed they wouldn't until morning. But back roads were often least attended to, especially during a snowstorm. The main streets through the city were always tended to first. Allison didn't care. It was cold, and she was tired. Tonight, she risked it and turned onto the back road.

She slowed down as she turned. Much more snow accumulated here than on the city streets, but soon, the back road gave way to a portion where trees on both sides of the road made an overhead canopy, bridging the snow from falling so quickly onto it. She would remember this fact in case she ever had to argue against Frank's wrath. The night wasn't as dark as usual. Allison noticed how the snowfall cast a pale-blue shadow everywhere, confusing the twilight and mimicking pre-dawn. The night remained lit only by the moonlight and the snow's blue shadow, making her relax and unwind while she drove.

She turned on her radio and listened to her Oldie's station. Her favorite music brought back childhood memories and burst from the dashboard. Silently, she sang along with Sam Cooke and drove her usual route unhindered by the falling snow. About a mile from

Eagle Rock Mountain, something along the side of the road caught her attention.

She gasped at what she saw. As the mini-van idled by, Allison spotted a small boy walking hand in hand with a younger girl. The boy couldn't have been more than five or six, the girl not more than twelve. Ahead of them walked another young boy, though slightly older than the first, also walking and clutching hands with a younger girl, who appeared no older than her early teens. In front of them, two equally adolescent boys lumbered through the snowy roadside. All of them appeared to be desperately off to somewhere in the freezing night, and not all of them seemed to be properly dressed for winter.

Something must have happened, Allison thought. She'd seen such things before as a nurse, kids leaving home because of fighting parents, house fires, even homelessness. There could be any number of explanations as to why these kids were out walking around in the dead of a cold winter's night. Allison was nothing else if not a dedicated nurse. She was obligated to stop and learn their situation and help if she could. She dreaded to think that one of them might be hurt. She slowed down and pulled over on the side of the road, not far up ahead from the two boys who led the small and surely freezing parade.

She watched them through her side mirror, but the minivan's exhaust billowed out and blocked her view. She wound down the window as the girl and the small boy from the end of the line ran ahead of the others and approached her window. The boy jolted ahead of the girl, who seemed to stumble in her attempt to catch up with him.

"What on Earth are you kids doing out in this cold? Are you all okay?" Allison spoke first, taking the initiative to ascertain the situation.

The small boy appeared moderately bundled, unlike the girl who wore merely a hooded sweatshirt, the hood draping her long blondish hair that hung over her ears. As the boy's face came clearly into her view, Allison noticed his growing fatigue but most of all, the fear in his eyes seemed to fight back frozen tears. When he spoke, he sounded like a lost child searching for home.

"Please, Ma'am, I want to go home to my mom and dad."

The girl planted herself directly behind him and clasped her hands to his shoulders.

"Could you please ride us all to Eagle Rock? Our parents are waiting for us there."

Something wasn't right to Allison. Something about the way the girl spoke sounded strange. Not only was her speech off, but her voice sounded measured somehow. Allison didn't like how she'd kept her head down as she spoke, hiding her face so she wouldn't see it. Besides, why would parents wait for their children at a mountain this time of night, this time of year? Something was going on here. Allison decided to discover what it was.

"Did something happen tonight? Was there an accident? I'm a nurse. Let me come out and get a look at you all."

Allison shifted the minivan into a parking position and started to open the door. Before she knew it, one of the older boys bolted to the driver's side and pushed the door closed again. He loomed in front of the driver's seat window, blocking out the boy and girl and taking control of the situation. Allison could see his face right in front of her, slightly gaunt with a pale complexion and cold black eyes that contained no irises—just black pupils gazing into her soul. She felt a great dark hand reach inside and take hold of her. The feeling of being frozen overpowered her even as the heater continued to blast.

"As she said, our parents are waiting for us up on Eagle Rock. We need you to take us there." The black-haired boy's voice was even toned, but straight and demanding. Underneath it lingered the slightest sound of a threat.

Allison glanced out the window back to the girl. She saw her face for the first time as the girl looked up. Her eyes were black also, but the small boy desperate to get home had normal eyes. The older kids were different somehow in a way Allison didn't understand. As she tried to piece it together, the boy spoke again, this time louder and more forceful.

"Take us to Eagle Rock Mountain. Now! We are pressed for time. Our parents are meeting us there."

A thousand typical responses Allison would've uttered to such a little smart-ass punk erupted in her mind, but her lips, like the rest of her, remained frozen. This kid was no normal punk. Something was definitely different about him, something inherent that made her unable to reason. She'd never seen anything like those black, menacing eyes that now bore down on her. Off to the side, she spotted the others coming closer, crowding around him as he framed himself steadfastly within her driver's seat window. A wave of fear rippled through her. She felt it grip her inside and tingle her spine all the way up to the nape of her neck. She heard a sound coming from her, the only sound she made, a moan of fright and frozen shock.

A sudden wave of images flashed in her mind. She saw him pulling her through the driver's window and tossing her out onto the road. She envisioned them taking off with her vehicle and leaving her behind, freezing and bleeding to death in the plunging temperature. Her eyes turned once again to the little boy. He appeared just as scared as she was. Then, Allison spotted another boy, one slightly older than the younger but not by much. The look on his face alternated between deep concern and alarm. Regardless of what kind of threat the black-eyed kids presented, she had to get the two boys out of the cold. Allison also thought of driving away as fast as possible and then calling the police, but a sudden and overwhelming feeling told her that within the time it took her to shift into drive and step on the gas, she would be sorry.

The thought of never seeing Frank, her children, or her grand-children again became an overpowering reality. Her mind showed her images of them without her. She wondered if what she was seeing were the manifestations of her own imagination, or if the black-eyed boy was planting them in her mind. The latter explanation felt like a foregone conclusion. She didn't resist any further; she couldn't.

"Get in," she said.

The black-eyed boy motioned behind him, and then crossed in front of the vehicle. Allison automatically unlocked all the doors and allowed him to hop into the passenger's side. The back doors swung open, and Allison saw the young man with reddish hair climb into the far back. Then, the girl who initially approached the minivan climbed in just behind the driver's side, holding the frightened boy's hand. Another girl with red hair followed and got in with the older boy. There were six of them in the vehicle with her. God help her if she made the wrong move or said the wrong thing.

She eyed her phone plugged into the Bluetooth system in front of her. Allison did her best to sound normal as she reached for her phone and spoke.

"I'm just going to call my husband and let him know I'll be a little late. If I don't, he'll worry about me."

Just as Allison's hand neared her phone, its screen went blank and dark, void of the electronic life that kept it glowing in the dark. Allison lifted her phone from its holder—dead.

"Your phone will not work right now," the dark-haired boy said, sitting next to her. "You don't need to call your husband."

Allison swallowed hard. She heard his voice more clearly now, strange and warped somehow, like an old record playing too slowly. "Please don't hurt me," she said to the boy, but she kept her eyes straight ahead on the road.

"No one is going to hurt you," he said. "Just drive us to Eagle Rock."

Within the next mile, the mountain appeared, silent and snow-capped in the darkness. The boy dictated where she should drive, while the others remained silent.

"Not too far up the mountain," he said. He led her up the mountain a short distance, and then ordered her to stop right along the roadside.

"Right here," he said. "From here, we will hike up a short distance. This is where our parents will meet us."

Allison peered ahead through the blue-tinged twilight. She caught sight of a path that led a short way up the mountain to a point where several caves sat slightly hidden by the trees but still remained visible. Allison felt a slight revival of her determination, a reigniting of that spark that made her a dedicated nurse.

"You all go on ahead," she said. "I'll stay with the two younger boys. I want to check them out and see if they're alright."

"You'll do no such thing," the boy next to her scolded. "You are not staying here with them. Like them, you are coming with us."

Now, the feeling of paralyzing fear that ravaged Allison Prescott quickly turned to one of impending doom.

23

ON THE MOUNTAIN

Leah gazed at the great snow-covered mountain once it came into view through the van's rectangular side window. Locking it into her sight, she closed her eyes and let her third eye gaze even farther. Dylan noticed her actions through the passenger's side window.

"That's it, Leah," he advised. "Try to see where they're nesting. Search for them."

Leah's third eye roved like a moving camera in her mind. She saw the snowy crags of the mountain, the frozen foliage, and the snow's moonlit blue tint revealed footprints in all directions. Leah focused on the footprints, her chakra showing her the hooded figures that made them, all moving in the same direction while the moonlight guided their path. She directed her sight to move swiftly ahead of them. Where were they headed? She saw a cave, the entrance to which appeared purposely covered in what little brush could be mustered. Her sight moved away and on down the western side of the mountain, down to the roadside where a minivan had been pulled rashly to the side, seemingly abandoned in the cold night.

"Take the road to the western side of the mountain." She spoke quickly with a tone of authority, and Sidney jerked the steering wheel just as fast. "They're there, not far up the mountain. I see a cave. That's where they've been hiding. Keep your eyes on the road. You'll see an abandoned minivan. I think they have a hostage."

"Dylan, call Brett, Nadine, and Brad," Sidney said, as he drove studying the road before him. "They need to know where to meet us."

But Dylan was already dialing.

————

WHEN HIS PHONE LIT UP AND RANG, BRETT ANSWERED. He then let Dylan's voice blare from the speakerphone.

"We're on the western side of the mountain," Dylan reported, "on the road just above the main one, several hundred feet in. We just found an abandoned minivan, parked slightly askew along the roadside. Leah thinks they've taken a hostage."

Brett spun the four-wheel drive around and faced the opposite direction, causing Tahoe and Susan to grasp onto the nearest safe hold.

"I've turned around. We're on our way."

Brett's vehicle took to the snowy, slickening mountain roads without even sliding. Within five minutes, Sidney's van and three other vehicles came into view. Brett spotted Sidney shining a flashlight through the interior of a crookedly parked minivan. The other vehicles belonged to Nadine and Brad, who had already made it to the rendezvous point. Brett parked on the opposite side of the road and now he, Tahoe, and Susan climbed out to complete the small gathering crowd.

"I don't see any signs of a struggle," Sidney announced as they approached.

Leah pointed to the minivan, adamant in what she obviously knew. "They've coerced and taken whoever was driving this minivan. I see a woman." Leah closed her eyes and held her right hand out in front of her. "Dark brown hair, middle aged or older, they forced her to drive them here." She turned and pointed to the mountain behind her.

Tahoe stepped forward. "Follow their trail, Little One. We will do so together."

Leah stepped off the road, inching closer toward the great mountain's base, her eyes wide open. Then, she closed them again and envisioned, tilting her head slightly backwards, scanning the mountain and the darkness. She reached outward with her hand, which moved not far to the right. She opened her eyes.

"That way," she said. "We'll find a path, one that leads to a cave. They're waiting."

"Let's go," Dylan said.

Feet moved and trudged through the snow. Brett and Tahoe accompanied Susan on both sides. Dylan trekked alongside Leah, as she led the search party forward.

———

THEY WALKED LESS THAN A HUNDRED FEET ALONG THE winding mountain road before a footprint laden path became apparent. In Leah's mind, she saw feet making tracks on this same path, and now they all were about to do the same. Overwhelmingly, she knew it to be the way forward.

"This is it," she pointed. "This path leads upward to a small clearing. The cave is up there."

Dylan and Sidney flanked her on each side as if to guide her.

"Thanks, guys, but I'm the one wearing boots," she said. She turned to those behind her. Tahoe, Susan, and Brett stood waiting, yet Brad and Nadine appeared fretful within the small crowd, anxious to find their children. Leah spoke to them frankly. "I know you're both anxious to find your kids. Don't worry. They're here. I've seen it. We *will* get them back. But please, let Dylan and I handle this. We're not yet fully aware of what we're dealing with here, but I promise you, we're not leaving this mountain without your children. Trust us."

Leah purposefully failed to mention the deep-rooted fear the Black-Eyed Kids instilled at first sight. Now was not the time, especially after they'd taken their children.

"These kids claim to be ours also, remember," Nadine interjected. Leah had no response. "You said they've taken a hostage. Are these kids armed?"

"They're not armed," Leah replied. "They're using their hostages as bargaining chips. We're about to discover why."

As Leah turned away, the group began to trudge through the snow. Dylan whispered in her ear. "They *don't need* to be armed. Let's pray we don't find out why."

Leah shushed him over the steady crunching of snow beneath boots and shoes. The mountain path became narrower as they hastened upward on a slight incline. Now, hands began to help one another and guide each other's bodies forward as the path ascended to a small clearing. Sidney shined the flashlight beam forward, but the iridescent moonlight needed no help. As they reached the top and gazed out over the vast clearing, a blast of icy wind blew stinging sleet at their faces. As it passed, a clearer view emerged.

Snow covered a vast stretch of land where grass and foliage normally thrived in the sunshine. Trees stood bare and stripped of life, wooden skeletons frozen into threatening stances. Above, the sky appeared more immense here on the mountain; it always had. Now, the sky appeared almost apocalyptic in its appearance, a vast violet sea spinning endless spirals of white downward to amass indefinitely.

Leah moved her head left to right, her eyes searching the mountain around her. About a hundred yards away, between two trees, a pile of brush appeared to be hastily collected in an attempt to cover a dark opening in the mountain itself. She pointed towards it.

"There, that's where they are. I'm sure of it."

Sidney shined the flashlight in that direction. "Looks like a cave."

"Let's approach it, slowly," Dylan advised.

Their small crowd began to move once again. The sound of feet crunching snow recommenced, but with it also came the resonance of caution and apprehension. The assemblage stopped merely feet from the cave's entrance. Sidney stepped forward and circled the flashlight's beam at the small mouth of the cave. Within the light, figures moved.

———

DYLAN GAZED AROUND HIM, HIS EYES RECOGNIZING THE familiar scene. He clutched Leah's hand for just a moment.

"Let me go first," he said. "I think I know what's about to happen."

Dylan let go of Leah's hand and stepped closer to the cave's entrance. The others stood still behind him. Enrapt and mesmerized by the recurring sense of déjà vu; Dylan's heart pounded while his legs shook. Surely enough, the color red came closer and closer to his eyes. The boy walked toward him through the snow, red hood pulled tightly over his head with black bangs jutting out from underneath, just like in the dream. Within so many countless steps, they faced each other.

Dylan saw the boy's face for real now, a pale white countenance sporting eyes like big black marbles that gleamed against the moonlight. The boy's expression appeared emotionless, cold like the wintery wrath that assailed them now. For eternal seconds, neither of them spoke. Then, as in the dream, Dylan heard the one word that had continuously haunted him.

"Papa," the boy called him, right on cue.

Stepping forward another few inches, Dylan's heart reeled as he noticed a quick and slight resemblance. Something about the boy's face just underneath those huge eyes and above the cheekbones, something he recognized as his own. He ignored a passing ache in his chest and stuttered as he spoke.

"M-My s-son." In his mind, Dylan questioned the boy's age versus the short time ago when he was abducted. How was it even possible?

"You know how it's possible," the boy said, his tone warped and mechanical, causing Dylan to feel a momentary sense of madness. "As far as my age is concerned, there are things you and your friends don't understand. You all are mostly limited, but not all of you."

The boy looked past Dylan to Leah, and then back again.

Telepathic, Dylan thought. The boy read his mind. Dylan thought of the one thing he hadn't vocalized to the rest of the team, the one thing that troubled him throughout. It was time to ask that question, no matter what it made him sound like, no matter how he was supposed to feel inside.

"What is it you want from me?" Dylan felt the fear the boy emitted like a wave, but his tone remained strong and in control.

"The same thing we all want," the boy replied. Dylan noticed the others emerge from the cave and suddenly they stood behind their leader. He heard the team move in closer behind him. To the boy's right stood a boy and a girl, and on his left, another girl. "We want to learn. We want to discover our origins. That is why we're here."

"And so you terrorize and kidnap others into getting what you want?" Dylan's loudening voice echoed across the mountain.

"We don't mean to harm." The girl with the reddish hair who stood next to her male counterpart spoke now. Her voice, similar in its mechanical tone, sounded less rigid than his son's. "We've spoken through dreams, but we remain unacknowledged."

"Those who brought you here, have they told you how you came to be?" Nadine stepped forward and stood to Dylan's left. Her voice seethed in anger, a burgeoning shout in the whistling wind. "I want my son, now!"

The girl's male counterpart stepped forward and faced down Nadine. "Am I not your son as well?"

Dylan noticed the combination of hurt, anger, and pain on Nadine's face. He watched her fight back against the overwhelming fear she felt. Nadine lifted her hand in the air and touched the side of the boy's face, tears streaming from her eyes. Then, she quickly withdrew her hand, as if she touched something she shouldn't have. Dylan knew her next words would be rooted in that same pain and anger.

"I want no parts of you!" She pointed at the twins. "Bring me my son!" Tears drenched her face.

Dylan watched the expressions on the twins' faces—emotionless like that of his son's but with a slight streak of anger and mild confusion seemingly repressed but lingering just underneath. What he saw was direct proof that they were human, but not completely human. But whatever minute trace of humanity their expressions held quickly turned into a fixed and ominous stare at Nadine, one just as icy as the wind that swept all around them.

———

BRAD FELT AND UNDERSTOOD NADINE'S WORDS. GOD help him, but he agreed. The fact that this was real was enough to bear, but the thought of this ongoing nightmare being a permanent and recurring chapter in his life was worse. He would never fully comprehend what they did to him aboard that UFO. He was not responsible for what had occurred. The creation of this malignant female child who stood not far from him was not his choice, not his doing, if she truly was his daughter. He had an obligation to his five-year-old son, the boy she kidnapped from his home. In light of Nadine's reaction, Leah's admonition to stay put no longer seemed relevant. Brad stormed his way to the forefront, to Dylan's right, and faced the girl who claimed to be his.

"Where's my son! Tell me, now," Brad yelled. Brett rushed over in an attempt to pull him back, but just as he grabbed onto the back of his jacket, Brad stopped in his tracks. The girl lifted her head briskly and faced him, but something about her face disarmed him. The lower part of her face and his were the same, and it drove something like a knife through his chest. At first, he wanted to grab her and throttle her, but a quick vibe struck him, one that told him not to even attempt it.

Gazing deeply into her eyes, he saw nothing but blackness, black impenetrable orbs that dissuaded him. His best attempt at reading her was by the expression on her pale face, a sardonic semblance that appeared to taunt him now, almost daring him to lay his hands on her. She stared him down before uttering one word in a tone that seemingly elicited and awaited his next move.

"Daddy," she said, tauntingly.

Brad ripped himself away from Brett's grasp. His eyes never left the girl's face, and in this moment, he felt not only the anxiety she provoked but pain, anger, and, most of all, repulsion. He kept his focus on her black eyes, where his frenzied reflection stared back at him.

"Don't ever call me that." His angry breath billowed out in a cold cloud. "I'm taking my son home. Go get him, now."

She turned her head and glanced at the boy with the red hoodie, who now walked in front of the other kids. He stood at her side.

"As I've said, we wanted nothing more than to learn and experience, but your anger and resistance show your ignorance and your hatred. Your fear overwhelms you." Discreetly, Brett and Susan had been recording video from their phones the whole time. Now, Brett stepped closer to the boy to catch him on camera as he spoke. The boy turned his head toward Brett. "Your contraptions will not work for the time being, but it is your wasted effort."

Brad and the others watched as Brett and Susan checked their phones, saw nothing wrong with their camera functions, and continued undeterred. Just then, Dylan held out his hands in an attempt to broker a solution.

"Alright, listen," he said, his voice sounding desperate.

"There's nothing I can give you. I'm not sure what to do here. You're making it impossible for us to understand each other, so what is it you want? What can we do in this moment? Because we're not leaving here without those kids and the woman you've taken."

The boy who claimed to be his son stared him down, and then moved those black eyes across the lot of them with a frightening pause.

"The girl with the third eye," the boy finally responded. "I want to see her up close. I want to know why she is so different. I want to learn the extent of what she is."

"Absolutely not," Dylan said.

Her boots trampled the snow underfoot and made a crunching sound as she stepped closer.

"Yes, Dylan," Leah said. "I'll do it."

———

"No, Leah. I'm not going to let you do this." Dylan tried to stop her. She ignored him and kept moving. Closer now, she faced the boy in the red-hooded sweatshirt, close enough that she could see the ashen pallor of his stone-like face and the opaqueness of his eyes, like gazing into black mirrors, perfectly hiding whatever existed behind them. She noticed his slight resemblance to Dylan, and it shook her. Up close the face appeared strikingly similar, even the eyes in a way, but the eyes were shaped differently, curved upward like no other humans. Leah felt fear all around her, but she realized that in her short life, she'd faced down fear many times. The true identity of Leah Leeds suddenly overrode the dark foreboding attached to these young beings.

"Go ahead," she prompted him. "Take it. In my life, it's been just as much of a curse as a blessing. That is what you want isn't it, to take my foresight?"

"I wish to take nothing from you," he replied. But Leah didn't trust the sound of his voice, that awkward mechanical drone.

"Why would I do that? I see as well, if not farther than you. I wish to know why you do, and they do not."

"Wait," Tahoe's voice thundered from behind. He maneuvered his way through the small crowd and stood at Leah's side. "Stop this now, I urge you. I also possess the foresight. I come to you now, sent with a warning for you. I was told that you must not engage in that which is forbidden, if you have not already." Tahoe stared at the four Black-Eyed Kids, one by one. Then he looked upward at the sky. "Otherwise, your elders will leave you behind."

The boy's eyes pierced Tahoe. Leah watched as anger flashed across the boy's face. Obviously, Tahoe had struck something, as if he'd taken a pickaxe and plunged it through the mystery the dark kids desperately clung to. The boy's solemn stare now fixated on Tahoe.

"Old man," he said, "or is it young man? Yes, you see as she does, though your third eye is keener and more experienced. And there is more. There is another person inside you—two beings in one. I wish to know why."

"Something we may have in common, my young friend." Tahoe's response was quick but cordial.

Then Leah decided the time was now before she relented.

"So, what are you waiting for?"

The haunting resemblance to Dylan came closer as the boy approached her with his hands held out in front of him.

"Wait." Raising her index finger in the air, Leah stopped him in his tracks. "First, bring the woman and the two boys forward. I know they're in the cave. Bring them out—now."

The boy turned around slowly and faced the direction of the cave. Leah and the others watched as he lifted his hands into the air and slammed them together, creating a thunderous double clap. Within seconds, three figures emerged from the mouth of the cave. A woman stood in the middle between two boys on each side of her. She held both of their hands. Then they trudged forward through the snow. Feet away from the gathered crowd, they stopped when the black-eyed boy held up his hand. Silently,

Leah raged as she glimpsed the gripping look of fear on their faces.

———

ORION TURNED BACK TO HER. HE FELT HER FEAR lessening. Maybe, somehow, a chance existed of making them understand. If so, that chance resided with her and the strange older man whose body housed two souls. But first, he must understand her. He gazed into her eyes, marveling at the brilliant shade of blue they bore, unlike so many other pairs he'd seen so far. Cautious and careful, he took another step toward her. Gently, Orion laid his long, lanky fingers on Leah's face and allowed them to creep to the center of her forehead, to her chakra. Suddenly, a barrage of images invaded his half-human mind.

He saw her as a child, a small girl playing beside a rocking chair and talking to an old woman who was there, but not there. A ghost she was, someone who'd left this realm and returned in spirit form to lay claim to a world that no longer belonged to her. He saw the little blonde girl playing in a big house, where blackened figures moved threateningly around her. The little girl could see them, but she failed to understand. Orion witnessed her parents fighting; their anger and their hatred exploding as the blackened figures secretly fueled their tempers and triggered their emotions. The parents ignored their child, leaving her to wander off alone and play with her only friends—the undead. Then, the spirits began to taunt the child, to frighten her, to try and claim her. They'd recognized her third eye. He saw her father carrying her away in the middle of the night. He saw her mother swinging from a noose attached to a stairwell, her neck viciously and swiftly broken.

Another man entered the vision, a man with darker-colored skin, the same man who just warned him of being left behind. He had known her as a child, guided her in this life, and understood well the extent of what and how she saw. The man didn't appear to have aged since then. Or did he? Orion envisioned the house again, though in this latter vision it appeared older and in decline. The girl, also older, had returned to confront the blackened figures that remained.

They tried to claim her once again, but they'd failed. As Orion witnessed the past, he saw another man erupt into flames, touched by the hand of a blackened figure, a hand that was meant for the girl with the third eye. Then, the great house was consumed by flames. Windows broke. Spirits cried out. Demons scattered.

Then the man he'd ignorantly called "Papa" yanked her from behind and whisked her away from the touch of his fingers. "Enough," he said. "You've learned enough. All of this has been enough. It's time. We're taking the boys and the woman back with us now."

Orion stepped even closer, not intimidated in the least. He felt his so-called father's fear, his ignorance, and most all his loathing. He could see it in his eyes, heard it in his voice. "Is that all you have Papa, fear, hatred, and ignorance?" He spoke directly to Dylan. "Is this what you choose to do, run away rather than understand?" Seconds of silence passed. "You're not the investigator you pretend to be." Orion turned his head and scanned them all with his eyes. "None of you are."

Then Orion watched as the man named Brad charged at him again.

SUSAN CONTINUED TO HOLD UP HER PHONE CAMERA, unabashed by the boy's admonition that their gadgets would prove pointless. She witnessed Brad run toward the boy again, but suddenly, Brad stopped still, frozen in his tracks as the boy lifted his hand upward. Susan maneuvered herself through the others, convinced that she'd recorded it all on video. Brad stood immobile, seemingly paralyzed by an invisible grip wielded by the black-eyed boy. One of the smaller boys began whimpering. Susan noticed it was Brad's son, Adam.

Then, the leader addressed her. "I told you your gadgets would not work." Suddenly, Susan's phone rang, causing the ID screen to temporarily block her view of the camera shot. Jamie's name flashed on the screen. Susan attempted to press the answer button. Then her phone completely shut off. She glared at the black-eyed boy, knowing he'd done it using his telekinetic weapon. "The call was from Jamie," he said. "But there's no point now." He turned his black eyes up toward the sky and back again. "They will be coming for Jamie shortly. You cannot save her. You never could."

His black eyes penetrated her, piercing her like knives. He spoke as if he knew her, her past, her history.

"You son-of-a-bitch." Her words were automatic, and her fear ushered them out in a whisper. "Let him go, right now. Damn you!"

Orion stepped toward her. From behind, so did Tahoe, taking his stand beside Susan. But suddenly, a flood of green light exploded all around them. Heads turned upward as the light came from above. It distracted Orion from Susan. Like the others, he now gazed up at the sky and at the great metallic object that hovered high above them.

———

TAHOE STOOD MESMERIZED BY THE OBJECT IN THE SKY. It appeared just the same as it did in the dream he had of the chief. The infamous phantom in the sky, as they called it here in Green Valley, lingered with its brilliant green light blinding them, but not enough to make its presence hidden. Tahoe had seen many things in his life, but now his once aging eyes saw clearly through younger ones, and now at last he felt like he'd seen everything.

Silence befell those who'd gathered on the mountain. Mesmerized, they watched in both fear and awe, waiting for some unprecedented action to come from the rotating object, but there was none. It simply hovered in the sky, silently watching them.

"The Star People." Aghast, Tahoe whispered. Then, he turned away from the sight in the sky and directed his attention to the boy, who now watched the object expectantly, but with an expression of confusion and unreadiness. "They are here, young ones!" Tahoe's voice became a shout that echoed across the mountain. "And they are not happy. Secretly, you have done what is forbidden. Stop this now and go back from whence you came!"

Just then, Brad unfroze from his trance and dropped to his knees. Dylan and Brett rushed to help him stand. The weeping boy ran away from the woman and past the Black-Eyed Kids who stood in front of them. He ran to his father.

"Daddy!"

Leah snatched the boy up in her arms, as Sidney pushed his way past the kids and ushered the woman and Nadine's son over to his mother. Nadine grabbed her boy and held him close to her. Sidney cradled his arm around the woman and brought her to safety with the team. The Black-Eyed Kids simply watched the object in the sky.

Dylan faced his son. "I suggest you take Tahoe's advice. There's nothing here for you. Never contact me or any of us again and leave these boys alone." He stepped back along with the others who began to make their way back down the clearing and onto the path. Dylan glanced at all of them, who now turned their attentions from the sky and watched him back away. The fear they wielded continued like an unending wave. *All of you!*

———

DYLAN WALKED BACKWARDS, KEEPING HIS EYES ON them the entire time. Slowly, the green light lessened, the emerald tinge it made in the snow gradually turning white again. Once he felt he was far enough away, Dylan turned and ran to catch up with the others, who'd made quick progress through the clearing. Soon, they arrived back at their vehicles.

"My name is Allison Prescott," she said after Dylan asked her identity. "I'm a nurse at University Hospital."

"Allison, do you know Dr. Susan Logan?"

"Yes, I've met Dr. Logan."

Susan stepped forward. "Yes, I recognize her. Allison, tell us what happened tonight."

Flustered and shaking, Allison quickly relayed the night's details, leaving the hospital after her shift, then seeing the kids walking through the cold, snowy night.

"I couldn't leave them," she said. "I'm a nurse. I thought something happened. On the way, I could see the boys and two girls were different. The younger boys were freezing, wanting to go home. I knew something was wrong, but they made me so afraid. I felt this fear, like my life was in danger." She gasped. "Those eyes, I'll never forget those evil black eyes."

"All right, Allison," Susan said. "We can talk more about this later, but right now, we've got to get out of here, as quickly as possible. I think it's best if Sidney and Dylan drive you home. You can come back for your vehicle tomorrow."

"No," she said, her voice adamant. "I don't want to do that. Besides, Dr. Logan, I'm fine now, a little cold, but I'm okay to drive. I'm worried about the boys. You need to get them to the hospital. Have them checked out for hypothermia, and the man who fell to his knees, where is he?"

"I'm alright," Brad assured her, now holding his son up in his arms. "Just a little dazed is all. I assure you, I'll have him checked out."

"I agree, everyone," Susan declared. "But please, no cops. This is a paranormal investigation. If you tell the cops what happened tonight, do you think they'll believe you? Trust me—you don't want to put your families through that."

Nadine and Brad hurried their children into their cars and left the scene. The team waited for Allison to retrieve her minivan out of its skewed position from the snow. She left hurriedly, as advised. Then, Tahoe gazed above them, up toward the small field they had just fled.

"Look," he said. "The green light is gone." He closed his eyes and envisioned. "And so is the phantom in the sky."

———

THEIR PLANS HAD FAILED. THEIR QUEST FOR knowledge had been pointed with too sharp of an edge. Now, the feeling of fear they once wielded surrounded them in a wave like the one they'd previously and maliciously projected. But the fear was only partial. The other half of what they felt in this moment was pure indifference.

They stared at the sky, believing yet disbelieving. The green light was gone and with it the prospect of returning.

"What now, Orion?" Iona's tone was indignant toward him. She stepped closer to where he stood, his back to her, his head still turned up at the sky that had darkened once again. He lowered his head and then turned to them all. The expression on his face was as equally indignant as Iona's tone.

"Don't worry," he told them and gazed up at the sky once more. "They'll be back."

Orion sounded convinced, but Iona knew better. Just like the wise man with two souls had predicted only moments ago, they'd been abandoned.

24

BREATHE, JAMIE, BREATHE

DYLAN APPROACHED SUSAN JUST BEFORE SHE'D CLIMBED up into Brett's Range Rover and told her that he'd also received a call from Jamie while he was driving but hadn't noticed. Nadine had also received a call but couldn't answer. Now Susan started her phone back up and checked to see if it remained in working order. Seeing that it was, she redialed Jamie's number, but the connection went straight to voicemail.

"Brett, I know it's late, but we have to check on Jamie. I can't help but feel that something's wrong. What the boy said about 'them' coming for her is alarming me."

"We can do that," he replied, "but the way the roads are worsening we may not make it there for at least twenty minutes."

"By then, I'm afraid we may be too late," Tahoe warned. His cryptic words elicited a dead silence. Brett stepped on the gas pedal and drove as fast as he could on the slippery roads.

———

NO ONE COULD HELP HER NOW. SHE'D BEEN A FOOL TO think that anyone could. "Call me anytime, day or night" was just a feel good phrase, a way to calm a person's fears, a hypothetical lifeline, but it was never truly meant. When she'd called in the night, no one answered. Dismayed, Jamie shut off her phone. It was too late now, anyway.

She hadn't been able to get back to sleep after dreaming of the red-hooded boy and the cave. The bundle he'd put in her arms, the baby with the blackest eyes. She didn't want it; she knew that now. Mother's words had proven to be unbearably true.

The boy's warning made it impossible for her to close her eyes again. *"They will come for you soon, Jamie."*

His words had caused her to awaken, screaming.

They would come to abduct her again from the privacy of her home, the sanctity of her bedroom. Then, they would crudely invade her once again and take the fetus she carried within her. It was part of them. That was the message of the dream. A Black-Eyed hybrid had been implanted inside her, and soon they would steal it from her womb and send her back. Would she then continue to be their specimen, forever breeding for an alien race that refused to show their faces? She would not. Tonight, she would see to it that it would never happen. She refused to be taken as their subject ever again, and they would never get whatever lay sleeping inside her.

She would end it tonight, once and for all. Jamie glanced around at her humble abode. She was alone in this life, outside of Misty who simply watched her now, curious as to what was coming next. Jamie had no one. No future existed with Sam. Just as she'd feared, he discovered her to be exactly what she'd always felt like—a basket case. Mother was gone. Jamie hadn't seen her father again since the day he walked out the door. She was an only child, and now having remembered a secret part of her mother's history, she felt she understood why.

These strange beings had tortured her mother for years, and Mother kept it a dark secret all of her life. They'd taken them both when Jamie was a child. She would never know the reason why. Was she now their focus because they'd failed to get what they wanted from her mother? It didn't matter anymore. All of it would end tonight. After tonight, there would be no more unanswered questions.

Years of being a Girl Scout and attending summer camp regularly taught her how to make a noose. She made one at the end of a rope she'd stashed away in the garage. Ironically, she once thought she'd never have any use for such a rope. At last, now she had. It opened and closed perfectly as she tested it in her hands.

She turned and glanced at her beloved Misty one last time, petting the back of her small head soothingly. She would miss her, but cats had nine lives. Someone would take her and give her a good home, and Jamie strongly suspected who that might be. She gazed out beyond her bedroom and turned her attention to the front door, which she left unlocked. Someone had to find her. She didn't want to be found later, stinking and rotting in her quaint little abode.

Jamie rose from the bed and walked to the center of her bedroom, where she'd placed a chair just underneath the ceiling fan. The fan, often the first thing she saw after waking from a dream, would now be one of the last things she saw in this world. She stood atop the chair and affixed the rope tightly to its base just above the blades. Then Jamie looped the noose around her neck and affixed it snuggly in a strong potential grip. She'd already tested the chair earlier, ensuring it was set in the right proximity for when she finally kicked her feet away.

She took one final look around her room and outward at her small apartment. It would be the last time she would see it. She glanced down at Misty again who simply watched her. Jamie hoped that curiosity wouldn't kill the cat but her instead. Then she gazed up at the ceiling fan. Soon, she would be reunited with Mother. All would be over.

Jamie kicked the chair away. It tumbled over on its side. As the rope dropped from the ceiling fan, so did her body. She felt her neck crack and the rushing shock of hot fluid pulsating through her body. The noose clenched her throat in a stranglehold and spread a burning fire across her neck. She couldn't breathe, and the slightest inkling of regret entered her final thoughts. Her body fidgeted. Her legs kicked. Her eyes filled with tears, and the room grew dimmer and darker. Colors flashed before her eyes, stunning reds, greens, and blues, just like the painting in Susan's office. Her heart pounded, her lungs gasped for air, the absence of which made her less and less conscious.

One final thought entered her mind—*Breathe, Jamie, Breathe.* But she could not. Then the world grew dark and cold around her. Her body stopped moving and simply swung from side to side. Misty jumped down from the bed and raised a paw, touching Jamie's foot, but Jamie would no longer respond.

———

ABOVE JAMIE'S APARTMENT HOUSE, A BRIGHT, circulating green light remained unseen—that and the disc-shaped object that hovered just above it. The object waited expectantly in the stillness, seemingly with an intended purpose. Then abruptly, it vanished.

———

"JAMIE," SUSAN CALLED AND POUNDED ON THE FRONT door. "It's Susan. Please, open up."

Tahoe, who had stood with his head slightly bowed and his eyes closed, looked up. "The door is unlocked, Susan. We must go inside."

Susan turned the knob and opened the unlocked door. Cautiously, the three of them entered Jamie's apartment and stood in the living room.

"Jamie, are you here? It's Susan." Susan called out again, but only the maddening reverberation of dead silence responded. Susan took a few steps more and noticed that the bedroom door remained open. She motioned for Brett and Tahoe to follow her as she walked toward the bedroom. Then she pushed the door open wider, wide enough to see inside.

Jamie's body hung from the ceiling fan. Susan's heart skipped as her eyes caught the unthinkable. Just as she did, Jamie's cat ran over to Susan and stood placing her paws on Susan's left knee with a silent and seemingly desperate plea.

"Oh. Dear God," Susan exclaimed, her hands quickly fixed in a steeple over the lower part of her face.

"Jesus!" Brett cried out, quickly turning his back.

"No, Jamie, no," Susan sobbed. Tears welled in her eyes and now rolled down her cheeks.

Tahoe simply stood and lowered his head, closing his eyes once again. "As I feared, we are too late."

25

APOCALYPSE

During the weekend, Troy had decided to visit his parents back in Allentown. It had been awhile since he'd been home. Now, he'd returned to Green Valley late in the dark of night. He felt tired from the four-hour drive and thankful now that his house finally came into view.

After such a close call recently, he felt the need to see his family again, especially his parents. He would never reveal the extent of what happened to him to his family; it would remain his secret. He'd often thought of going back home; he'd missed it just as frequently as his thoughts reminded him of its simplicity. Green Valley harbored too much mystery, too much mayhem for a place that appeared quaint and quiet and beautiful with its bountiful green surroundings.

He parked the car in the driveway and then retrieved his overnight bag and briefcase from the backseat. As he slammed the car door shut, that's when the green light splashed down from above, immersing him in it and rendering him unable to move. His eyes became inexorably drawn to the familiar shape in the sky, the gray metallic craft that wielded the great green beacon. His bag and briefcase slipped from his grip and dropped to the ground. But

Troy felt no fear, only confusion. Whoever they were had saved his life. He felt as if he owed them.

Troy then felt himself being lifted off the ground. He felt weightless and unafraid, lost in a trance as a magnetic grip pulled him upward to the sky. Two sides of the craft's bottom opened up like steel jaws and awaited his passage through. As he was pulled into the craft, the green light disappeared, replaced by a blaze of white light that blinded his eyes completely closed.

Troy felt the familiar touch of lanky fingers caressing his face and forehead, a touch that sent him deeper into the trance. This time, there was no gurney. He felt himself reclining backward in a cold metallic chair, while the familiar sun-like heat warmed his face once again. The caressing fingers continued their trek across his scalp. Steel utensils of some type plunged into his nostrils and gently lifted his head up. They were checking his brain once more, searching for signs of what had previously ailed him.

When it was over, Troy sat upward and awake in the chair. The initial blurriness in his eyes lessened until his vision sharpened, making the whole experience seem less like a dream and more like reality. Before him stood several of the lithe, shadowy figures, but Troy saw them more clearly this time. Bulk-shaped heads protruding in the back and big oval black eyes, they were not from this world, but this he already knew. In front of him stood a female figure, obvious by her rounded shapely breasts, which appeared to be the most human attribute he could discern. Two male figures stood to his left and another to his right, all of them regarding him as if he were a specimen.

Troy thought it best that he speak first, a secret attempt to gauge their intentions and find out what was happening here. "The last time I was here, you saved me." The female figure simply nodded her misshapen head. Troy noticed how impossible it was to ascertain any emotion or reaction upon such faces. Their features appeared almost still and unreadable. "Thank you," he added.

The female nodded her head again and blinked. The others

stood and awaited her initiation. Troy was about to ask why they'd come for him again. Had the tumor returned? But before he could speak, he heard the female's voice in his mind.

"We have brought you here so that you may see." Her lips never moved as she spoke.

As the female stepped aside, Troy saw a small dais and upon it, an image flickered into existence. Much like a screen, only not a screen, he saw no frame, no stand, just a wavering image. Suddenly, the screen became one, filling a space the size of a small television.

"You must see what is before you." The voice belonged to one of the males who stood off to his left. "You have been chosen to see."

Troy then saw a clear image of people, like a video. The people were wearing masks around the lower part of their faces, covering mouths and noses. He saw them arguing, some ripping masks from their faces and throwing them to the ground. Others ran for cover, fearful of what looked like infection. Troy saw a sign that read "QUARANTINE." He saw others yelling in protest, marching in the streets. Others were coughing, dying as the hospital workers inserted tubes within them. Troy saw another sign. This one read, "HAZMAT." He saw Hazmat workers in full gear, spraying resistant humans with large rifle-like weapons meant to cleanse them. He saw dead bodies, coffins, and children crying.

"The plague you see is one of many," the female said.

Troy kept his eyes on the image. Then, he saw riots in the streets, fighting, bloodshed, bullets fired and bodies falling from acts of mass murder. The fact that he was being shown the future became undeniable. Troy saw images of massive flooding every-where. Buildings and street signs halfway underwater, people escaping or making their way on makeshift rafts, some with life vests, and some without. He saw people drowning, others being rescued, cars floating downstream.

Then, the image changed. There in the frameless rectangular space, the live images changed to a map of the world, with the

United States poised perfectly in his frontal view. The image began to shake just to the right of the U.S. Troy watched closer to try and discern what he was seeing. The shaking was not of the image but of what existed within it. Troy traced it with his eyes and saw that the northern coast of Africa was quaking. He watched as the sea level on the map rose up into a giant tidal wave, a result of the quaking. Troy sat amazed as the tidal wave moved forward on the map, straight toward the United States.

A hand of one of the male members behind him touched his shoulder. "You must watch closely."

Troy watched the tidal wave grow in height and crash into the southeastern coast of the U.S. He felt his heart exploding in his chest. A trickle of sweat ran down his face. Blue filled the lower half of the eastern U.S. coast, all the way to West Virginia. Then, the map moved slightly to offer a better view. He saw in main focus the Midwestern U.S. states, and there he witnessed another trembling, though this one appeared different somehow. Suddenly, a plume of black and orange erupted from the Midwest, spewing black and gray as far north as Canada and beyond and engulfing the rest of the U.S. with its blazing breath.

The words that entered his mind sounded almost aloud—eruption—volcano. The female turned to him and nodded. The catastrophe that befell his country appeared to spread to other parts of the world. The massive plume stretched far and wide and engulfed an endangered globe. Troy watched an image of it blocking out the sun, and the sun's radiant light dirtied like sackcloth.

"No, no, no," Troy shook his head. Fear overwhelmed him to the point where he closed his eyes. He didn't want to watch any more.

"Open your eyes," the male behind him said. "There is more."

Troy reluctantly opened his eyes and watched as something moved upward through the air in the area of Washington, D.C. A missile; it was obvious by the way it moved on the map, a perfectly simulated reproduction. Then, the map changed and showed Russia, where the missile had hit and exploded. Another missile shot out from Russia and detonated in the United States. And more missiles fired from different spots on the map as war reigned majestically. When it appeared to stop, Troy noticed fire almost everywhere on the map. Still, it was not over.

This time, the shaking encompassed the entire map, a world-wide earthquake. Then Troy saw the images. Different parts of the globe have fallen, people screaming in terror, roads opening up and falling away, swallowing houses and buildings—total destruction. Troy cried out and again closed his eyes.

"What you are seeing is the future," the female confirmed. "It is the apocalypse."

Troy opened his eyes back up, tears spilling from them. The next thing he saw was a giant rock, an asteroid, barreling toward a devastated Earth. Then, the screen went blank, leaving nothing more than empty space it once held.

"Will I be there?" Troy asked. The female nodded. "So what am I supposed to do?"

"You can do nothing to stop it," she said. "But you are one of few who will understand the part you will play when it occurs. You will know what to do at that time."

She touched her lanky fingers to his forehead. "Calm yourself. There is one more thing you must see before you go."

He felt his breathing relax and slowly, he slouched in the cold metal chair. Before Troy knew what was happening, he found himself raised from the chair, as if uplifted by an unseen force. Then, he realized he was walking with the female and two males down a long metallic corridor. A door at the end of the corridor opened vertically, with a *whooshing* sound. The female extended her hand, inviting Troy to enter inside first.

Troy stepped inside, and the others took their places alongside him. The room was cast in the same luminous green light that had sucked up him up through the sky. Before him he saw rows of small tanks with glass windows set in the front of them. A bright, luminescent liquid glowed from each of the tanks, but within them is what caught Troy's attention. Floating inside were sleeping bodies of children, but not ordinary children. He turned and glanced at the female leader.

"Go ahead," she said. "You may look closer. It is why we've brought you here."

Troy stepped as close as he dared to one of the tanks on his left. The body inside was infantile, a mere fetus being incubated in a vastly different way than what he'd known. He could see that the child's face was human, but different like those of his hosts. Troy could not stop staring at the big round eyes, and as he did, the eyes opened briefly, causing him to jump backward. The eyes appeared black, like marble or onyx. Then, the eyes softly closed again. These beings, these children were not only alive but waiting.

"They are waiting to be born," the female said, as if she had read his mind.

"What," Troy stammered. "Who are they?"

The female turned her head, glanced at the sleeping children, and then turned back to Troy.

"They are who your world has deemed "The Black-Eyed Kids," but what remains unknown to your world is the fact that *they*," she pointed to the glass tanks, "are the future of your world."

Troy stepped forward to the tanks and gazed even closer at the sleeping children inside. Human-alien hybrid faces with huge eyes and lithe, straggly bodies. They sported a perfect combination of both humanity and those who stood with him now. Troy closed his eyes and let the telepathic thoughts of the others fill his mind. Finally, he understood and opened his eyes.

"They will replace humanity," he said.

He noticed the others nodding. "So that humanity will not completely die," the female said. "Although they age at a faster rate than humans, we've narrowed it down to approximately seven years to one human year. But one day soon they will become the next form of humanity."

Troy stood aghast, simply staring at the beings who would one day rule the world. They floated in their infancy now, but one day they would run governments, the law, the culture, the arts, the sciences, and build back what their predecessors had obliterated. This was real. Everything he was seeing, hearing, was no illusion, no hallucination, no dream. He felt his heart beating, his sweat dampening his temples, his breath running away and then calming.

"You will play an essential and key role in your world's future," one of the males said. "But you must wait and be patient until that time has arrived."

"And now that you have seen," the female said, "you must return. You will know your place when the time comes. You will remember everything, and you will be ready."

Troy witnessed walls shifting around him so fast it created a dizzying effect. He saw a bright flash of blinding white light, and then he was engulfed in the green glow once again, descending closer and closer to his driveway. When the green light disappeared, he stood at the side of his car, where it seemed like he had just slammed the door shut. The frigid cold gripped him, as if he'd just walked out into it. With his hands held outward as they were when he dropped his bags, he slid down to his knees as tears of helplessness burst from him in a fit of sorrow.

26

WHAT TOMORROW MAY BRING

THE FOLLOWING DAY ARRIVED WITH A QUICK FLASH OF blue dawn but bringing a subtler, gentler morning. Icy winter winds had persisted, and cold remained, causing restless bodies and tired eyes to sleep little or not at all. Any and all schedules or appointments were cancelled, dismissed because of the previous night's mayhem. A morning meeting in room 208 became impertinent. Now, everyone connected with the previous night's events was present. Susan decided early on that this meeting must be video recorded. The old-fashioned recording of minutes was not acceptable for everything that had transpired. Brett had set up the video camera just as she requested, and a meeting of somber hearts and confused minds began.

"Thank you all for being here on this awful morning, after everything that's happened," Susan began. "I just want to state for the record that all are present, that is, the society's investigators, as well as Brad Byers, Nadine Parks, and Allison Prescott. Troy Adler has phoned me. He will be a few minutes late, but he's assured me he will be here. Apparently, Troy was abducted last night and has quite a story to tell."

Sounds of astonishment came as no surprise. Susan continued.

"I especially want to thank Brad and Nadine for being here when your children need you most. Would both of you mind giving us an update on the boys?"

Brad spoke first. He'd been consoling Nadine by holding her hand, and as he let go, she wiped ongoing tears from her eyes.

"The boys were kept overnight in the hospital for observation," he said. "My son, Adam, is suffering from slight hypothermia, but they say he should be okay to go home tomorrow."

"Todd is okay, they tell me," Nadine said with a weakened voice. "I may be able to take him home later today."

"Our boys are okay," Brad said, turning to Allison, "because of you. We both would like to thank you, Allison, for picking the boys up as they were walking. If you hadn't stopped, our boys may be dead right now. You risked your life without knowing. We are so grateful to you."

"Yes, I'd like to second that," Dylan said. "If you hadn't stopped for them, we may never have found them. It was because we discovered your vehicle that we knew where exactly to locate them."

"No, no need to thank me," Allison deferred. "I felt obligated to stop for them. I saw children walking through the cold night. I assumed something had happened. We'd seen things like that before in the ER, everything from house fires to domestic disputes. I thought something like that happened. I should be thanking you all for finding us so quickly."

"And Allison, I want you to tell your whole story of what happened last night," Susan said. "But first, I need to begin the meeting with the awful news of what occurred after last night's confrontation on the mountain. Some of you already know." Susan took a deep breath and continued. "Last night, Brett, Tahoe, and I drove to Jamie Cohen's residence. We were concerned about her." She paused. "We found her dead, hanging from a makeshift noose in her bedroom."

Nadine heaved and cried out further. She'd already heard the news from Dylan. It was why Brad was consoling her. "She tried to call me as I was driving, trying to find Todd. I didn't answer her."

"You're not to blame, Nadine," Susan said. "This is not your fault. Jamie tried to contact Dylan, as well as myself last night. It was she who called me on the mountain, but the black-haired boy stopped my phone from working. That's why we went over there. You had an emergency. Your child was missing. Jamie was likely unaware of this. The boy on the mountain warned me that her abductors were coming for her. I have a feeling Jamie knew this."

Susan paused again, swallowed hard in trying to collect herself for what she was about to say. "If anyone is to blame for what happened to Jamie, it's me."

The word "No" felt like it was assaulting Susan. It had come from Dylan, Brett, and Sidney.

"Yes, please, don't," she responded. "It *is* my fault. I failed her. She was my patient and I failed her, and this is not the first time I've failed a patient in such a way." She looked at each of the investigators. "And you all know what I mean. That's why I've decided to retire from the field of Psychiatry, effective immediately."

The others gasped in sorrow, making failed attempts to protest.

"I feel it's time anyway," Susan continued. "Besides, I'll be able to dedicate more of my time to this society and to the field of Parapsychology. I think maybe I was always best suited here. Last night taught me many things, one of which is that we know nothing in this world, and therefore the need for discovery is even greater than before. So that's where I'm going to position myself, permanently, here under the stars and wait for what presents itself next. I thank all of you for your concerns about me, but I'll be fine." She paused, took another deep breath, and went on. "Now, I'd like to hand things over to Dylan."

Dylan thanked her before turning to Brad and Nadine. "I'd like to begin by thanking you both for reaching out with your stories, but I would also like to apologize. I feel like my dilemma has caused harm to your children, and this I never wanted."

"That's just it, Dylan," Nadine interrupted. "You don't have to apologize. Apparently, the story of our children is not limited to our boys in the hospital. It's our other children that brought us here. Children we and you knew nothing about."

Brad clutched her hand again. "But we had to choose, Nadine. And we chose."

Nadine used her other hand to wipe away more tears.

"Understood, Nadine," Dylan continued. "But if things had ended worse than they did, I would've never forgiven myself."

"It was not your doing," Brad claimed. "It was theirs. You remembered what happened to you, Dylan, but so did we. We needed your help, and you responded."

Dylan nodded. "I know what you're both feeling right now, that mixture of fear, repulsion, and unexpectedly, love, a strange love that we have no justification for. A love that somehow needs to be acknowledged and accepted but cannot be." Nadine shielded her eyes with a tissue. "I don't think I'll ever see my son again. I doubt it. But I'm perfectly okay if I don't. I can't get past the fear that emanated from them. I can't erase the feelings of being cruelly violated and manipulated. I'm sure you both feel the same." Dylan paused, allowing his words to sink in. "Now, I'd like to hand the discussion over to Allison." He turned his head toward her. "Allison, the society would greatly appreciate your testimony of what happened, that is, if you're up to it."

Allison nodded in agreement. She began by telling them how she left work and took the quicker route home, even though the back roads may have been more hazardous. If she hadn't, she would've never encountered the group of kids trudging through the bitter cold. She reiterated how unusual they looked, walking through the cold, dark night. Allison had noticed two smaller children within the group. That compelled her to stop and intervene. Then she described how the other kids were dressed.

"They appeared to be dressed for October or November, not the dead of late January, certainly not for an arctic blast. And the clothes they wore were shabby, drab, almost worn out. Flimsy hooded sweatshirts when they could have been dressed more warmly." She shook her head. "That was part of what convinced me that something was wrong, that they needed my help." Allison recalled the two older boys approaching the driver's side window. "They approached, and I felt suspicious of them. Something seemed out of place, but I was worried about those two smaller boys and the girls. So, I let them in."

Allison stuttered, wrung her hands, and inhaled deeply.

"It's okay," Dylan said. "You're doing fine. Take your time."

"When they got in, and the black-haired boy sat next to me, he turned and looked right at me. Then, I saw those eyes, those big black eyes." Allison described the fear. "I felt afraid like I'd never been before. The fear came from that boy. He exuded it. I was so scared out of my wits that I couldn't think. I honestly wasn't sure what was about to happen to me, but I knew they would be the cause, the older kids. That's when he threatened me." Allison struggled for words. "If I didn't do what he said, I *knew* I would never make it home. So, I did as he asked. I drove to the mountain, and when he told me to park, I made sure I parked recklessly. I was hoping it would serve as a signal to someone that something wasn't right in the area."

"A brilliant move," Sidney said. "It stood out to us as possibly abandoned. We noticed it immediately."

Allison continued. "We walked a bit up the mountain. Then, the boy directed us to a cave. We were told to stay there and wait. They knew you all were coming, you see. They were waiting for you. The black-haired boy maintained that their 'parents' were coming for them. At some point, he turned to the others and said, 'They're here.' He ordered me and the boys to stay put and to come out only if he motioned for us. He said that I would know when. Then, well, you all know the rest."

"Thank you, Allison," Susan said. "I'm not sure if you've been able to piece together the identity of these kids or not, but they are infamously known in the paranormal community as 'the Black-Eyed Kids.' We've been investigating them and have ascertained that they are the offspring of UFO abductees. Therefore, through genetic manipulation, they are alien-human hybrids."

Allison's face sunk into blankness.

"I'm sure you recall the Green Valley UFO event that erupted in our town a few years ago. In case you didn't know, Dylan here was abducted. What we recently learned is that Brad and Nadine were among several others who suffered the same situation. The kids that took you last night are their offspring, and their intent was to contact those with whom they share human DNA. But it came to everyone's attention that the ways and methods of these kids were sinister and threatening. Their agenda is something we haven't quite completely uncovered. These facts are about to be confirmed by our friend Troy. He claims that as a result of his abduction last night, he knows who these kids are and why they're here."

"Well, it was obvious that they possessed some sort of top-notch psychic ability," Allison said. "I knew there was *something* about them, something that wasn't natural."

Leah and Sidney sat next to each other, all talk of demons and vampires long behind them.

"You're right," Leah insisted. "And top-notch is the best possible phrase. When he laid his hands on my head, his fingers caressing my eyes, we saw what each other saw. He probed my mind, my third eye, and I saw what he saw, though very quickly. I saw a million images I couldn't decipher within a matter of seconds. He possessed a second sight neither myself nor Tahoe could ever imagine. He perused my entire life in a matter of seconds. All memories of my childhood and Cedar Manor flooded my mind before I could stop it. He saw all of it and didn't stop. He watched everything as it happened. Then it was over before I could resist. Several of you have asked already, and I thank you, but yes, I'm alright since he touched me. He didn't harm me in any way. I'm fine, but I'm left with the strangest, unsettling feeling that his psychic ability, his foresight, was inherited from his alien DNA, not his human side. This is something I know I'll never stop thinking about."

"Their abilities are more than we could've ever imagined," Susan said. "We have proof of it." Susan directed everyone's attention to the giant overhead screen that hung from the wall. "Last night, Brett and I attempted to capture video images with our phones. When we were discovered, you all remember the boy's admonition to us. Now, I want you all to see the end results of those attempts."

She motioned to Brett, who sat ready with his laptop in front of him. After a few keystrokes, an image appeared on the screen.

"This first video was shot by me," Brett instructed. Quickly, the snow-covered ground could be seen after a fast flash of whiteness. Footsteps were heard in the background as the video drew closer to the cave's entrance. Then, a mixture of light static and blackness interrupted, and the outdoor image was no more. "This continues the rest of the way through, almost ten minutes." Brett exited the video and produced another. "This is Susan's footage." There on the screen, the same blank blackness played out uninterrupted. "Nothing of what Susan attempted to capture recorded. They, or he, wiped out our tech capabilities effortlessly."

Silence ensued.

"Then last night, he gave us a warning about Jamie," Susan offered. She paused before her tone issued the sounds of deep hurt and regret. "But Jamie would not be taken again. She fought back in the worst way possible."

Nadine hung her head and continued to sob.

"The boy said quite a few things to me last night," Tahoe said, "many of which hit home. But I was struck by something he said in particular. It was what he said to you, Dylan. He asked if hatred, fear, and ignorance were all you had. He accused you of running away rather than understanding. I'm brought a little closer to the chief's admonition of them being dual beings, but I don't understand the darkness they wield combined with their wanting to be understood."

"Agreed, Tahoe," Susan said. "Could we, in some way, still be held accountable for our reactions? Possibly. This fear we speak so freely of is confounding. It goes back a long way. It is fear of change, which is fear of the future, which is fear of the unknown, which always leads to ignorance. Are we guilty of such reactions? How can we not be?"

"I warned them," Tahoe said. "They had indulged in that which is forbidden. I remain unaware of what this means, but I fear the price they will pay for such an infraction."

"Or a price we all may pay," Sidney offered.

Heads turned to the hissing sound of the heavy door opening. Troy had arrived. He apologized for being late.

"No need, Troy," Susan assured him. "Thank you for joining us." She then directed him to an empty seat next to Sidney, meant for him. Troy sat, and then listened as Susan quickly caught him up on all that was discussed. He hung his head and extended his condolences over Jamie.

"We all are devastated and mainly shocked, Troy," Susan said. "A shock that never seems to end, but we're here, and I believe you have something extremely important to tell us."

"I was abducted again last night, right from my driveway as I arrived home." Troy began quickly, not wasting any time. "I stepped out of the car, and the green light engulfed me. It all happened so fast. I was sucked up into the air, paralyzed and endlessly floating. Then, I found myself inside that thing once again."

Troy described the quick examination of his brain and the affable words exchanged with his captors, those who had saved him. Then, he told them about the screen he was made to watch and the images he became forced to endure. Troy lowered his head and stared at the table before him, obviously contemplating his next words carefully.

"They showed me the future," Troy revealed. "I saw it come alive, as if it had already happened, and to say it's bleak is an understatement." He told them about the impending plague, the riots and unrest, the public violence. Then, he talked of fires, floods, weather catastrophes, specifically the great tsunami that swallowed the south-east coast of the United States. "States that we see on the map now were no longer there," he said, aghast in disbelief. "I saw a future map of the U.S. There were many changes. Many states were just gone, sunken underwater."

He told them about the volcano and how its outpouring affected the rest of the globe. "I watched the sun get blocked out, just like it's described in the Bible." He described a virulent nuclear war that followed and worse, a worldwide earthquake that literally shook the globe. "Everything was destroyed. Human existence, as we once knew it, became a thing of the past. The female who tended to me described it as the apocalypse. She confirmed that I would be there when it happened, and that I would be part of a surviving existence, that I would know what to do 'when the time came.' That was the hardest thing I've ever had to watch. It was all so real, and they assured me it was real. It just hasn't happened yet, but it will." Troy recounted seeing the plummeting asteroid before the vision ended. "And there's more, so much more."

He described being taken into another room and the large canisters perched high in the air. "Inside those things were those kids, the Black-Eyed Kids, all of them in their infancy. Those canisters were basically incubators. Apparently, they age differently than humans, but I was told they would replace humanity. That's their purpose. That's why they're here, to replace us after the apocalypse, to fill the void we will all leave behind."

Shock lingered throughout the room and created an invisible thickness, the weight of which was felt by all. No one doubted Troy's words. Here sat a man once described as a skeptic, now providing them with the missing yet unexpected piece of a baffling puzzle.

"Then I found myself back in my driveway, crying like a child in the freezing cold." A somber, sobering silence followed Troy's words. Susan broke that silence.

"Strangely enough," she said. "It all sort of makes sense now, doesn't it? A fear invoking remedy to the world's inevitable conclusion?

"If those kids are the remedy," Sidney noted, "I fear for tomorrow's world."

"Ultimately, no one knows what tomorrow may bring," Susan continued. "We don't even know if we will be a part of that tomorrow. The chances for me are much less than for you all. But as you were advised, Troy, we can watch the world's events unfurl and hopefully be prepared for when and if the time comes. After all, we have no other choice."

Susan continued to ask Troy questions about the time he arrived home versus the time he found himself back in his driveway. As expected, Troy suffered from missing time, at least an hour or so. Then Susan handed control of the meeting over to Dylan.

———

DYLAN SAT AT THE OPPOSITE END OF THE LONG conference table, his elbows touching the table-top, his hands clasping each shoulder. He struggled in thought, contemplating where to begin.

"My life was turned upside down a few years after being abducted. I spent years not remembering. Then, I remembered and wrote a book. I'm not so sure I don't regret that decision now." He paused. "We all knew there had to be others who were abducted, just like me. We decided that you all would come forward in time, but each of you came forward because of my book. I may be wrong, but I will always feel guilty about that. I feel as though I dragged you all with me on this journey, but you were victims the same as I was. If I endangered your lives, I'm so sorry. If I brought you to face a truth you didn't want to face, I'm sorry. I will forever be grateful for your bravery and your persistence for the truth. My heart will remain eternally broken over Jamie's sacrifice. I wanted to learn the truth so badly. Now, a big part of me wishes I had never learned that truth."

Dylan glanced at Brad and Nadine. "I feel what you both do, a feeling of shock, devastation, repulsion, and love, all at the same time. I feel a need to be there for my son, but I cannot. The bigger part of me tells me, as I'm sure it does you that it's not meant to be. I am not responsible. Right now, I wonder where to go from here. The world, for me, is no longer what it used to be. What do we do next? How do we go on living, as if none of this ever happened? What is the best way to continue? So much is going through my mind right now."

Dylan thought back to effortless abductions done in the dark of night, the personal invasions against their wills, the feeling of helplessness on the cold gurney, the manipulations of both the body and the mind. Hybrid children wandering through the night searching for their parents, parents shocked and devastated by their existences. He thought of the threat toward human children who already existed, children taken from their beds and into the cold night. He thought of how his predicament had endangered his friend, Leah, but how she risked her life for him. He thought of poor Jamie swaying from a noose she'd hung from the ceiling fan in her bedroom. Then he thought of the apocalyptic visions shown to Troy. He imagined the destruction of the world he now sat in.

"What *will* tomorrow bring, I wonder?" he said. "But right now, I also wonder, does it even matter?"

27

THAT WHICH IS FORBIDDEN

Later that night, after the sun went down, darkness descended quickly over Eagle Rock Mountain and all of Green Valley. The wicked winter wind had died down, but the bitter cold remained like an unwelcome visitor. The vast expanse of starless sky from the more prominent view on the mountain seemed endless and almost threatening. Devoid it was of any strange objects or powerful green lights. The only sound on the mountain was the soft crunching of snow beneath feet, trampling the ground.

Orion led the aimless way ahead of the small group, while the remaining three lingered behind him. Iona watched everything transpire in front of her. She noticed Orion's patience begin to wane. He became more adamant, more restless, as he guided them across the mountain. She felt herself steaming inside, but she was just as angry with herself as she was with Orion. She'd been too passive, allowing Orion to appoint himself as the leader of this earthly excursion. She should have taken over the entire operation. If she had, they might be back where they came from by now, rather than stranded here on this mountain. It was his fault they were stuck here. The need to unleash her ire upon him bubbled just beneath the surface like lava pulsating beneath a volcano.

Orion lifted his hand and motioned for them to stop. He turned his head up toward the darkened sky, as they all did, and hopelessly scanned for miles with their eyes. They had been searching for hours, only to be met with the blackness of night staring back down at them. The sky produced no sign of the elders. Orion had been wrong; they had not returned for them. Orion dropped his hand in frustration. From behind, Iona watched as his upper torso heaved up and down in anger. They sat on the mountain, continuing to watch the sky as it grew blacker and ultimately became lighter.

Then Orion let loose of his anger with a fitful scream that echoed across the mountain. Iona stood from her sitting position and kicked a foothold of snow in front of her.

"Damn you, Orion! All of this is *your* fault!" She stepped forward and faced him down, her big black oval eyes gleaming and glaring into his. "We were warned not to interfere, especially with those with whom we share a biological connection. We were told only to watch and learn, or we would be lost. Now look at us, Orion! Look at the sky above you. The elders have left us, abandoned us here with nothing other than our own limited resources, all because of your single-minded, arrogant belief that we would prove the elders wrong. You're a fool, Orion, a fool to think our parents would want anything to do with us, to think that they don't lead their lives with their ignorance and their indifference. You are as ignorant as they are! You were warned not to do that which is forbidden, yet you made us do it momentarily to steal those two boys away from their world! *Look again, Orion! We are lost and left behind!*

Her mechanical voice blared at him in the cold night, creating a strange sound through the mountain air. Orion breathed heavily, attempting to subdue his rage. Then he turned his back to her. She, Indrid, and Medea watched as Orion seemed to change before their eyes. Something was happening to him, and Iona guessed she knew what it was. Then, he turned back around.

When Orion faced her again, he was different this time. His face was that of a normal human adolescent with regular brown eyes and the same black hair. His complexion appeared less of their typical gray pallor and of a more tan-colored flesh tone. He had done that which was forbidden, and he now appeared as one of "them."

"So because of their ignorance and hatred they will not accept us?" Even his mechanical tone was gone, replaced by a normal human timbre. "Then we will live out our existence as one of them! After all, we *are* one of them. They are us, and we are them. We will live in their world, and they will never see us coming. Then they will have no choice but to accept us."

Iona closed her big black eyes as tears streamed down them. When she opened them again, her eyes became a perfect shade of hazel, her face strikingly similar to Nadine's. Indrid and Medea induced the same change, and now the four of them stood together on Eagle Rock Mountain as regular human adolescents. They glanced at each other, knowing that what they'd just done would seal their fates forever on this world.

"Then together we will go bravely into this new world," Indrid declared, his voice the same as any common eighth-grader.

And there, beneath the moonlight, they moved forward.

———

THE MORNING SUN AS IT ROSE OVER GREEN VALLEY WAS bright and powerful, diminishing the frigid temperatures and rising thermostats to at least 40 degrees Fahrenheit and becoming the first sign that Spring lay just around a long awaited corner. Icicles that hung from eaves dripped, and then slowly crashed to the ground. Those who had sheltered inside from the nearly week long spell of an Arctic blast rejoiced and gratefully shoveled their walkways. Winter had not much longer. Green Valley celebrated. The snow was melting, rudely awakened by a deceptive sunshine.

———

Don't miss out on your next favorite book!

Join the Melange Books mailing list at
www.melange-books.com/mail.html

AFTERWORD

Hello Friends and Readers! Thank you once again for joining me on what I hope has been yet another wild ride through Green Valley with the paranormal investigators. This one has been a long time coming, so I thank you for your patience. In this book, as I often do, I have tied together two paranormal phenomenon into one story. This time, it was alien abductions and a subject I have always been interested in, the Black-Eyed Kids.

Rude Awakenings came about because in 2015, I published the fifth book in this series titled, *Phantom in the Sky*. In "Phantom" the Green Valley UFO made its debut and Dylan was abducted for a brief period. I had suppressed Dylan's memories of what happened during his abduction for the sake of the next book in the series, which I began immediately writing. But I knew he would remember at some point and given that I didn't go into the subject of alien abduction as much as I'd wished in that fifth book, I was well aware that "Phantom" would spawn a follow up when other abductees from Green Valley came forward.

The problem therein was that after writing "Phantom," I felt that writing about this subject was vast, endless, and complicated in its own way. At that time, I vowed never to write about this subject again, but as those of you who are writers know well, that vow was pointless. I had wanted to delve more into alien abduction, and I wanted to write about the BEK as well. They have always fascinated me. Stories of them have persisted throughout Pennsylvania and other parts of the country since 2006. Many theories surround them. The most popular conclude that they are either vampires or demons. I don't agree with either of those theories, as you may have gleaned from Leah and Sidney's argument. But another theory struck me; one that I felt had more plausibility. Some have speculated that these kids are alien-human hybrid created beings; the offspring of abductees since they bear a resemblance in many ways to the Grays, the most often described alien beings. I felt that if I could work this theory in, I may have a story that incorporated both alien abductions and the BEK. And that is what you have just read.

Stories of the BEK continue to persist, and I have found what I feel is the most bountiful source of them, which I will share with you now. Since many BEK stories come from Pennsylvania, there is a local paranormal investigator who is responsible for a website that contains innumerable eyewitness accounts. His name is Lon Strickler, and no, he is not any of the paranormal investigators fictionalized in this book. I want to direct you to his website called phantomsandmonsters.com. There, eyewitnesses are invited to submit their accounts of all types of phenomena, and stories about the BEK appear from all over the world. Here, one can find and read up on the stories of these beings, as well as learn about all the most reported phenomena occurring here in Pennsylvania. It is a trusted site from a well-documented and respected investigator. Find out for yourself.

As far as alien abduction, many reports and accounts exist and have persisted for years of people being abducted and experimented upon physically and biologically. Many women from around the world have reported being used in reproductive experimentation, being impregnated by their alien abductors and later either experiencing a miscarriage or yet another abduction, after which time, they were no longer pregnant, and no evidence of a fetus could be found. Many of these women claim their unborn child was taken from them by the aliens. For those of you who are unfamiliar with the 1965 case of Barney and Betty Hill, they were a married couple who reported being abducted one night on a drive home. Under hypnosis, Betty recounted being experimented upon much in the same fashion as that of Nadine and Jamie in this story. Men have also reported having their DNA taken from them in such experimentations. Travis Walton, a reported abductee in 1977, details his own experience in his book, *The Walton Experience*. It is the claims and beliefs of these abductees that the aliens are creating a hybrid race of beings using human DNA. I encourage all of you to research this matter further.

On that note, I will conclude. I would now like to thank my publisher at Melange Books, Nancy Schumacher, for her patience and understanding and her avid interest in this subject matter. I would also like to thank cover artist, Caroline Andrus, for another outstanding cover. And to you, dear readers—thank you for being here once again. May your unpleasant dreams be purely fictional and your pleasant ones a reality.

Thank you once again,
    With Love,
    Chris

Christopher Carrolli
February 2, 2023
10:43 pm.
(EST)

THANK YOU FOR READING

Did you enjoy this book?

We invite you to leave a review at the website of your choice, such as Goodreads, Amazon, Barnes & Noble, etc.

DID YOU KNOW THAT LEAVING A REVIEW...

- Helps other readers find books they may enjoy.
- Gives you a chance to let your voice be heard.
- Gives authors recognition for their hard work.
- Doesn't have to be long. A sentence or two about why you liked the book will do.

ABOUT THE AUTHOR

Christopher Carrolli is a fulltime writer, who lives in Western Pennsylvania. He is a graduate of University of Pittsburgh at Greensburg and holds a BA in English Writing, and an AA in English. He has also won the Ida B. Wells Prize in Journalism.

www.christophercarrolli.blogspot.com
carrollic@aol.com

 facebook.com/ccarrolli

ALSO BY CHRISTOPHER CARROLLI
WITH MELANGE BOOKS

The Paranormal Investigator

Pipeline

The Listener

The Third Eye of Leah Leeds

The Skinwalker's Tale

Phantom in the Sky

Black Mirror

Shadows Among Us

Malevolent

Rude Awakenings

www.ingramcontent.com/pod-product-compliance
Lightning Source LLC
Chambersburg PA
CBHW022029260626
47156CB00017B/958